AMREEKIYA

AMREEKIYA

AMREEKIYA

A NOVEL

LENA MAHMOUD

UNIVERSITY PRESS OF KENTUCKY

Scholarly publisher for the Commonwealth,
serving Bellarmine University, Berea College, Centre
College of Kentucky, Eastern Kentucky University,
The Filson Historical Society, Georgetown College,
Kentucky Historical Society, Kentucky State University,
Morehead State University, Murray State University,
Northern Kentucky University, Transylvania University,
University of Kentucky, University of Louisville,
and Western Kentucky University.

Editorial and Sales Offices: The University Press of Kentucky
663 South Limestone Street, Lexington, Kentucky 40508–4008
www.kentuckypress.com

Library of Congress Cataloging-in-Publication Data

Names: Mahmoud, Lena, author.
Title: Amreekiya : a novel / Lena Mahmoud.
Description: Lexington, Kentucky : The University Press of Kentucky, 2018. |
    Series: The University Press of Kentucky New Poetry and Prose Series
Identifiers: LCCN 2018027377| ISBN 9780813176376 (hardcover : alk. paper) |
    ISBN 9780813176383 (pdf) | ISBN 9780813176390 (epub)
Subjects: LCSH: Palestinian Americans—Fiction.
Classification: LCC PS3613.A3493353 A85 2018 | DDC 813/.6—dc23

Member of the Association of University Presses

For my mother, Debra

CHAPTER ONE

Though he wasn't a real uncle, I still called my father's cousin Nasser my amu, uncle, and his wife Samia amtu, aunt, because they had told me to do so when they took me in at eight. I figured it was best to do what they said. Back then, after my mother died and my father decided he couldn't take care of me, I had no place else to go. But now, nearly fourteen years later, they made it clear that I had overstayed my welcome.

As family, they had to find an honorable way to get rid of me: find me a husband. But after nearly two years of lining up men, they were still unsuccessful, growing impatient with how selective I was. Why didn't I want to marry a man who was pushing forty and already graying or a man who had been divorced and had three half-white kids? Those kids would just love me as a stepmother. Having an Amreekiya mother myself, I would be able to understand them.

It also helped that, at twenty-one, I was only ten years older than that man's eldest child.

When I told Amtu Samia that the last thing I wanted was to be a stepmother or a trophy wife, she replied, "Is better to marry older man. This one with kids, you don't have expectation to have many children because he already has some. With this gray-haired man, he will think you are pretty and forgive your mistakes fast, if they are not too bad."

Most of all, she said, an older man's mother was either dead or on her way out, so she wouldn't be much trouble to me.

That was pretty much who came for me: older men. I guess I wasn't the most desirable woman to have as a wife. I had a reputation for being short-tempered, and guys around my age didn't want to have that struggle; it was too much work. Older men liked spunk; it made them feel young, alive.

I wasn't convinced. Older men were never my type. I didn't like that they always thought they were right and dismissed me as an inexperienced young woman. If I wanted to live like that, I might as well stay in Amu's house, cooking and cleaning for an old guy but at least not having to sleep with him.

Amu rarely came home before eight, so whenever I saw his car parked in the driveway, I knew that he was early so he could introduce me to a man. Today there was an older Nissan parked at the curb, my usual space. I parked behind it and looked in the windows. An enormous biology textbook lay on the front passenger seat, an undershirt in the back, and some used napkins and wrappers and bags from fast food restaurants barely hidden on the floor. This man's car was only a step above my fifteen-year-old Toyota Camry. I wondered why Amu Nasser even had him over.

I turned the doorknob slowly to catch Amu and Amtu off guard, but I was the one to be surprised when I stepped inside. I kept myself from blushing when he came to shake my hand, thinking of how bad my messy bun and drab clothes made me look in front of my latest marriage prospect.

Amu talked more about himself than Yusef did over dinner. It was typical for Amu—when he was around—to talk about his colleagues and clients as if we knew them all personally, though there were long periods of time when we heard nothing about them because he worked late most of the time. The information Amu gleaned from Yusef was that he was almost done with a master's program in biology and working part-time at a research institution and a community college, as well as teaching a lab at the university. He had moved out of his parents' house almost three years ago and lived on his own with various roommates over the years, but he was living alone now. His apartment was just north of campus, a complex I passed every time I did the grocery shopping after school.

"Well, Yusef, you sound like a diligent young man. You believe so, Isra?" He looked over at me, a stiff smile letting me know there was only one acceptable response.

"No," I said.

Amu glared and pursed his lips. "Why is this?"

"Scientists strut around school thinking they're better than everyone." I rolled my eyes.

Yusef looked from my face to Amu's and laughed. Amu Nasser followed suit uncomfortably; Amtu Samia elbowed me under the table.

"Tell me how to impress you." He looked me straight in the eye, challenging me.

He had me there. I took a minute to think of a response. "If you can cook and clean for yourself, I'll be impressed."

Amu shook his head. "No, she jokes. Be nice, Isra."

Yusef stayed until almost eleven. I kept the tea and sweets coming on Amtu's orders, and it felt like the evening would never end. Amu Nasser droned on about his work as a lawyer, and Amtu Samia kept nudging me to do things that she believed would make me more desirable to Yusef.

My cousin Hanan came home from a choir recital in the middle of the visit, the only relief. She changed clothes and helped me with the trays of sweets and fruits. While we were both in the kitchen, I told her, "Shoot me now. I can't take this for one more second." I let out a long sigh. "Actually, just shoot your parents. That'd be better."

She giggled. "I know you have a crush on that guy. Yusefee! Yoo-see-feee! Don't take your green eyes off me!" she sang quietly.

I rolled my eyes. "Shut up."

Yusef tried to catch my eye the whole time, but I kept mine somewhere else, on the armrest of the couch or on my tea or on Amu's stiff face. I wouldn't give him confirmation. I wouldn't make it easy for him.

On the way out the door, he smiled at me. I found myself smiling back.

I had missed him so much.

Amtu lectured me about what a catch Yusef was and how lucky I would be to have him, even though I knew they wouldn't even think of him as a candidate for Hanan, not only because she was sixteen but because his family was too poor and uneducated for them. That didn't matter in my case. Baba, my father, came from a refugee camp in Ramallah (Amu came from a family who were slightly better off in Jerusalem), and I was practically an orphan living off Amu Nasser's charity, so I had no right to expect better. I tried to drown out the sound of Amtu Samia's voice as I cleaned up the house.

"Listen to me, Isra. You are acting as a child!" She went on to say she didn't know how exactly I met this boy before and why he wanted to marry me, but, knowing me, something indecent went on between the two of us, and I was lucky that he was still willing to commit to me.

I slammed a soaped-up dish back in the sink and turned around to glare at her. "Calm down! It's not like I said no."

"You want him as husband or not?" She put her hands on her hips and straightened her back, her eyes narrowed.

"I'm thinking."

"What? You think he wait around forever? Or that you have many men to choose from?" She threw her hands up in frustration. "Have there been that many men here since you've been a woman?"

Amu Nasser was usually gone by the time I got dressed, but the next day he stayed a half hour later so that he could talk to me over breakfast. His approach was different from Amtu Samia's: he spoke in a reasonable tone and presented the advantages I would have if I made such a marriage. "Yusef does not come from much money, but he is hardworking and has a good education, and he will be able to give all you need and most of what you want." Then he inserted further persuasion. "You must know this: You have come from very little, and look at what you have made of yourself. Yusef is a young man as well."

"I know. I'll have to spend the rest of my life with him, so I need time to think."

"But life will not stop for you, Isra. You must not take too long."

"He can give me a few days. I'm sure he had longer when he decided that he wanted to ask me."

He sighed. "You do not know what he has done to come here. His parents did not think we would consider Yusef for you, so they did not want him to come. If you agree, he will bring his mother and father."

I should have been touched by that, but I found it funny instead. Yusef's parents should have seen all the old and/or divorced men who had come for me. It seemed like almost everyone we knew was aware of the way Amu Nasser and Amtu Samia regarded me. "I wouldn't want to seem desperate by accepting too quickly."

He shook his head and sighed again. "Have your time."

I thought about it during all my classes and later at the doctor's office where I worked, thinking about what it would be like to be a wife. Yusef's wife. My parents never married; Mom didn't see the point of it. It wouldn't have made Baba any less of a deadbeat or her family any more accepting of the fact that she had a child out of wedlock with an Arab.

Then there was Amu and Amtu's marriage. They could barely stand each other and hardly spoke. Amtu Samia still did things for Amu Nasser sometimes, like having Hanan and me help her cook up big breakfasts on the weekend, but he never noticed or even said thank you, especially for the last few years.

At the end of the day, Yusef showed up just before closing with flowers and a smile on his face. The waiting room was empty, but the nurse was filling out some charts in the office with me. "Isra, you didn't tell me you had a boyfriend," she said.

"He's not my boyfriend," I whispered and stood up to meet him at the window.

I opened it and thanked him for the flowers as he handed them to me. He reached in to squeeze my arm. "Sana told me when you got off, so I thought, if you had the time, we could talk."

I nodded, unable to fully meet his eyes. "Sure."

He rested his hand on mine for a few seconds and then settled himself in a seat while I finished up my work for the day. I set the flowers on the table away from my area so they wouldn't get in the way, but I kept glancing at them, and I knew he saw me each time.

Yusef took my hand in his on the way to my car, telling me how happy he was to see me after all this time. He got in on the passenger side of my car and made small talk at first, asking me how things were going, how I liked my job, but it didn't take him long to get to the point: What did I think about his proposal?

I took a deep breath. "I'm still thinking about it."

He reached over and took my hand. "I thought we were . . . you know . . ."

"I'm not sure about marriage in general."

He laughed. "Isra, who doesn't want to grow old together and have babies and all that good stuff?"

Did he think it was that simple? His parents' marriage must have been perfect, or else he was completely oblivious, or maybe it was just that much easier for men. I never saw Amu or Baba stress or suffer because of the women in their lives. I would never be able to make him understand. "It's not so perfect." I paused and set the flowers down on the dashboard. "I would think you'd understand. You've lived a lot more life than I have."

He blew air from his mouth and tapped his fingers impatiently on the dashboard. "I know that, but things get complicated anyway."

I wanted to ask him what he knew about life's complications. He was the cherished only son who had the support of his family for nearly all his endeavors (except for those related to marrying rich girls, apparently). His family didn't seem to have a lot of money, and he'd always had to work hard in school. But that was far from being complicated.

And what if I had a different vision of my life? What if I didn't have room for him in that? "I said I would think about it, and I'll take my time. I gave you yours. It took you long enough to even ask."

He raised his eyebrows and grinned. It lit up his whole face, showing his white teeth, his green eyes sparkling. "So you wanted me to ask?"

I folded my arms and looked out of the window.

He pried my right arm from the other, took my hand in his. "You should have said something. I would have been here in a minute."

I wasn't in the mood to argue, but I refused to agree with him. "I can't help that I need time to think."

He reached over and kissed my cheek softly.

If I had known that Yusef had daisies waiting for me when I came home, it wouldn't have been so hard for me to leave the roses to wilt in the car so Amu and Amtu wouldn't see them. Amtu Samia had set the new bouquet on the coffee table in the living room. She was sitting on the couch watching television, and she reminded me that this sort of behavior wouldn't continue in marriage. "But is nice he took the time to do it before," she said, her arms crossed, her gaze turned right back to the TV. I expected to hear another lecture, but she must have been absorbed in her show, because she said nothing else.

"So are you going to marry him?" Hanan asked, reading from a textbook on the loveseat. I had told her all about him the night before. Well, at least about how I knew him through my friend Sana, and that we went to high school together for a year.

"I don't know," I said reluctantly, dropping down next to her.

"Imagine you as a wife," Hanan said. "And him as your husband." She must have been the only one who didn't want me to get married. She said that I would be leaving her alone with her brother Rasheed because he'd probably never marry, or move out, or even graduate from college (he was already in his sixth year).

"I was her age when I married, and your father was not many years older than Yusef." Amtu wagged her forefinger. "In Amreeka, you girls have too long to grow up. You have too much time to think, 'I cannot do this. I will have to be woman.'" She shook her head.

She was exactly the reason why I would never want to grow up fast, the way she did.

"Going to college is grown up," Hanan said.

Amtu dismissed the idea with her hand. "Laa, no, it's only more school. You don't have to be adult in schools, not at these American ones where the teachers spoil their students."

CHAPTER TWO

I found out that Amu was having an affair when I was fourteen.

On Saturdays, I had to wake up early to help Amtu Samia with the big breakfast and do chores until four or five in the evening. I started with Amu and Amtu's laundry, sorting the clothes from their hamper into whites, delicates, and colors.

One day I noticed that Amu had left his briefcase on their dresser. Normally, it was either with him at work or in his office here at home, so I had never got the chance to go through it, the way I did with everything else in Amu and Amtu's bedroom every weekend.

The briefcase mostly had boring stuff—thick manila folders, chewing gum, some cash—but I found something to make my time worthwhile.

It was a picture.

A woman stood in a white bathrobe, exposing her whole sprayed-tanned left leg, almost showing her crotch. She held a wine glass in one hand, and she had thin, messy, reddish blond hair. I stared at the photo for several long minutes, finding her startlingly hideous. Her orangey tan and pinkish hair almost blended into the same color, and though she was probably in her mid-thirties at most, she had a gaunt face and body. She was practically a bag of bones, with a flat chest and chicken legs; girls my age had more developed bodies.

Amtu Samia wasn't the most attractive woman in the world: she aged before her time, with lines around her mouth and eyes, and up until the year before, she had been losing weight at an alarming rate. But even she looked better than this woman.

Ever since Mom's death, I had heard how everyone deemed her an immoral Amreekiya, not only sleeping with Baba before marriage, as most white women did, but having a child with him without a wedding. Amtu Samia was the worst about such insults, and I had countless arguments with her about Mom, usually with me ending up in my bedroom crying tears of anger and sorrow.

Amu Nasser wasn't above it, though. When I first came to live here, he cast his judgment about my mother: being involved with a bad woman had pushed Baba over the edge and made him crazy and useless. Amu Nasser also didn't like me to ever talk about my mother, especially in front of Hanan—as if Mom's immorality might rub off on her from my words.

How could Amu Nasser judge? At least Mom wasn't wrecking someone's home (not that there was much to wreck here). At least she took care of her child when she could, unlike Amtu Samia who lay in bed all day, lost in her depression, leaving a child to take care of her house and letting her own children practically run wild.

Once I came back from my thoughts, I read the back of the picture, clichés that made my nose wrinkle in disgust. At the end she wrote, "I do for you what your wife can't and won't do, habibi."

I put the picture back in Amu's briefcase just the way I found it, but the image kept sneaking up on me for the rest of the week, and I had to stop myself from cringing each time.

By the middle of January, Amtu Samia's father was close to death from Alzheimer's and old age, so she went to Jordan with one of her friends to see him for a month. Amu Nasser said he couldn't get the time off work, and he didn't want to have to buy the plane tickets for all us kids to go. Rasheed and I were teenagers, and I could take care of Hanan. I already did that while Amtu was here, anyway.

I basked in the time without Amtu home watching her soap operas on satellite TV and berating me for every little thing. Amu Nasser and Rasheed were hardly here, and Hanan was old enough not to be a ton of work anymore.

Suddenly, though, after Amtu Samia had been gone a week, I had an epiphany during a class discussion on *Jane Eyre*. Someone said something about Rochester's crazy wife basically being absent, so he has no problem bringing Jane into the house, and I realized that Amu Nasser was going to bring that woman into the house. Maybe he already had her there now, while we were all at school.

At first I was appalled, then excited. I had a half day every third Wednesday of the month and felt certain that Amu had no idea of that; I would be surprised if he even remembered I was in high school now. I usually took the school bus, and since I went to a school about fifteen miles from the house, I was dropped off at the bus stop at two. Combined with the walk, I'd be home around two-thirty. They'd already be gone by then, because Rasheed would be home within an hour, and I was sure Amu would bring this woman home on his lunch break. He worked just four miles from the house, and that was the only time none of us kids would be around.

I had to find a way to get home earlier. I had made friends with two girls, but they were both my age, so they couldn't drive yet. But there was Yusef. Sometimes I spent my lunch with him, or he'd spend his with me and my friends. He had a license and a junky car that broke down every few weeks. When it was working, he offered me rides, but I refused each time. He had given me a ride from Sana's house the summer before and dropped me off at the end of the block, but even then, I saw Imm Samir, one of our neighbors from across the street, a moment after I got out of his car. She said hi to me, and we made polite conversation for a while. I couldn't tell if she just saw me get out of a boy's car. A couple weeks passed, and I figured she probably didn't see anything, because I knew she'd say something to Amtu Samia right away. Still, I'd better not take the chance again.

In a second those concerns vanished. I hated asking for things, and I had no explanation for why I wanted to go home early on Wednesday, but luckily Yusef accepted right away with no questions.

Yusef drove fast and got me there in less than twenty minutes. He parked the car at the end of the block and kissed me on the cheek. He moved his lips to mine. I backed away before we kissed, but my lips tingled with anticipation. We had an awkward silence, not making eye contact. I leaned over and kissed his cheek, but that wasn't enough. He gently pivoted my head and kissed my lips. I pushed him away from me. "No, I don't want to do that!" I got out of the car and slammed the door. "You better not follow me."

Though I was tempted to run to make sure I didn't miss Amu and his girlfriend, I walked so I wouldn't stand out. When I reached the driveway, I saw the Acura that Amu drove. My heart beat in my head and chest. He was home! I had packed him a big lunch in the morning, so he had no reason to be here. No one was in the living room, but I heard voices and footsteps upstairs. I wondered if I should go up there or not. The room Hanan and I shared was downstairs, but I wanted him to know that I was here. I wanted proof that he had a woman here. I guess they were so absorbed in what they were doing, they didn't even hear me come through the front door.

I walked to the kitchen and got something to eat, momentarily distracted by my thoughts of Yusef. Maybe I did lead him on by asking him for a ride—boys always had the idea that if we initiated anything with them, it meant we wanted to make out or have sex—though he should have realized he assumed wrong when I turned from his kiss. But even if he seemed nice, Yusef was still a man and would do whatever he wanted regardless of anyone else's feelings. I felt stupid for being blinded by his charm, especially while I was in the middle of trying to catch Amu in his lies.

I was so lost in my thoughts that I didn't realize I had left the jam jar close to the edge of the counter, and I elbowed it when I picked up the peanut butter. It fell to the floor and sprayed my pants and the bottom of my shirt, even though I jumped away as soon as I knew I wouldn't be able to catch it. The noise was too loud to be ignored, and I heard Amu charging down the stairs. From the corner of my eye, I saw Amu look toward the front door. He thought someone was trying to break in the house. My lips trembled as I stifled laughter.

I had scared him.

And now I would shame him.

"It's me, Amu," I called out after a few seconds. "I broke the jam jar."

His head whirled to the kitchen before his body did, and he saw me squatting and picking up the big glass pieces. He charged toward me like he was still after a thief, his brown eyes bright and enormous. "What are you doing home, Isra? You should be at school, not breaking things in the house!"

His temper was out of character. Amtu Samia was the one who flew off the handle over broken jars and dishes, not Amu. "I have a half day today. I just came home and made a snack."

He stared at me a few more seconds with his arms crossed. "Clean the mess and go to Imm Samir's to tell her she will not have to pick up Hanan and watch her today after school."

I nodded. Trying to get me out of the house. That woman must be inside. "Okay, I'll call Imm Samir."

"No, she only lives across the street."

"Yeah, but I need to hand-wash my clothes soon so the jam won't stain." His wife was stingy enough about getting me any clothes, even the ones from the bargain stores and thrift shops.

He was at a loss. He needed me out of the house. His lunch break was probably going to end soon. He must have already been home for a long time. "You will at least pick up Hanan, himara?" As if that was his concern.

"Yeah."

"And make sure to tell Imm Samir."

"Mm-hmm."

He left and walked back up the stairs. I threw the glass in the garbage and went to the laundry room. There was a window that showed one side of the driveway, and if I tilted my head, I could see Amu's car. More footsteps, going down the stairs, I was sure. The front door opened. My heart beat inside my throat, and I craned my neck to see who was leaving the house. She wore a long, flowery skirt and a black coat that practically drowned her in fabric, and she looked so young and tiny that I thought she might be a different woman, but when she turned around, her face confirmed her identity. Her lips were pursed, making more lines around her mouth. Amu was saying something to her, probably about pesky nieces or cousins' daughters or whatever I was to him.

I wondered what she was thinking then, for the whole time that she was here. Did she expect a nice, quiet afternoon alone with her married lover and feel pissed that I interrupted it? Did she love Amu or did she just enjoy the thrill of an illicit affair? Maybe she worked in his office. She might be a lawyer or something.

She must have been easy, docile, desperate; those were traits any man valued in a mistress.

Valued in a wife, too, except for the easy part.

CHAPTER THREE

I had imagined what Yusef's mother looked like on several occasions. She didn't differ from my expectations exactly. I thought she would wear a hijab over her hair and a jilbab on her body, because Yusef said she was conservative. She was only about five-one or five-two, with a slightly weathered brown face, thick eyebrows, and olive-green eyes like Yusef's. She gave me a tight bear hug and pulled me down by the neck to give me three hard kisses on both cheeks, right, left, right.

She insisted that I should address her as Amtu Maryam, or Auntie Maryam, but I didn't want any more fake amtus, so I stuck with the more formal Imm Yusef.

We sat down for tea. She and Amtu talked most of the time, inquiring about each other's families and talking about home in Palestine and, in Amtu's case, Jordan. Amtu must have really wanted me to get married, because she was on her best behavior, listening to a poor, religious woman like Imm Yusef. Amtu didn't wear the hijab, and she thought the women who did were haughty and ignorant. She was a modern woman, and the poor bumpkins wouldn't keep her back and call her a sharmoota, a whore.

"Do you read the Qur'an, Isra? Do you speak Arabic?" Imm Yusef asked, sipping tea in the dining room.

Amtu answered ahead of me. "She can read a little. She knows some Arabic. We took her to a Sunday school to learn when she was younger."

I bit my lip. I only went to Sunday school for six months when I was twelve to learn how to read the Qur'an; I barely knew more than the Arabic alphabet.

"I teach Yusef the Qur'an when he was a boy. His older sisters did as well." She went on about how he was their only son, and he came after she had been married for over ten years. I knew he was the only boy and the youngest, but his mother worshipped him even more than I expected (and I had expected a lot).

Later she asked about what happened to my parents, and Amtu said, "Her mother died when she was a little girl. She was Amreekiya, and my husband offered to let her live here when her father went back to Falasteen. You know how it is hard for these American kids to live back home."

Imm Yusef shook her head and clicked her tongue before she put her sympathetic eyes on me. "Does your father come to see you, Isra?"

"No, not really."

The corners of her lips turned down in disappointment, and she shook her head again. "It is hard for men to have children alone. He has not remarried?"

I shook my head. "He doesn't want to." I doubt he ever wanted to marry anyone in the first place.

But who knows? Baba could have gone back. As far as I knew, he wasn't a citizen, and his green card could have expired at any time. Maybe I wasn't telling a lie.

Now that Yusef and I were engaged, the real trials began. Planning the engagement ceremony took almost as long as I expected a wedding to. Imm Yusef drew up a long guest list and so did Amtu, including everyone she had ever met, even if I didn't know them that well. Imm Yusef rented a party hall and was meticulous about how everything had to be set up: she wouldn't budge on the number of tables, the amount of food she would order, and the gaudy decorations she would put up. She and her husband argued a lot about these things, mostly bickering that neither took seriously because they both knew that Imm Yusef would get her way.

At first Amtu and I would go to Imm Yusef's house to see the progress of her plans. After a couple of uncomfortable sessions, I ended up driving there by myself and lied about Amtu being sick. I said she had a lot of ailments, but I didn't specify that most of them were mental.

Imm Yusef used my visits as an investigation, because she didn't care about my ideas for the engagement party or the wedding. Her questions usually centered on how Yusef and I met and how well we knew each other. I suppose she wanted a good Palestinian girl for her son, one who would never be alone with a man before marriage, who would never let his lips touch hers; a girl who didn't have an American mother, who wasn't born out of wedlock. I kept insisting that I met him at Sana's house while her parents were there to supervise the children; we hadn't talked much then and not at all in the last seven years. When I lied about our history, I realized that we didn't have much at all. Less than a year of lunchtime meetings, a few car rides, two flower deliveries.

"Have you put on hijab?"

I never even considered it. "No."

"It will be very good for you."

"Oh, well. . . ."

She ran her fingers through her thick black hair, focusing more on the few gray strands she had. She didn't wear her hijab in the house; it was only her husband and me around. "My son may have not notice you if you have the cover over your hair," she said. She looked at her rough, dry hands. I expected her hands to be veinier, but she only had a couple of sunspots and cracks. "I started wearing after I got married. It is very good for marriage. Your husband will feel like a man."

If she wasn't my future mother-in-law, I would have laughed at her. She emasculated her husband more than any other woman I knew, regardless of her hijab and jilbab.

And it wasn't so important that I cover my hair. No matter what, men found something to lust after in a woman. If she covered herself from head to toe, a man would drool over the way she walked or how her feet looked in closed-toe shoes, but I imagined Imm Yusef wouldn't appreciate hearing these thoughts. "I don't know. It hasn't ever come up."

"Your amtu does not wear one, and your mother did not? What about your amtu's mother?"

"No, neither of them did."

"You must give it thought. Your husband will respect you much more."

She might have had a point there: she had much more control over Abu Yusef's life than Amtu Samia had over Amu Nasser's, but I doubted the hijab was what made the difference. Amtu was a lot more weak-willed than Imm Yusef, and Abu Yusef didn't seem nearly as self-centered as Amu. Besides, I was enough of an outcast in American culture with my dark curly hair, olive skin (even if it was light), and dark eyes, and enough of one with Arabs because of my white mother. Why exacerbate my situation for something I didn't believe in?

Like the sharmoota that I was, I called Yusef as soon as I left his parents' house that day. I was at a stoplight when he picked up, and he insisted that he didn't care about hijab or anything like that. "Don't you think I would have said something before? I know you don't wear a scarf. You know, only my oldest sister Khadija wears one. The other two don't even wear it." He laughed. "I think Khadija just started wearing one because she doesn't comb her hair anymore. I didn't think you were so vain about your appearance."

"It's more than appearance, Yusef."

"I know, I know, Isreenie. I won't make you do anything you don't want to. Mama is just a little conservative. She doesn't mean anything by it."

"What does she know about how we met?"

"Uh . . . I don't think she knows anything. She never asked."

Our engagement ceremony turned out to be even more elaborate than Imm Yusef made it sound. Gold banners on both sides displayed our names in huge letters, Yusef Isa Mubarak and Isra Munir al-Shadi, the left in English and the right in Arabic calligraphy, just over the two buffet tables. The love seat for Yusef and me had jewel encrusting and purple cushions, reminding me of those movies about royalty where they hold court over their subjects, arrayed in jewels.

I was decked out the same way, wearing all two pieces of jewelry I owned (silver earrings and a silver bracelet) and half of Amtu's jewelry (she was wearing the other half). Still, Imm Yusef didn't think it was enough. Though she wanted a good girl for her son, she demanded that I wear a stronger shade of lipstick, kohl, and more eye shadow. She had me sit down at one of the tables and pulled the needed items out of her bag and applied them to my face herself, even after I tried to at least put the kohl on myself. "See, you are very beauty girl." She pulled a compact out of her purse and handed it to me.

"Yes, she is, Mama." Yusef smiled in agreement, looking down at me.

My appearance startled me. There was no time to look at myself before I left the house; we were running late. Amtu ironed my hair straight; Imm Yusef put a deep red on my lips, which washed me out, and a lavender eye shadow on my lids; my eyes were rimmed with thick kohl. I was as made up as an actress on an Egyptian soap opera. I didn't look bad, but I might as well have worn a mask. I was surprised Yusef even recognized me.

"It look good with your dress," Imm Yusef said defensively when I stared at myself too long.

Amtu sniffed and looked the other way.

"She's nervous about today." Yusef took my free hand between his.

"No, I think it looks good. I'm just a little pale."

Instantly she used both hands to pinch color into my cheeks. "Eh, do you know how many women want to have this skin?" She wrapped her arms around one of Yusef's. "Habibi, don't hold hand during the ceremony. Not until you give ring to each other."

Now she was a stage director as well as a makeup artist. Most of her time was taken up giving orders to caterers, though. Yusef held my hand as we walked up the stage, and I heard Imm Yusef whisper to Amtu, "My son is such a kind man."

"Let's try this thing out."

I sat down, forgetting to smooth my dress. It bunched up in the back, so I stood up again to straighten it out. I apologized for my awkwardness, and he laughed. He ran his fingers through my hair. "It's so soft, but I like the curls better."

I nodded, recoiling from his touch in front of Imm Yusef. "But straight hair make me look like movie star," I said with a Palestinian accent.

A photographer arrived, and we took pictures before the party began. According to Yusef, his mom was big on pictures, and she ended up arguing with the photographer a couple of times about what sort of poses he wanted. She objected to having us kiss in a photo—even on the cheek— or having his hand on my lower back, but most of the time we had our arms around each other's waists and smiled stiffly into the camera. It was odd being so close to him for so long in front of all these people. Taking pictures usually made me self-conscious, but it was like we were an island unto ourselves for that time, even for the group picture, with my family on my side, his on the other.

Sana arrived early with her parents and her younger brother while we were still taking pictures. She clapped at the end. "You two are the most beautiful couple ever." Her mother agreed and said that we had better put a blue stone up in our house to protect against the evil eye. I hugged Sana and her mother. Sana's mother kissed me on both cheeks. "I always thought that you two would make good husband and wife," she said.

The men all congratulated Yusef with hugs and kisses, except for Sana's younger brother, who only shook his hand. All the women congregated around the three of us, and the older women exchanged stories about their weddings and engagement parties and how they were so much different back home. They had no say in the weddings or anything else; their mothers-in-law chose everything. The conversation turned, as all discussions of the Old Countries inevitably did, to the excitement of coming to America, of seeing all the sights they saw on TV, and soon being terribly disappointed by Amreeki decadence and immorality.

"Ya Sana, when will you be married?" Imm Yusef asked suddenly with a teasing smile.

She shrugged. "I wasn't as lucky as Isra. I don't want to marry some hairy bear." Sana and I laughed, but the older women didn't.

"Sana has a new job as a nurse at the hospital, and I'm so very excited, but, Sana habibti, every woman needs a husband and every man needs a wife," her mother said, placing her hand on Sana's back, sorrow in her eyes.

With her back to the other women, Sana asked to see the ring I got for Yusef. Once we were a safe distance away, Sana whispered in my ear, "If this is the engagement party, what's she planning for the wedding?"

"It's her only son. He came to her when she was in her thirties, after being married for more than ten years and three daughters," I said.

We giggled quietly, though I felt cruel for mocking Imm Yusef in such close proximity. I suppose it was payback for what she said to Sana, what she did to my face, and her controlling behavior.

"How you have not killed that woman yet is beyond me," she said. "I guess your temper is getting better." She reached for the ring I had for Yusef and opened it. "It's nice." It was a simple gold band, the manliest ring I could find.

Imm Yusef soon interrupted the conversation by telling Sana about her nephew who had immigrated from Falasteen a few years ago and looked almost exactly like Yusef and was the sweetest man and not yet thirty. She offered to show Sana pictures of him later and kept on saying, "You must find a husband when you are young and can have children. I was younger than twenty when I married and didn't have a son until I had more than thirty years." She went on with a catalog of young men (and some who were well past being young) whom she knew, and while I looked at Sana sympathetically, I felt immense relief that I wouldn't have to hear this anymore.

Yusef and I spent the first half of the ceremony sitting on our love-seat-throne while Arabic music played in the background and guests arrived in groups. Most were late and seemed to be in the midst of intense conversations. There was so much noise that my head started to beat like the drums in the music.

Yusef leaned in next to my ear and asked me what I was thinking about.

I shrugged. "Nothing. Just our throne." I squirmed in my seat. "The couch is so uncomfortable." My butt was already asleep. I might as well have been sitting on a hardwood floor.

Before Yusef could answer, Amu came up to the stage and asked how we were. We both said fine, but Amu had much more to say, to Yusef in particular, about marriage. He told him how this was a big step in both our lives and truly made us adults, and we needed to take this seriously in order to be happy. He also talked about children, but I had stopped listening by that time. This whole event was a way for Imm Yusef and Amu to glorify themselves by displaying Yusef and me for all their friends and acquaintances. For Imm Yusef, it was her production of such a fine son; for Amu, it was his generosity in taking me in from a life of sin and making a good Palestinian Muslim girl out of me. I should have stormed out, but I sat there and let Amu—and now Imm Yusef—get away with it.

"Cheer up, Isra. Be happy. This is your engagement party." He smiled to instruct me, showing no teeth like a modest girl. He usually smiled widely, letting all his front teeth show.

"I am happy. I'm just not one for big displays of it."

He rubbed my shoulder. "This is a day for displays. It does not hurt so much to have a little smile."

"Okay." But I didn't smile. I couldn't. I didn't know it had to be part of my accessories like my gaudy makeup and flattened hair.

He left the stage and went back to his seat in one of the front tables. Yusef squeezed my hand and asked me what was troubling me. Didn't he see just half of what made me angry? I opened my mouth to say something, but I was too nervous and angry to speak. "Isra, it wouldn't be so bad if you did smile."

The party hall was about half full, but that didn't keep me from throwing my arms out in frustration. "I guess that's what you guys have been talking about when you and your father meet with him."

He sighed. "Whatever. Let's drop it here." But he lied. "Why are you so mad, Isra?"

"I already told you." I kept my face averted from his, feeling childish. We were up on a stage, what did he want me to do, reveal my deepest feelings? "All this has been taking orders, orders, orders. From Amtu Samia, from Amu Nasser, from your mother."

"Is this about the makeup?" he asked, exasperated.

"You don't get it! All you had to do was put on a goddamn tux and come over to my house a couple of times."

"Isra, let it go."

Right then I saw a woman in her late thirties or early forties in hijab coming up to the stage. I turned away from Yusef and faced her, trying to keep anger out of my face. "It's my sister Khadija." I had met the other two, who were both married with children, but Khadija was very busy because she had five boys.

She gave Yusef a hug and congratulated him. "So you are Isra!" She hugged me and told me I looked beautiful. "I knew Yusef would always get a pretty girl, the way all the girls go crazy over him. I'm so happy for you two. He is a good man, and Mama has been telling me what a nice girl you are." She apologized for not being able to meet me earlier, and while she talked, I couldn't help but try to peek into her purple hijab to see if she combed her hair. I saw only a little above her forehead, dark brown and smooth enough to look brushed, but today was a special occasion. Yusef was honest about her being the only one who wore the hijab at least, so maybe I should take his word on the rest.

Abu Yusef finally came up to the stage with a microphone and made a short speech about how the two of us would be married at the end of May. "Inshallah, Yusef and Isra will be blessed with many children and a happy, healthy life together," he said at the end. Everyone clapped; someone even ululated, causing a roar of laughter and a round of ululations. Amu came up with the cushion that held our rings. Yusef picked up his ring for me first, and it took several seconds for him to slip it on because our hands were shaking. We stabilized ourselves by the time I took the ring for him. The clapping started again, and the music resumed.

CHAPTER FOUR

Before I met Sana, I dreaded summer, with its promise of endless days with Amtu and her complaints and orders. Rasheed also drove Hanan and me crazy with his antics. Sometimes he would shoot tiny wads of spit-soaked paper through a straw or pick his nose and flick the boogers at us. Hanan was small then, so on occasion he even picked her up above his head and spun her around while she screamed in protest. I usually had to hit him and hurl insults to get him to stop. Amtu had enough energy to make my summers hellish, but she wouldn't do anything to Rasheed until Hanan ran to her crying. She never did much more than pull his ear and tell him that he was acting like a hiwan, an animal.

But I escaped by going to Sana's house a couple days out of the week; my chores could wait till the evening sometimes. I felt bad for leaving Hanan at the house, but Amtu didn't want her taking the city bus with me or staying at Sana's house, because she believed any friend of mine would make unsuitable company for her little girl. Nothing really went on there, even though Sana's parents both worked, and we were free from adult supervision. Sana and her siblings did violate their parents' rules by having the brothers' and sisters' friends over at the same time. She said her parents were worried that something indecent would happen if unrelated boys and girls mixed. Her brothers were unwilling to compromise on which days Sana and her older sister brought friends over, so all her siblings had friends over whenever they wanted, and just made sure that everyone cleared out by three-thirty when their mother got off work.

There was no risk in having us mix because we—boys and girls—knew to keep our distance from one another as if the adults were still in the house with us. Even her brothers' friends who weren't Muslim knew to keep away from us. None of the guys were anything special. Sana didn't think any of them were worth a second look, and we both agreed that her brothers hung out with ugly guys to make themselves look better.

Toward the end of June, Sana and I were in her room, sitting on the bed while she told me about some guy she liked at school. "I don't know how I've survived almost the entire summer without seeing him!" She looked up at the ceiling with her hands out in supplication. This was nothing new—she had crushes all the time and claimed that when she was eighteen she'd move out and have lots of boyfriends. Who cared what her parents thought? Didn't all the Arab boys do that? But once she tired of talking about this boy and her parents being unfair, she asked me, "How come you never talk about boys, Isra? There's gotta be someone."

I shook my head. "No." Occasionally I saw a boy I thought was cute, but I never had a real crush—no one I wanted to be my boyfriend anyway. At my middle school, the boys were just as overprivileged and snobby as the girls; I hardly talked to anyone there. That was why I decided to transfer to a GATE school all the way across town. Those rich kids would never take me in as one of their own with my cheap clothes and less than cushy life. I had spent about six years among them but never became a part of them. I didn't want to have anything to do with them.

"It might be better once you start high school, even though it's definitely overrated how hot the guys are." She looked down and giggled. "You know my brothers' friend? The one with the eyes?"

"They all have eyes." But I had noticed him a few days before. He wasn't one of the regulars, because he had a summer job that took up most of his days. I caught him staring at me while Sana and I scoured her back issues of teen magazines for ideas on how we could style her hair and do her makeup once she saw her latest crush again.

"You know who I'm talking about." She paused and grinned. "Do you like him?"

"I think I weigh more than him." He was so skinny that his head kind of looked like a balloon on top of his body.

"At least he won't suffocate you with his fat stomach."

"I don't want to be the one to suffocate him." But he did have striking eyes, lots of wavy black hair, smooth honey skin, and full lips for a boy, the kind I imagined would be good for kissing.

"You know what? He told my older brothers that he thinks you're hot. He said he loved all your curly hair and big boobs. He'll probably try to rub his face in them." She simulated the movement, her hands as my boobs, and threw her head back to laugh.

I rolled my eyes. "Now I know you're lying about that."

"Hey, I got two older brothers—that's how dudes are. Even my younger brother probably already thinks that way, he's just not joining in on it. Yet."

Did Rasheed say those things? Not in front of me, probably not even in the house, though I could believe him saying such things with his friends. He was crass and annoying. But hearing that a boy like Yusef said those things about me—that made me feel nauseated and yet flattered. Then I thought about Amu and Baba being that way in their youth. I couldn't imagine either Baba or Amu with a sex drive, despite all the havoc they wreaked with their libidos.

Sana suggested that we go out past the living room to the kitchen, where we could look his way without the boys noticing us if we were discreet. I thought it was a good idea except that Sana was far from discreet. She'd giggle and whisper too loudly about how Yusef looked at me, and talk about how the two of us were meant for each other. She was so in love with love and anything resembling it: crushes, lust, all that. To Sana, love was attention and pleasure. Though Sana was two years my senior, I felt old and bitter compared to her. I wondered how she would cope when she learned the truth.

She found a board game in the storage closet in the hall so the boys could see us doing something besides looking at them. She motioned with her forefinger for me to follow her down the hall, then stopped at the end, watching the TV for a few seconds. I didn't get why she was waiting, but at a critical point in the boys' video game, she walked in front of the TV with me in tow. I heard her brothers groan and protest; even the little one made a ruckus.

Sana turned around and glared. "Shut up. Is it a crime to walk in my own house with my friend? It's better than sitting around all day, being couch potatoes like all you guys."

The oldest one, Bassam, made some remark about how she walked in front of the TV intentionally. "I need to see the game, not your ass." Yusef said it wasn't that important, and it's not like it messed up the game. Sana's older brothers both laughed at him. "We're not pussy-whipped like you," Bassam said with the smugness of an oldest son, and all the boys laughed. I was already wishing that we'd stayed in her bedroom when I saw Yusef give Sana's brothers the finger.

"God, brothers suck. You're lucky you only have to deal with one," she said. She assumed that Amu and Amtu were like parents, Hanan and Rasheed like siblings, despite all I told her.

She calmly set up the game like she hadn't had a tiff with her brothers. It wasn't anything unusual. Sana and her siblings constantly bickered. I had dinner with them a few times, and each time her parents ended up yelling over their kids and threatening to pull their ears or worse if they didn't shut up. It kept them quiet for the rest of the dinner, but there'd be another argument to settle within an hour.

Sana leaned toward me. "He's looked at you at least three times," she breathed.

She'd told me often before that crushing on Muslim boys was dangerous territory: if his parents saw him with a Muslim girl before marriage, they'd freak and make sure her parents found out, even if those parents spoke on no other occasion. That sort of informing was hardly a risk with other boys, whose parents usually didn't care if Muslim girls kissed or touched boys. I reminded her of what she'd said. "So why're you trying to set me up with a Muslim boy? Do you want me to get in trouble?"

She snickered. "Well, I know that you'll resist temptation. It'll be fun for you, an innocent flirtation."

"With who?" Yusef asked when he came up behind me, startling me so much that I nearly pushed my chair back against him.

Even Sana was a little flustered. "No one you know," she said, crossing her arms and looking away.

He held on to the knob on the back of my chair. Sana's cheeks twitched. He introduced himself, holding out his hand. I took it and gave him my name.

He smiled. "That's a pretty name."

I didn't know what to say.

"Isra's going to the same school next year," Sana said. "She's going to be a freshman."

"Then I'll get a chance to see you."

"Yeah." I had to say something.

"I'll let you guys get back to your game."

Once he was out of sight, Sana turned her face to the side and laughed silently, her face still twitching and reddening with the effort to muffle it.

When the time came for me to leave and Sana showed me out the door, Yusef offered me a ride. Sana's brothers, who had been absorbed in their video game, tore their eyes completely from the screen and looked over at us for a few seconds, then went back to the TV, waiting to see what would happen from the corners of their eyes. I hesitated and had difficulty saying something as simple as "No, thanks." Why couldn't everyone just look away while I turned Yusef down? Tekken had to be more interesting than this.

"Are you sure? It's no trouble for me."

"Isra's family is really strict," Sana said.

"Okay, then. Thanks." I don't know what it was that made me accept: it could have been the desire in his eyes, the slight sad slackness of his lips when I said no, or my fluttering heart.

Sana's eyes almost popped out of her head, and she mouthed, "What are you doing?" I shrugged and walked out the door Yusef was holding open for me.

Yusef wanted to know why my family didn't attend the masjid that was only a couple of miles from Sana's house. I turned my eyes to the road and swallowed hard. "We're not very religious," I said. I couldn't imagine us all going anywhere together except an occasional visit to a family friend's house. Most of the time Amu didn't have dinner with the family; I saved him a plate in the refrigerator.

"But they're strict?"

"About some things."

"So you live with your aunt and uncle?"

"They're relatives. He's my dad's cousin."

Halfway there, Yusef's car started to overheat, which must have been a regular occurrence, because he didn't seem alarmed. We had to drive the rest of the way with the heat blasting, though. We were both sweating profusely. "Man, your house is far away," he said, wiping his forehead.

"Sorry." *You didn't have to offer me a ride.* At least the city buses had air conditioning. I leaned my head further out the window in a futile effort to cool down.

"It's worth it."

About twenty minutes later we got into the neighborhood. "This is a pretty nice area," he said. "Must be good living here."

It wouldn't be so bad if I had the house to myself and didn't have to go to school or interact in any way with the spoiled kids around me. "It's all right." To avoid the subject and to be polite, I asked him about school, to see if I made a good decision transferring.

He parked the car a block away from the house and told me it wasn't too difficult, but it took a while for him to get used to the amount of work he had in his honors classes. Also, it was in the ghetto; there was a shooting in the area at least once a year, so they put the school on lockdown as a precaution. Cops had been on campus a few times. This terrified his mother, and she sometimes tried to talk him into going to the neighborhood school, which was a lot safer, even if it didn't have such a good academic program. What was the point of them moving across the world if their children were still going to be in danger? He dwelled on the danger of the area, and I knew it was no exaggeration. My father used to have an apartment less than a mile from the school, the last place where Mom and I lived with him. Yusef took the same concerned tone he described his mother taking; he was scared that I'd be too ignorant of the circumstances and end up getting hurt.

"I don't think I'll be in that much danger," I said. "I can blend into a crowd." Nobody knew I was alive at my middle school except to sneer when they were forced to talk to me.

"You haven't seen the crazy chicks at this school. They always get in fights because their boyfriends were looking at some other girl. 'Bitch he's mine!'" He pointed his forefinger accusingly at the windshield.

We both laughed. He threw his head back and opened his mouth wide when he did.

"I won't worry about stupid girls." I already had to worry about a stupid woman.

"I would. I think you'll get a lot of attention."

I looked away and stared at the part of his car door that was starting to come off at the top.

"I don't want those girls' boyfriends to look at you either."

I snorted and laughed. "Will you get into fights with them, too?"

"If it comes down to that."

Lena Mahmoud

I woke up late the first day of school, a regular occurrence for me then. I had time to put a stick of gum in my mouth and tie my hair back without combing it; if I missed the bus, I was screwed. The last thing I wanted to do was ask Amu or Amtu for a ride. If I got one of them to do it, I'd hear a lecture the whole way there about how stupid I was to transfer to a school so far away when the schools in this area were some of the best in the county, at least as good as the program for the gifted students at this low-class school that had gang fights and lockdowns all the time.

The adrenaline rush and the walk to the bus stop kept me up at first, but after sitting on the bus for ten minutes, the stuffy air and exhaustion got the best of me. I slept until someone nudged me when we stopped in front of the school. I reluctantly opened my eyes and saw loud crowds of teenagers in front of chain-link fences.

I tried to find Baba's apartment in the background, but I couldn't see it past the school's two-story buildings. By the time Mom and I moved here, she was so sick that we didn't have any walks together like we did before, so the scenery wasn't that familiar. Besides, she said, this was no place to take a leisurely stroll; it was too depressing. The only things to see were decaying buildings, scared people keeping alert, and fierce guard dogs in front of the houses or in the backyard, ready to gobble you up if you got too close.

Disorganization and crowds were the first things I noticed when I got on campus. The line for schedules stretched from the cafeteria to the amphitheater. I unsuccessfully looked for a sign that showed who had to go where, so I assumed the order was alphabetical and took my place in the last line since we only used Shadi instead of al-Shadi on our official documents.

I stood there impatiently, my legs aching. I scanned the area for possible seats, but if I sat down, I knew someone would take my spot in line. Already a few had tried to edge their way in, so I made sure to keep as little space as possible between me and the guy in front of me, even though he had atrocious body odor.

I felt a hand on my shoulder and heard my name, "Isra" pronounced perfectly. He had to be an Arab boy, but I didn't know many and not any that would come up to me at school. Yusef. I thought about him quite often, but in my rush to leave the house this morning, the possibility of seeing him hadn't entered my mind. He looked handsome and fresh-faced. Seeing him so close, I could tell he already shaved; he had short coarse whiskers in his pores.

I was embarrassed about my hair and my greasy skin. I managed a "Hi."

"How's your first day?"

"It hasn't really begun. I've been here since eight." I eyed the front of the line resentfully.

He nodded. "That's how everything is here." He looked ahead of us. "You know what? They probably didn't have half the schedules printed until nine, and they're coming out with more."

I sighed. "Why did they have us even come here this early?" The thought of lying in bed was almost too much to resist. If it didn't take so much energy, I would have started walking home.

"When you're a senior, they just mail your schedule to you." He stepped closer to me, close enough I could feel the heat coming off his body. "This will be here for hours. We can just go and hang out until it clears up."

"Okay." Even I couldn't believe how readily I accepted this time.

Once I sat down, my nerves calmed. His car was far from comfortable, but I felt ready to curl up in the passenger seat and fall asleep. Yusef suggested getting something to eat, so we stopped at one of the nearby fast food restaurants and ordered some breakfast. The building looked decayed, and one of the lowercase letters had fallen off the sign, but the food was edible and Yusef paid for it. He talked about his new job as a busboy at what he called a "hick diner." He felt grateful that he wasn't a waiter, because he couldn't understand half of what his clientele were saying. "People say we can't speak English just 'cause some people have an accent. At least my parents move their lips. But whatever—it's money." He laughed at his own statement and took a big bite of his hash browns. "Can you believe they hired me? I said I was Arab, and if there's something in Spanish, they still ask me to translate it for them." He shook his head and snickered.

I tore pieces off my wrapper and smiled for his sake. That struck me about him: how open he was about these things, even to someone he barely knew.

"What about your . . . your amu and amtu? How do they speak English?"

"Amu's English is better than Amtu's, but they speak pretty well." Amu had some schooling in English back in Palestine, and Amtu in Jordan, but it seemed like her English never improved the whole time I lived with them. I chuckled. "They're horrible at idioms and slang or anything like that."

He smiled and looked out the window. "My parents haven't been here that long, or, you know, they were pretty old by the time they came. Only me and Lubna were born here. Mama always says that American water's what made her finally get pregnant with a boy."

From what I gathered from Amu's stories, Baba was twenty-one when he came and Amu twenty-four, both with college degrees. They lost touch as Amu assiduously worked at his law career while Baba was unruly. Somehow Baba met Mom—I didn't know the story about that. Neither of my parents ever talked about it. Amu Nasser went back home to find a wife.

Yusef looked back at me. "You're quiet," he said.

I shrugged. "That's the way I am." If he had a problem with it, I didn't care. He could find some other girl to hang out with if I wasn't to his taste.

He picked up his cup and swirled the straw in there, making the ice cubes clink against each other. He sank back into his seat and looked ahead at me. "You're beautiful."

I looked down at my hands, at the leftover wrappers, at the ads beneath them. I couldn't have blushed more deeply; I felt it throughout my whole body, and I had no words to say back to him. You are, too. I like you. It was true but so hard to admit. I said it, though, after a long pause, and he took my hand and kissed my fingertips.

CHAPTER FIVE

Imm Yusef insisted that I have my dress made by one of her old friends, whose family was responsible for introducing Imm Yusef's family to Abu Yusef's when they finally found a permanent settlement in a village right outside Nablus. Imm Yusef gave me a more detailed history of her meeting her future husband and of this seamstress, but she kept referring to people and situations I had never heard of, so it didn't make much sense. I just knew I needed to go to this woman to make the dress.

I had no problem with the decision before she gave me an extensive history of the dressmaker. As for the dress, I didn't have my heart set on anything or any ideas about what I might want other than something that made me look slim and attractive.

But I knew I didn't want Amtu there, though this was the only aspect of my wedding she seemed to care about.

On the way there, I could only think about the old days when I used to have to go clothes shopping with Amtu. Once I got a job of my own at the end of high school, I started buying my clothes myself; all she'd ever buy for me were bargain-store clothes, and she always claimed that they never fit right because I was too fat or too tall for women's clothes, even at ten or eleven years old.

I braced myself for the experience during the fitting, comforting myself with the fact that this would be the last time I would ever do this. Just as I expected, once the old woman took my waist measurement of thirty-one inches, Amtu suggested in her sweetest tone—one I only ever heard in front of people outside of the family—that I should lose some inches before my wedding.

Imm Yusef was sitting next to Amtu, saying something to the seamstress in Arabic. She interrupted herself to say, "That is not so very big." I appreciated her defending me, but I wasn't sure if it was because Imm Yusef liked me or because she hated Amtu a lot more than me. The seamstress also chimed in, claiming a real man wanted a woman with a bit of meat on her bones so she could handle his "manliness." Imm Yusef and Amtu stood with their arms crossed, each refusing to look at the other in a sort of reverse staring contest, but the seamstress threw her head back and showed her dentures as she laughed at her own comment.

On the way out, Imm Yusef invited Amtu and me to Yusef's apartment to give me a chance to see it before the wedding. "It is so very small, but he will move out soon for when there are children," she said. "You can invite your husband, yes? Abu Yusef maybe come a little late. He watch the store until after dinnertime."

Amtu smiled and agreed to come, but she doubted Amu could be there on a Saturday evening. We gave hugs and kisses as we left, but before Amtu and I got to the car, she leaned in close to my ear, nearly spitting on me. "I will not go there," she said. "Imagine what such a place looks like."

"I'll go by myself." I didn't like the idea of being alone with Yusef and his mother, but it was a lot better that I only had to worry about my behavior instead of mine and Amtu's.

Because only Hanan and I were going to Yusef's apartment, he came to the house to pick us up to make sure we wouldn't get lost on the way, though it was just a few blocks from the university I had been going to for four years.

"Why would Mama be mad that I'm going with you?" Hanan asked while I was putting on makeup in the bathroom.

"You know how your mother is." I pressed my lips together and looked at the brown-pink on my lips, deciding if it was right, if it made me look put together but still conservative enough for Imm Yusef's taste. She'd probably prefer some red or even purplish lipstick, from what I saw of her taste in makeup at the engagement ceremony.

The doorbell rang while I was brushing my hair. Hanan went to get the door, and I closed the one to the bathroom, considered locking it. I didn't know why I felt the butterflies in my belly all of a sudden, but I continued brushing my hair. I heard his voice, then Hanan's, though I couldn't tell what they were saying. I sat down and tied my hair in a messy bun. *It's not like today is the wedding. We're just going to his apartment for dinner.*

I composed myself and met them both by the door. Hanan said she had to go to the garage to set the security alarm before we left, leaving Yusef and me alone. "So there's no one else in the house? What about your other cousin?"

I shook my head. "He's never here."

He reached into his back pocket and pulled out a dark velvet jewelry box. With all the money he and his parents were spending on our wedding, I wondered how he could afford to buy jewelry. I smiled and opened the box to find a gold necklace with a heart-shaped locket. "Thank you so much." I hugged him and kissed his cheek.

He held me close and kissed my hair, let his nose linger for a few seconds, tickling my scalp. He pulled away to put the necklace on. "Mama told me that'd be a good choice. You could put one of our wedding pictures in there."

"Your mother picked it out?"

He rested his hands on my shoulders. "Yeah, I needed a woman's opinion." Yusef had three sisters, yet he always went to his mother to get a "woman's opinion." I didn't mean to, but I asked him why he never wanted his sisters' opinions.

"I used to, but they're all so busy now that they're married—taking care of their kids and all." His face fell into something that was not quite a frown but not the bright smile he had on before. "You like it?"

"Yes, I just wondered."

He gave me a soft kiss on the lips. "I know Mama's intense about the wedding and everything, but she'll calm down. She's usually not like this." He parted his lips and leaned in for another kiss.

I heard Hanan's footsteps approaching in no time, but I couldn't pull myself away until she opened the door from the garage to the kitchen, making enough noise for Yusef to hear because the door always stuck. When she came into the living room, I noticed that all my gloss was on his lips with a smear on his two front teeth. I wiped it off with my palm, and Hanan averted her eyes like I was undressing him. "I need to get my purse," I said.

He nodded vigorously. "Uh, yeah, that's fine. Take your time, Isra. Mama's still cooking."

Hanan opened and then closed her mouth without saying anything. She went into the kitchen for no reason.

I got my things quickly, and we were on our way out. The silence was too much for me to handle, so I thanked Yusef for coming out of his way to pick us up. "No problem. It's a relief. Mama gets pretty crazy when we're expecting company. She's gotta clean every crevice in the house, make sure everything looks new and the food's perfect."

"My mama's like that, too," Hanan said. Except Amtu Samia hardly did any of the work herself. She only criticized.

Yusef opened the backseat door for her. "Yeah, it's an Arab woman thing."

"Of course. Everyone will judge you if it's not perfect." I folded my arms and felt my stomach turn.

"Women are always hard on each other." He placed a hand on my lower back and opened the car door.

Yusef's apartment smelled like meat stew and cumin. The apartment's appearance was no surprise to me: bright white walls, brown carpet, tiny kitchen, and a narrow hallway. Inexpensive one-bedroom apartments had not changed much in the last fifteen years. I had lived in two with Mom that could be mistaken for this one, but ours rarely had such a strong food smell. When Mom was healthy, she worked all day as a clerical assistant, sometimes Saturdays, so she never made anything too complicated. Most of it came out of a box, spaghetti with premade sauce, macaroni and cheese, tuna sandwiches. Yusef's bedroom reminded me of the rooms I slept in with Mom; we shared a bed until Mom got too sick and we moved into Baba's apartment with its dingy walls and more cockroaches than I'd ever seen in my life.

I sat down on Yusef's lumpy full-size bed and tried to keep the tears from coming to my eyes, knowing that he would interpret them as those of a spoiled rich girl, one who could not stand the thought of the demotion in status by having to live in such a small, plain place. That was how little he knew about me, and our wedding was only a month away. "I'm so tired," I offered as an explanation, which was not a complete lie. Memories were always draining.

He put his hand on my shoulder. "Why?"

I stared ahead at the wall. Imm Yusef came to the door. "What are you childrens doing in here?" She was already mad that the only chaperone we had for our car ride over here was a teenage girl; she had expected Amtu to come at least.

"Nothing. Just looking, Mama."

She told us the food was almost done, and Hanan was out there waiting. I wanted to lie down on the bed and sleep, but I got up and left the bedroom under Imm Yusef's suspicious eyes.

Abu Yusef arrived for dinner, and Imm Yusef kept on insisting that everyone eat more all the way through dessert. Abu Yusef didn't have dessert; he couldn't wait to sit on the couch and smoke. He must have smoked at least four cigarettes while we ate, and Imm Yusef kept on complaining to him in Arabic. She even got up once and put one of his cigarettes out, and their argument intensified for a few minutes. He lit another as soon as she walked away. "Welcome to my childhood," Yusef whispered to me and put his hand on mine.

"He smokes right in the house?" That was the only thing that surprised me. I'd been spending hours every week at his parents' house. I had seen plenty of these disagreements before.

"He's old."

"Take more dessert, ya Hanan," Imm Yusef said, already spooning another square of it on her plate. "Abu Yusef has no manners, smoking right in the house with guests! 'Ayb, 'ayb." She clicked her tongue and went about making more tea.

I was sleepy by the time we got home, so I changed into my pajamas and took off my makeup, and lying down made every muscle in my body gradually relax itself. These days were so exhausting for me; I had finals and papers coming up, work, visiting Imm Yusef so I could watch her plan the wedding, and family visits with Yusef. On top of that, Yusef asked me as soon as Hanan got out of the car if we could meet alone. "Without my crazy parents," he said, grinning. And my insane relatives, too, he probably wanted to add. I felt the temptation to say yes, but I only gave him a maybe. At this point, it seemed like another obligation that I had to fulfill.

And anyway, I had no time to squeeze in meeting him without looking suspicious to Amtu. Normally she didn't care about what I did as long as I cooked and cleaned, now that Hanan didn't need to be watched all the time, but ever since my engagement, she kept her eye on me to make sure I didn't mess anything up. She kept track of my work schedule to make sure I wasn't staying out later than I should be, and when I went to see Imm Yusef, she always called their house to make sure that was where I was going and that I came back in a reasonable amount of time.

I had tomorrow to think of these things, though.

I was just about to doze when Hanan quietly called my name.

"Yeah?"

"Are you really going to, like, go through with it and everything?"

"Umm . . . of course. I mean, it's only a month away. It seems a little late to break it off." I sighed. "Why?"

"Oh, you know, are you really going to live in that apartment? His dad smokes in there, and it's so small."

I turned over on my other side so I could see her. She had her knees to her chest. "Well, it is only a one-bedroom. Those are usually small."

"I was just wondering."

I turned back over on my other side, keeping my back to Hanan. I suppose I had some time every other morning to see Yusef. Nothing could get Amtu out of bed early unless it had something to do with Amu.

Yusef had coffee ready for me when I arrived. It was strong instant coffee that needed more sugar or milk, but I thanked him. We sat down on his couch, his hand on my knee. I faintly smelled his father's cigarettes from a couple of days before.

"I would have made some food, but I noticed this morning that I didn't have anything to make." He laughed and took a drink from his coffee cup.

I didn't imagine Imm Yusef's only son cooking for himself, the prince she considered him to be, but it was something that he knew how to make a decent cup of coffee with the help of a machine. I'd be surprised if Rasheed knew how to operate a coffee maker or fry an egg.

"What about you? Do you cook a lot?"

Maybe this was an interview to see how good a wife I would make.

I stirred the coffee with the spoon and sipped some from that, focusing on a water stain right in front of me. "I cook almost every day. I don't know if it's that good." I did know that Imm Yusef's food was better. A lot better.

He put his arm around my shoulders, shaking me up enough to almost spill coffee on the front of my shirt. We laughed and kissed; he tucked a lock of my hair behind my ear and caressed my cheek with his thumb. We ended up talking most of the time, and I rested my head on his lap. Our conversation turned to children. It had to be the first time I ever discussed this with anyone, and I always went back and forth on whether I would want to have some. "Two would be good," I said.

"A girl and a boy?"

"No, two girls. Boys run around the house naked and pee in your face."

He chuckled. "Come on, boys aren't that bad, but I like girls, too. They're so cute and sweet." He went on about his three nieces, about how much he loved them, how much they loved their khalu, their maternal uncle. He took me to his bedroom and showed me a box he kept of drawings and other crafts that his younger nieces and nephews made in school or at home. One was him as a stick figure in red crayon with his name misspelled on the top, "Uncle Useef."

I held on to his arm and smiled. "How old is she?"

"Three. She's my youngest niece." He raised his eyebrows mischievously when he looked over at me. "Two boys and four girls would be good for us."

"Six?"

"Yeah."

"Maybe you need a second wife to have the other four."

He laughed. "Why'd your aunt and uncle only have two?"

I hesitated. "Amtu had some trouble with pregnancies. She had a miscarriage when Hanan was four or something, and they found something wrong with her uterus."

"Cancer?"

I kept my eyes down on his niece's drawing. "I don't know for sure. I was pretty young, and they didn't talk about it."

"That must be hard."

I went to his house every Monday and Friday morning for a couple of hours, and Amtu didn't seem to take note of this change in my schedule.

I left before nine, so I doubted she was even up, but I asked Hanan a few times about anything she heard her mother talking about when I wasn't there. I also looked in my rearview mirror for almost the whole drive to his apartment, making sure that no car was following me. Hanan said I was paranoid. "You're acting like Mama's a secret agent or something," she told me. "She wouldn't follow you in a car. She hates driving anyway."

At first I thought it was ridiculous that everyone kept such a close eye on us to make sure that we didn't do anything haraam. I mean, we were going to be married; the wait wasn't that long. We could resist temptation.

But lately when I was around him, it seemed like all I could think about was how warm his skin felt against mine, his hands that were just rough enough to be manly, and the way his eyes softened when he looked at me. When I was at work, too, or in class, or finishing up my last assignments as a college student, my mind would wander to Yusef. I wasn't this bad even as a teenager. Probably because we were better at keeping our hands off each other back then.

After that first day we rarely had any serious conversations. We kissed and explored each other's bodies. I could always feel his hard-on pushing against me and the pulsating wetness between my legs, but we both kept our clothes on.

"Imagine what it'll be like when we're married, when we get to see each other every day. None of this sneaking-around bullshit." He stroked the back of my hair while I snuggled up to his neck, breathing in his musky scent on his bed.

"What made you ask for me?"

His eyes met mine, and he grinned. "Because I had to have you."

"But why right then? Why not wait until the fall, when you're graduating?"

He sighed and ran his fingers through my hair. He gave me a few syrupy and vague answers: he couldn't stop thinking about me, he lost a piece of his heart every day he was without me, blah, blah, blah. Eventually I coaxed the truth out of him.

"I was at Khadija's house for dinner one night, and her husband had this friend over. You know Abu Bilal?" He examined my face for a reaction.

"Should I?"

"It's good you don't remember him—he's not much to remember. But he wanted to marry you. He was going on about how you were such a 'rose,' and then when it was just us guys, he was talking about what a 'womanly body' you had, and a 'beautiful face.'" His mouth tightened, his tongue moving over his teeth underneath the skin. I had never seen that expression before. He shook his head over and over. "I almost killed that guy. I wasn't going to let him take my woman just 'cause he's got a four-bedroom house and a nice car."

"Oh, he's the one with the white ex-wife and the three kids?" That was what Amu and Amtu kept on repeating: he has big house and nice car, and he was married to an Amreekiya before, so he'll be okay if you don't always act like a lady because you know Amreekiyaat don't know how to act like proper ladies the way Palestinian women do.

"Yeah, he's got an American ex-wife. I think he has three, yes . . . I know he's got kids at least. He's forty-five or something." He kissed my neck and ran his tongue down the middle in a way that made me moan while he cupped my breast. "He can't do this for you. You don't want some old guy, popping Viagra pills just so he can enjoy your 'womanly body.'"

CHAPTER SIX

I had been up nearly the whole night, scrubbing the kitchen and the living room walls. We were having company the next day, which we did at least once or twice a month back then, but something about this company coming over was different. I wasn't sure why, but Amtu Samia was even more insane about having every inch of the house clean. Earlier that night, when we had come back from a family friend's, she screamed in my face that the house looked like a pigsty. She claimed the walls and kitchen floor were filthy, and she hit me upside the head and told me to get it done.

"It's not even that dirty, you crazy bitch!" I yelled in her face.

That's when Amu Nasser intervened and twisted my ear so hard I thought it'd fall off. My eyes filled with tears.

"Don't talk to your amtu this way. What is wrong with you, ya hiwana, you animal?" He ordered me to clean the walls and floors until my hands were so tired they fell off. If I mouthed off again, he would do much worse to me.

"You came from trash, so you don't know cleanliness," Amtu Samia added.

Hanan's six-year-old eyes were wide and her lower lip was trembling; even Rasheed looked a little frightened, but he went right up to his room to avoid any trouble. "I'll help, Baba," Hanan offered.

He pointed to the room we shared. "No, you will go to bed. It is a school night."

Never mind that I had school the next day.

I stormed off and changed into my cleaning clothes, banging anything I could the whole time. I did the same when I made the soap mixture, and the real noise started when I was cleaning the walls with the adjustable mop. With every stroke, I made sure to slam the mop against the wall, and not long into my cleaning, Amu came down in his pajamas and yelled at me to keep it down. I was already steaming, and seeing his anger only fueled mine. "I can't get it clean without touching the wall, you know."

He slapped my face and told me to drop the attitude. And then I heard the lecture I knew so well: he saved me from the streets and gave me a good home, and all I did was complain when I had to give anything back. "I am finished," he said. "I am done with your shit."

I wanted to throw the bucket of soap at him, and I was tired enough for my self-control to be at a minimum. He went back up the stairs. I left the mop in the laundry room to dry and stood in the garage, thinking about leaving in my cleaning clothes, saying goodbye to no one, taking nothing with me. It's not like I had much of value: no money, a few outfits, letters from my family in Ramallah, and a small photo album from Mom. I couldn't leave without that, and getting that meant I'd have to go back to the room with Hanan and say goodbye.

And I had nowhere to go, no one to take me in. No friends at all.

On the way back in, I grabbed the stepladder and a dry squeegee to wash the walls, ignoring the tears running down my face.

I wasn't done until three in the morning, and I was too restless to go to bed, so I pulled out some books and the small photo album I hid in the slit in the box spring of my bed. I knew that Amtu often went through my stuff, and I didn't know what she'd do to it, the spiteful bitch. The only good thing I got out of that night was that Amtu Samia never laid a hand on me again. I suppose I scared her by my sharp retaliation, and I was already as tall as she was and probably twice as strong.

I made myself comfortable on the couch and looked through the photos. There were only five or six of Mom, but it was what I had left of her. She had some of her family, her parents' wedding and family vacation photos, two of her and Baba together. I stopped at the wedding photo of her parents, two twenty-somethings smiling into the camera, unaware that their only child would later have a swarthy, curly-haired bastard and that they would leave her to die practically by herself.

For a short second the thought that they might decide that they were wrong about distancing themselves from Mom and me and might take me in entered my mind, but it was so crazy that I shook my head and snickered at my own thought. I should have found them just to spit in their faces, to tell them that I'd rather jump off a cliff than have them in my life, call them my family. Call anyone my family.

I was exhausted the next morning and overslept, so I barely made it to school on time. The day dragged on, and all I thought about was sleeping. I didn't pay attention at all, just doodled on my notebook to keep myself up. The walk home from my middle school was slightly under a mile on flat ground, but it felt like an uphill journey that day.

When I finally got home, I listened to the message on the machine: Hanan's teacher saying that no one picked her up, or "Hannah" as she said; the school required her to stay in class until four-thirty, about an hour after school let out, but if there was some family emergency, she could stay longer. She'd like a call back so she and Hannah wouldn't be worried about what was going on.

I held myself back from crying out. The last thing I needed was to go pick up Hanan from school before I had to make a big dinner for our company, not giving me a second to take a quick nap. I was so tired that I was about to fall over.

No, I wouldn't take it. Amtu couldn't still be sleeping at this hour, and why the fuck did she need to be? She got to sleep all damn night while I cleaned up for her guests. I stomped up the stairs and went into the bedroom without knocking. I heard Rasheed's TV in the background. Typical: Hanan's teacher had probably called after he got home, but he would never be expected to pick up the phone or his little sister. I could have strangled him, too.

I saw just what I expected, Amtu sleeping in the bed, except her snoring sounded strange and uneven like she was having to catch her breath with each snore.

"Amtu?" I felt a twinge of embarrassment: that was the first time in a while that I called her Amtu to her face. Usually I didn't address her and avoided speaking to her at all costs. "Amtu? It's really late, and Hanan's still at school."

Still the same weird breathing sound.

My stomach turned in on itself. Amtu Samia had seizures—that's why she decided to get sterilized. But it had been a few years since her last one, and they were supposed to have been taken care of. I turned on the light and took the blanket off her. Her eyes were bugged out. It seemed like she was choking. "Amtu? What happened?" I saw two empty bottles of medication on her side.

I should have jumped to the phone and called 911 right away, but I hesitated. This woman had done everything to make me wish that I was dead and had taken out every bad feeling she had all these years on me. She'd live and never thank me and keep me as her slave.

I made the call anyway. The man on the phone told me an ambulance would be there as soon as possible, and to try and pump her stomach and make her vomit. As soon as I got off the phone, I yelled for Rasheed while I did the pumping, adrenaline the only thing keeping me going.

Amtu puked all over the bed right when the paramedics got to the door; the smell and the sight of it made me gag. Rasheed was still on the phone with his father, keeping him updated on his mother's status between sobs. I went down to let the medics in, and they quickly jogged up the stairs. I was only halfway up behind them by the time they had her loaded on the stretcher, Rasheed trailing, wiping his red eyes. When they left with her, he cried, sitting on the stairs, his shoulders sagging. I looked at the small clock on the living room wall; it was just after four.

"I'm going to pick up Hanan." I'd barely make it there in time, but leaving was better than staying there.

Once I fell asleep, I dreamed about Amtu's corpse: her severed head in the cleaning supplies beneath the sink, her body lying on a shelf in the pantry, in my bed, on the sofa. She was on the front lawn, splayed like the Vitruvian Man. Her face was pale, her lips bluish-purple, and her eyes open wide. I ran screaming down the street until I was out of breath and collapsed on the pavement. The pain of the fall was enough to startle me awake in my dream. Mom told me that I had been sleeping for years, and Amu Nasser and Amtu Samia and Hanan and Rasheed were all figments of my imagination. Baba had no family here in the United States, especially not in the same town.

Then I really woke up when Hanan opened the door. I yawned and asked her what time it was. Seven-thirty. I remembered I had already gotten the call about Amtu Samia being all right. They were just keeping her for observation and psychological evaluation. Also, Amu gave me all the names and numbers of the people I had to call to say that our dinner would be canceled. "Tell them that Amtu is in the hospital because—"

"—she's having an appendectomy?" I filled in right away, something my teacher had mentioned in my science class that day.

He paused for a minute. "Yes, yes, say this," he said absentmindedly. He ended the call with an order to take care of Hanan and cook dinner.

I made the calls and told Hanan her mom was in the hospital because she had gotten a little sick. Then I went to bed right away. The day had been exhausting, and it wouldn't kill Hanan and Rasheed to make sandwiches or ramen for themselves. There were things a lot worse than that, and they knew that now.

"Did you eat yet?" I asked Hanan.

She nodded. "I had three bowls of cereal. Each time I got a different one."

"Wow. Really?" I was groggy, but I humored her anyway. I was about the same age when we first found out Mom was sick, but the doctors said her chances of survival were good because she was so young. Life had a cruel way of misleading you.

I went out and had a bowl of cereal myself while Hanan talked. "Is Mama okay?"

"Yeah, that's what your dad said."

"You know, Rasheed gave me a hug today, and his eyes were all red, so I don't think she's okay."

I didn't want to have to keep pushing this lie, but how could I explain suicide to a six-year-old, especially her own mother's? "He was just surprised that it happened. He wasn't expecting it, and we were both together when we saw her fall."

"Oh." She bunched the bedsheet in her hands. "Did your mama get sick?"

"Yes."

"Did you cry?"

"Yeah, I cried a lot." I still cry. Just last night I did. Tears came to my eyes right then.

"Mama won't die, right, like your mama did?"

"No, I don't think so."

Amu came back early the next morning and made breakfast for us before he woke us all up. I didn't know he could cook. And instead of blaming me, he thanked me for taking care of Hanan and letting her sleep in my bed for the night. I also didn't know that he was capable of gratitude.

Rasheed and I were quiet at the table, only giving concise responses to something Amu said, but Hanan was excited to see her father again and kept talking to him. She was always a daddy's girl, something I found slightly sickening, but I guess I couldn't blame her for it. Though Rasheed had been the spoiled favorite since he was a boy, Hanan received most of the affection when Amu was around, which was less and less these days, and that change must have been what made her work harder and harder to keep him home. She was too young to realize how tenuous fatherhood—or, for that matter, life—was, but her parents were making their best efforts to show her.

CHAPTER SEVEN

The cosmetologist stayed away from heavy eye shadow and dark lips, but she still ironed my hair and put it up in a messy bun (the fashionable kind, not like the ones I did most days). I went back home with Amtu Samia and Hanan to get my dress, and then Rasheed and Amu Nasser joined us on the way to the mosque to have the imam marry us. I had never been to one of these before. Only immediate family were invited, or, in my case, the family I lived with. Basically, all the imam did was ask if Amu would give Yusef, who was standing by his father, my hand in marriage, and he agreed while I watched from the sidelines with Hanan, Amtu, and Imm Yusef. They shook hands, and Amu pulled Yusef in for a hug and kisses. "Mabrook, ya ibnee!" he said to Yusef, so elated that he'd finally found an acceptable way to get rid of me. Ya ibnee—what a crock! He'd never considered me his daughter, so how could Yusef be his son?

Abu Yusef and Rasheed gave their congratulations to Yusef as well, and Imm Yusef gave me a bone-crushing hug and a thousand kisses on the cheeks. When she was done, I looked over at Hanan, who was tearing up and wiping them away with her fingers. I knew she wasn't a happy crier, so I put my arm around her and asked what was wrong, though I didn't expect her to be honest in such a crowd. "Now you're going to leave," she said.

I could feel the tension in the room increase when she said that. "Bass, bass, Hanan," Amtu Samia told her. "This is what every woman does."

"My son is very nice man, habibti. He will be nice to your cousin."

"I won't hog her too much," Yusef said, laughing while he placed his hand protectively on my back.

"I'm okay. I know." She blushed and wiped the tears from her cheeks.

Amu Nasser pulled her close to him and told her that there would be a great party now and that I would be happy with my new husband and new life. Besides, she would still get to see me; I would still be close by.

It was a lot easier than the engagement ceremony; there was no stage, no ring exchange, only some pictures before the party. Outside it was hot and humid, and my dress felt sticky and heavy by the end of the night. Everyone congratulated me, and most gave me hugs. The older women had advice, stories, and praise. For a couple of hours I was caught up in the festivities, dancing the dabka with the women and children and being lost in the moment. I started to feel tired only after I sat down not long after dark, drinking some ice water and having some food. I hadn't had an appetite all day long and only ate a small breakfast, but now I could hardly keep myself from inhaling the food.

"Wow, you're really hungry," Sana said when I got up to go to the buffet table for thirds.

"I've had a busy day." I looked at the crowd to find Hanan, but I couldn't see her. Last time I saw her, she was meeting up with some of her friends. She seemed better once we got to the reception. Maybe it wasn't so stupid of Amu to comfort her with the fact that a big party would follow.

Sana tapped her heel against one of the legs of the table, scanning the crowds in front of us before she leaned in and whispered, "And a long night ahead of you."

It was past one in the morning by the time Yusef and I were on the road, heading to my new home. He drank coffee out of a Styrofoam cup and told me about his experience, smoking the arjila and shooting the shit with the other younger guys—apparently Rasheed wasn't "that bad"— and listening to the older men tell stories about their weddings. "You know, I can't believe this day has actually come," he said. He took his hand off the clutch, put it on mine, and smiled.

I smiled and nodded. I was relieved that it was over. No more parading, no more lectures, no more sneaking around.

Sitting down and taking off my heels was a short relief, but once he wrapped his arms around my waist, all the tension descended back on me again. I told him I needed to freshen up, take a shower, because I was so sweaty and caked with makeup. He nodded, pouty and put off. We undressed at the same time, but he was out of his tux in a couple of minutes. He came closer to me when he went to the closet to hang it up and cover it with plastic. I was trying to take my last sleeve off, but my skin was damp and the dress was a little too small in the first place, so that I nearly tripped trying to take it off. He caught me and laughed and asked if I needed any help.

I rushed to the bathroom and made the water as hot as I could, steaming up the tiny room instantly. I stared ahead at the wall and wiped the black eyeliner from my cheeks and eyes. It was much easier to do this unplanned, spur of the moment, so my body wouldn't clench like this. I dried myself off and took a long look in the mirror. I covered my body with the towel. I couldn't look at myself right now. How could I let him see me?

Thirty to forty minutes must have passed, and I just had to make myself go out there. I put my slip on and brushed my hair back, my stomach still in a knot when I walked out the door. Yusef was lying down on the bed, his eyes closed. I sat in front of him and hesitated before I rubbed his forearm. He opened his eyes and grinned, staring at my loose breasts. "I thought you escaped through the bathroom window," he said.

"I can't be a runaway bride; we're already married." If the days of planning with his mother, the engagement party, and the dress fitting hadn't run me off, Yusef's penis definitely wouldn't.

I leaned in and kissed his lips softly. He sat up and tried to pull the slip over my head. It caught a little on my arms because I didn't lift them high enough, so I finished the job and slid it off. We both laughed nervously, and he apologized as he kissed my shoulder and cupped one of my breasts. I closed my eyes and pulled him down on top of me. I clenched my teeth as he put himself inside me, and gasped when the pain was too much for me to hold back.

Yusef went to sleep not long after, clutching his pillow and snoring softly. My thoughts weren't keeping me up. My legs were. I was so bored I counted how many times Yusef's snore descended into a breath. When I got to 734, I decided I was too restless to sleep and quietly left the bed. It was so hot. His body spread warmth like a heated blanket. I needed some air, some space.

I went to the living room and opened the only window. The cool night air felt so good that my heavy eyelids closed, and I thought I might get some sleep while standing up, but as I leaned back, my head hit the wall and woke me up again.

I heard voices from the sidewalk, so I looked below. It was a group of three, and though I couldn't see them well, from the sound of their voices I guessed they were two guys and a girl, all drunk. No surprise. After all, it was a Friday night at an apartment complex right across the street from the university; three or four in the morning wasn't late. Yusef must have done that, especially when he was sharing an apartment with a college buddy, not even a year ago. Sana's oldest brother Bassam got his own apartment a few years ago. One time she and her parents stopped by, and they saw three empty bottles of Southern Comfort, a smoked roach, and his laundry scattered around the floor and countertops. Though Sana saw her father's face tighten, he only said through clenched teeth, "If your grades fall, I will snap you like a twig between my fingers."

"You know if it was me, or my sister, Baba would have snapped us like a twig right then and there," she said. We always did that: commiserate about how easy men had it.

I noticed a man staring at me from his window across the way, licking his lips. I was only wearing my slip, and my cleavage protruded while I was leaning over. I felt exposed. More exposed than when Yusef saw me naked. Was there any privacy here?

I slid the window shut, put the lock down, and closed the curtain. Windows scared Mom, too, at least when it came to me. Ever since I could remember, I made a habit of looking out of them, just watching the way cats do, even pulling up a chair when I was too short to see out of them, so Mom always made sure the lock was down. At Baba's, there was no lock, and Mom asked him several times to buy some because she was afraid that as soon as no one was looking, I might go to the window, reach my head out too far, and fall out. She kept nagging him for a couple of months, but chemo gave her a short temper. She roared at him, her face livid: "Why can't you just be a man, at least some of the time? That's all I ask!"

And he finally bought the locks.

CHAPTER EIGHT

During our trip to Falasteen ten years ago, Amu was embarrassed by how little we children knew of Arabic and Islam. Whenever relatives would meet us for the first time, they'd start talking to us in Arabic, and we'd have a blank look on our faces. Then they would look to Amu Nasser or Amtu Samia and say, " 'Ayb!"—For shame! (I at least knew that much Arabic)—and then something else, probably criticizing us for being too American. What made it worse was that none of us knew how to pray. It apparently involved a lot of kneeling, opening your hands, and looking to the side while reciting a sura; somehow you had to know when to do which. You couldn't just open your palms and look up at the sky and ask for things like Christians did, the way people did in movies. Amtu Samia didn't seem to care that much—she was pretty snooty around my family and Amu Nasser's and wasn't going to explain anything to these low-class people—but I saw the rosy tint of shame come to Amu Nasser's face every time he had to admit that all three of us spoke hardly any Arabic.

So within a few months Amu enrolled us in a brand-new Sunday school, located in an office complex, to learn about Islam and Arabic—at least Qur'anic Arabic, which would be of no use when speaking to modern-day Arab people but was better than nothing in his eyes, I suppose.

I wasn't against the idea of having another day of school like Rasheed and Hanan, but the thought of being around other Arab kids intimidated me. First, I couldn't speak Arabic, so the ones who did usually looked down on me for that. Second, I had a white mother. One more strike and I wouldn't be Arab at all.

It turned out that not many students at the school spoke fluent Arabic, and some weren't even Arab. Though we were taught that the prophet Muhammad believed an Arab was anyone who could speak Arabic, it was far from true, at least here. The non-Arab kids—mostly Pakistanis, Iranians, and a few black kids—were not berated too badly for their mispronunciation of Arabic words, because they weren't expected to know the language, but when it came to the Arab kids, color played a huge role in how badly you got nailed for such a mistake. If you were light, especially with a dark teacher, you had to pronounce all the guttural sounds perfectly, reaching deep in your throat to create the sound for the letters haa' and 'ayn and ghayn, or you were a miserable excuse for an Arab. But if you were dark enough, you didn't have to worry about how your vowels sounded and could say your haa' like an English *h*, soften your 'ayn into *a*, and make your ghayn into *g*, as long as you memorized the sura verse.

On our first oral quiz, the Arabic alphabet, I even heard one of the dark girls run all her letters together so that all twenty-eight of them sounded like one really long word. Our teacher said nothing, gave her a passing score without comment.

I only learned the alphabet and the Qur'an's opening sura "Al-Fatihah," which you were supposed to recite when you started a prayer (something I still didn't know how to do). My pronunciation was usually on the mark, except for a couple of times with my haa', when I only said it at the top of my throat like an Amreekiya, as my teacher, Brother Radwan, didn't hesitate to tell me before he snickered and mimicked me. Though they tried to advance us every three months depending on how many of the suras we knew, I didn't advance once in the six months I was there. But I didn't bear the brunt of the criticism: I was light-skinned, but I had dark curls and dark eyes to make me look Arab enough. Passable at least. The school had some students with light hair and light skin, some even with blue or green eyes—though most of them had two Arab parents, more Arab than me. Those were the kids who really heard it when they did not pronounce their consonants strongly or emphasize their vowels enough, and they tried harder to pronounce the words correctly. Of course, it wasn't all bad for them, either. They were always the most attractive unless they had some disfigurement like a harelip, and because most would assume they were white, it was probably easier for them around other people. They didn't have to explain what they were, because the other people thought they already knew.

Sunday school was like regular school: everyone broke off into cliques. We were separated by age and, of course, gender (the boys and the girls were supposed to sit at opposite ends of the class). Groups became more particular, though. The ones who spoke Arabic hung out together and felt like they were better than the rest of us, and we non-Arabic-speaking students came up with our own method for sorting people. The dark ones had their own groups and felt superior because they were true Arabs and knew more about their culture than we would ever know; the lighter ones formed a coalition and felt superior because we were more worldly and educated and attractive. I was surprised I made it into the "light" category. We were the darkest people in our neighborhood except for the Indian family that lived two blocks away.

It seemed like a lot of pointless work to remember all this, too, because once these kids weren't around a bunch of other Arabs, the lighter ones would pretend they were Greek or Italian or Eastern European, and the dark ones would suddenly become Mexicans. I recognized a few from my middle school, and I would never have known they were Arab, even if I came up to them and asked.

The only good that came of it was that I met Sana after about a month. During the lunch break they gave us between our grammar and religion lessons, I told everyone how much I hated Brother Radwan, the snickering asshole who had the nerve to say that I wasn't learning suras because I liked seeing his face every week. I was on guard while I spoke and kept my voice down, because he liked to walk around the small office complex and catch the students doing bad things, like an uppity half-breed girl talking shit on a great educator who donated his time to teaching Muslim youth about their religion. Sana was in the same class as me and responded loudly to my complaints: "I can't stand looking at that dude's feet. Seriously, if he's going to wear sandals, he's got to shave those feet. I just have a few stray hairs on my toes, and I get rid of them before I wear flip-flops. I thought my dad had some hairy feet, but that guy's got him beat. Ugh!" She shuddered.

Two of the other girls chuckled, but it sent me into a long belly laugh.

Amani, Sana's older sister who liked to brag about what a good Muslim she was by not eating pork or anything that may have been made from pork, like gelatin or Hot Cheetos, but wore tight jeans and green contact lenses, was not pleased with the comment. "Sana, that's so mean," she said with her hands on her hips.

"It's true. Those are pubes on his feet."

The other girls were scandalized, but I only laughed harder. From then on, if he passed by or quizzed one of us on the spot, Sana would stare down at his feet, and I'd fight back laughter. The other girls here were so prim and proper and pretended to be deaf to anything remotely lewd. It was the same way at regular school unless you were one of the slutty girls who already had sex or gave blow jobs. Even those girls hardly owned up to knowing those things around other girls. They just let boys use them so they'd be popular.

We had an amicable split from the rest of the group. We hung out, just the two of us, between two big trees for shade and talked. One day, totally unprovoked, some boy named Motabel came up to Sana and told her she was ugly.

She looked away. "Get the hell out of here."

He folded his arms and raised his chin smugly. "If I leave, it's not gonna make you any less ugly."

His reasoning, or lack of it, was funny to me, but I didn't laugh because it would seem like I was siding with him. "And you're the cutest guy in the world, aren't you, Pizza Face?" Sana responded. He smelled bad, too—a mixture of feet and moldy towels. I'd felt a little sorry for him before because he seemed poor and probably didn't get to wash his clothes often, but that vanished in a second.

"It doesn't matter. I'm a man."

She got right up in his face—her nose was maybe an inch from his— and laughed. "Man? You're just a scrawny little boy that's insecure 'cause your penis got chopped off in a botched circumcision."

His face scrunched up into an angry, hideous frown, and he stormed off as if Sana had uncovered the truth.

She rolled her eyes and muttered some insult I couldn't decipher. "Seriously, I can't believe these stupid guys. They walk around like they own the place!"

Everyone started heading back to class, and as soon as Motabel saw us come in the classroom, he picked up one of the desks and yelled obscenities at us in two languages: sharmootas, bitches, whores, cocksuckers. My blood pumped through my veins in violent spurts, and I clenched my fists. The teacher kept telling Motabel: "Oskoot! Be quiet and sit back down! Do not say bad words in class!"

But he wouldn't. He stood with the desk over his head and rage in his eyes. I was appalled. Amu and Amtu kicked me around emotionally and physically, insulting my mother for being a sharmoota and getting herself knocked up without a husband, and blaming me for basically anything that went wrong in the house because I was such a burden on them, but I wasn't about to let someone else get in on the fun and call me a whore. I barely even talked to guys and didn't want anything to do with them. Not the ones here, not the ones at regular school. I knew Motabel was a coward, and he'd eventually back down before he actually did anything to us. He deserved to be punished for threatening us with the desk and calling Sana ugly, though. I was sure Brother Radwan wouldn't deliver on that the way I wanted him to. What could he do? Suspend him? Kick him out? That seemed more like a reward to me, so I took matters into my own hands. I charged and crouched and pulled down on Motabel's balls, making sure to squeeze my fingers as hard as I could for maximum pressure. He dropped the desk on my back and cried out. The teacher ran toward us, but Sana was quicker and got to Motabel in time to slap him around before she tackled him and even pulled his hair. Motabel's scream was so high-pitched it hurt my ears a little. Brother Radwan tried to get Sana off him, but it took a couple of minutes before he stopped the beating. I noticed everyone else staring with their eyes wide, mouths gaping, while I rubbed the middle of my back.

When Sana calmed down, Brother Radwan managed to force her out of the class. Motabel tried to come back and get his revenge on me, but I got up and kicked him in the balls again before he'd even gotten all the way up. Brother Radwan was back in by then and tried to shove me outside, but I resisted, pushing his hands away from me. Brother Radwan only buckled—he didn't quite fall—but it was enough to excite Rasheed and the other students. "Aw, sweet, Isra!"

Once he regained his composure, Brother Radwan grabbed Motabel and threw him out of the classroom. Everyone was still quiet when he left, except for Rasheed. "My parents are gonna kill you!" he kept telling me, like I didn't already know.

On his trip back, Brother Radwan took Rasheed and me to the same office he took Sana to, the one where Amu and Amtu had signed us up to attend this hellhole. Motabel had been taken somewhere else. Rasheed sat down next to me and whined almost the whole time. "What'd I do? Why am I in trouble?" But once he got over the indignity of being sent here with me, he took the time, between bursts of laughter, to tell Sana what I did to Brother Radwan while she was gone.

She gaped like the kids in class. "God, Isra, you're majnoona to the core."

I was expelled. Brother Radwan wanted Rasheed reprimanded in some way for the things he said, but Amu and Amtu were too embarrassed to ever show their faces there again, so he and Hanan were taken out with me. It also made Sana and me minor celebrities among the Muslim kids in the entire county, or at least the ones who went to the mosque in town, where Sana told me it was talked about nonstop for at least a month and brought up frequently after that. She enjoyed the fame and laughed about it all the time when I went to her house in the summer to get away from Amtu Samia. Her parents weren't too pissed at her because she hadn't grabbed anyone's balls or gone so far as to trip a teacher. "See, I got so mad I beat him like this!" she would say and reenact the beating with one of the dolls she had packed away in her closet. But I could tell she was a little peeved by the fact that people talked more about her friend, raised by an Amreekiya mother until she was eight, who had the nerve to grab a boy's genitals right in front of a class and beat up a teacher.

Amu Nasser wasn't so amused by my behavior. I expected some ear-pulling, verbal abuse for weeks, maybe even a beating, a rarity for Amu because that would take too much energy, but I had never done anything this bad before. He did yell at me the whole way home, telling me the usual: I was ungrateful, I had been rescued from a kafir life to live as a good Muslim girl, and what did I do? I made it difficult for him at every turn. He had to spend more time cleaning up the messes I made than he did for both his own children. He claimed that now he and his wife were shamed in front of nearly the whole Muslim community here. All because of me.

He added a new twist to the attack, right at the end. "Your grandmother wants to see you be a good girl, and this is what you do for her? Wallah she would weep for days if she heard this. I cannot bear to look at you myself. There is not a girl more selfish in the entire world."

I figured if my grandmother could forgive my father for all he'd done—leaving his family behind without a word in nearly a decade and abandoning his own child—she'd be a hypocrite to judge me so harshly for merely defending myself and what I believed. I should be praised for it, but no one else seemed to feel the same way.

If anything, Amu Nasser was disappointed in me, not just angry like the other times, because he didn't speak to me for more than a month. I was relieved but also pissed that the worst thing I ever did brought me the least punishment. All I got was Amtu Samia's constant snide remarks about what a beast I was becoming, that I'd never find a husband with the temper I had and would end up spending my days alone. Then she'd gossip to her friends, especially Imm Samir, who said repeatedly that a man would take an obedient wife over a beautiful one, so my light skin wasn't going to save me from a life of loneliness.

Imm Samir would know about loneliness. She was about a thousand years old, and her husband had been dead for a while, but she refused to move in with any of her children's families like widowed women usually did. She went on living in her house by herself and did whatever she wanted, while Amtu Samia acted like she didn't know what Amu Nasser was doing when he stayed late at work or went to the office on the weekends.

What a sad, husbandless life I was doomed to lead.

CHAPTER NINE

I woke up to find my calves splayed across Yusef's thighs and Yusef eating a bowl of cereal that he balanced with his chest and other hand. The sun glaring through the thin patio curtain made the walls look more starkly white, making me squint once my eyes were all the way open. I sat up and pulled the straps of my slip up on my shoulders, and he startled, almost tipping the cereal onto me. His lips were still parted when he looked over at me, set the bowl down, and rubbed my calves. "You looked so tired, I wasn't gonna wake you up."

I was surprised that I had slept while he put my legs up and ate right beside me, but it was so cool and comfortable now after the long hot night. It took a minute to realize how I looked: dried drool on the corner of my chin and frizzy hair. I resisted the impulse to bolt and clean myself up, but I tried to subtly rub the drool residue from my face as I leaned in closer to the couch.

Most of my stuff was still in two suitcases and one raggedy duffel bag I'd had since childhood. Yusef had bought a small bureau for me, and he left some hangers free and half of the bottom shelf for my books.

It had been fourteen years since I moved from one place to another, and I couldn't decide how to organize my things. Dressy tops in one drawer and casual ones in another? I hung up my few dresses, including my wedding dress and the traditional Palestinian embroidered one Imm Yusef gave me, in the closet. Yusef had also brought me a pale blue cotton dress, fitted and sleeveless, which told me that he had picked it out without his mother. I put it on once everything was unpacked, and he grinned when I met him out in the living room. "Maybe I should have saved that for the house," he said. "You'll get more attention than all the girls in bikinis."

I nudged his arm with my elbow, hoping that the pink on my cheeks wouldn't be too visible. "You're such a liar."

We arrived in Avila Beach in the late afternoon, and though the sun still seared down intensely, groups of people were spread out on the sand with their umbrellas, towels, and lawn chairs. I had only ever been to the beach a couple of times, all before my teens, so the thought of wearing a bathing suit, even a one-piece, was mortifying. I had packed some capri leggings and a baggy shirt, but I felt a little anxious about wearing even those as I looked at the shirtless men and bikini-clad women. I leaned on the wooden fence just above the beach and wondered what it would be like to have that much of my body exposed in public; it was hard enough to let Yusef see me naked last night, and I had agonized about it our whole engagement.

But it was so nice to feel the cool breeze against my skin and to hear the waves as I stood against one of the railings.

Yusef wrapped himself around my waist with his cheek against mine. I put my hands on top of his. "It's so beautiful here," I said. I turned and gave him a soft kiss; he pressed my body against his and laid his cheek against my hair.

We checked into our hotel room, stacked the suitcase and bag in the corner, and browsed through the restaurant and bar brochures on the bed. I rested my head on his shoulder. "It's a little early for dinner."

He leaned in hesitantly and stroked my hair. We kissed and undressed; he ran his tongue over my nipples, the light stubble on his chin tickling my breasts. I moaned softly and caressed his back. I turned him over and got on top of him, letting him see my dangling breasts and the squished layer of fat on my belly. I almost lost my nerve when he took my hand and kissed the fingertips, his eyelids heavy and his lips twisted into a half smile, but he pulled my hips forward and put himself inside me.

Afterwards we cuddled for a little while, his breath coming in slow spurts against my hair, before he nodded off. He snored more quietly than last night, and the reverberations from his chest lulled me into a temporary stupor. Then something startled me, so I sat up. I was a little sore between my legs, but not nearly as much as last night. I checked for blood but felt only a sticky wetness.

Yusef turned over. His arm hit the empty bed and he mumbled my name. "Come over here, albi," he said as he pulled me down beside him again.

"I love you so much." I looked over as I stroked the arm that he laid over my belly, concentrating on the curve of his muscles at the top. He kissed the corner of my forehead and worked his way down to my cheek and then my lips. "I never thought that . . ." I felt my throat close up a little as I tried to finish my sentence. "I never thought that this would happen. That we would be together."

He raised his eyebrows. "Why?"

I didn't tell him that I thought we might be too different to be able to create a life together, to agree on anything. "Oh, I don't know. It seemed too good to be true."

He stared at me, searching for answers in my eyes. "It was hard when we were teenagers, and you were younger than me."

I snickered. "Three years makes such a difference."

"It did then. We were both so scared of each other." He rubbed my shoulder. "Remember when I tried to kissed you?"

I blushed even now. "I guess you weren't that scared."

He shook his head. "Nah, my stomach was doing back flips all day. When you asked me to take you home that morning, I thought, this was the day."

I rolled my eyes. "Of course you did."

"And when I got a little taste I had more courage than ever."

We were too exhausted to get ready and go out to dinner, and besides, all the socializing during and before our wedding had burnt me out, so we picked up some food from a local seafood shack and ate in our hotel room.

Yusef ate as ravenously as I did the day before, eating his entire steak meal and taking bites of my coleslaw and fries but steering clear of my shrimp and crab. "My mom was telling me that morning that we should go to Palestine on our honeymoon." He sat back in the chair and crossed his hands over his full belly, his eyes half closed. "I said, 'Mama, most women wouldn't consider visiting refugee camps and going through checkpoints a romantic destination.'" He laughed. "Besides, she wanted to go, too, with my father at least. That would cost a fortune, especially after the wedding."

"Which part? Nablus?"

"No, Hebron and Jenin, too. Also, we try to get into Jerusalem every time we visit so we can see al-Aqsa, but that didn't work out for us when we went the last time a few years ago." He started tapping his fingers on his belly. "They said there was something wrong with our passports, but they're full of it."

"I was in Jerusalem for about a week." That city unsettled me the most, especially when we visited the Dome of the Rock, seeing all those praying around us while I heard chants from the Jewish service beneath us. One of Amu Nasser's sisters said I should feel a special bond with the mosque because the name Isra referred to the journey that the prophet Muhammad—himself an orphan—made before ascending to Heaven from the Dome, but I only felt confused by the prayers and some residual fear from having to get past the guards at the entrance. "But I spent most of the time in Ramallah, where most of my dad's family lives."

He raised his eyebrows and parted his lips a little. "You've been to Palestine?"

"It's that surprising?"

He shrugged. "I just don't see your family as, uh, connected to the homeland."

I didn't know what pissed me off more: that he said it or that he was right.

"What, because none of us women wear hijab or read the Qur'an?" I crossed my arms in front of my chest. "Those are religious practices. Being Palestinian is an ethnicity."

He sighed. "Ah, Isreenie, it doesn't bother me that you're so Americanized. It's like being with two women at the same time: an American and a Palestinian."

He laughed at his own analogy, oblivious to or unconcerned with the glare I was giving him.

CHAPTER TEN

The summer I turned twelve, Amu finalized the plans for our family trip to Palestine, which he had been talking about for years. We'd go to Jerusalem, his hometown, and would visit some of Amtu's relatives in Jordan and a few people Amu knew there, but he never mentioned anything about visiting those relatives who were closer to me, like Baba's parents and his siblings, and his nieces and nephews. Almost all of them were still in Ramallah, in the interior of the West Bank. The Israelis had just set up a bunch of checkpoints going from Jerusalem to Ramallah, and Amu was afraid to face them. It was too dangerous. Not worth the risk.

But the whole time we stayed at his sister's house—which had been his parents' house—everyone pestered him about letting my other relatives see me. My grandmother was old, and she wanted to see her only grandchild from her youngest son.

Amtu Samia was opposed to the idea, too. She didn't like having to stay in this decrepit house, but she refused to stay in a camp for any amount of time. They were overrun with thugs and religious fanatics and regularly attacked by Israeli soldiers; also, the Arabic graffiti that defaced nearly all the buildings were just hideous. Her family had a two-story house in Amman. Just because she was Palestinian didn't mean that she would ever want to set foot in a refugee camp.

So, with pressure coming from both sides, Amu struck a deal. The day before we were supposed to leave for Jordan, he would drive me to Ramallah, drop me off, and rejoin the others in Jerusalem on schedule, inshallah (in Palestine, he was much more religiously inclined). He would come back for me the day before we were all to fly out of Jordan.

Everyone in the house, and some of the family that lived nearby, woke up

early to see me off. Amtu Fareeda, Amu's oldest sister, made a big breakfast to fortify us for the journey ahead, like we were going into battle. I
thought of my sixth-grade teacher who asked us to write and read a para-
graph to the class about what we would be doing over the summer. I wrote
about the trip we would be taking to Falasteen—which I called Palestine
in class, so everyone would be able to understand me. The teacher looked
stunned; I expected it. It wasn't the first time a teacher had gotten frightened at the mention of Palestine or Palestinians.

Amu wasn't exaggerating about the checkpoints. We were both American citizens, so it should have been easier for us to enter, but we looked
Palestinian enough to be delayed for hours. The brief morning cool wore
off thirty minutes into our nearly four-hour wait, and Amu and I rubbed
our faces with our increasingly lukewarm water bottles. Amu also used
the time to lecture me about how I should keep safe: avoid Israeli soldiers
and settlers; if I happened to encounter them, be respectful; under no circumstances separate myself from my relatives.

My mouth parched at the realization that Amu would be leaving me
here permanently. I couldn't believe I was blind to all the indications
beforehand: Amu helping me carry my things to the car, just like when
he picked me up from Baba's apartment, and dropping me off by myself.
How could he do this to me? Sure, Baba did it, and he had much more of
an obligation to take care of me, but Amu was supposed to be the honorable one. If I was shot, raped, or attacked, I hoped Amu would hear about
it and feel the sharp pangs of guilt—and Baba, too, wherever he was.

The soldier who finally came to Amu's window was young and pale
and skinny, with red pimples dotting his face. He had a machine gun
slung over his shoulder, resting close to his hip. He spoke the worst
English I ever heard, making it seem like a losing battle with his tongue
to form simple sentences. I was practically drowning in sweat, and the sun
blinded me more as the day pushed closer to noon. "What? You want us
to get out of the car to be searched?"

Amu glared at me and pulled my ear.

The soldier's lips were set to a thin line, and his blush not only covered his whole face but his neck as well. He tried to save face by deepening
his voice. "Yes. Get za h'll out of za ca.'"

He patted Amu down, and a woman soldier searched me, pinching my body more than patting it, and then ran a metal detector over me. She was done before the guy, so she went to search the car, but he said something to her in what I assumed was Hebrew. She nodded and walked away. He searched the car thoroughly, messing everything up, moving the front seats back and forward, and he especially took his time to be rough with the suitcase and duffel bag I packed. He even ripped the bag on the side, and he took the suitcase out and placed it on top of the trunk. He examined my bras and underwear, holding them up high, so maybe four or five of the cars behind us could see them.

"I'm not hiding bombs in those." I rolled my eyes and folded my arms, looked off into the hilly distance.

Amu pulled my ear again. "Ya Allah, majnoona, shut your mouth before I break it!"

But I figured if I was going to end up living here, I might as well learn to stand up to the soldiers now.

The soldier smiled, showing his front teeth. "Listen to you fazer, lee-tel girl." He shoved the clothes back in the suitcase so hard I thought he would dent the trunk. He threw it in the backseat and came over to escort me to the passenger seat, squeezing my arm hard. He shoved me in the seat and told me I was a desert bitch, no matter if I spoke English perfectly, and someday I would have a husband who would beat me in the ground, if my father didn't get to me first, and teach me some respect. He looked me straight in the eyes when he said it, and though I was trembling, I refused to look away.

I considered spitting on him, but the consequences that would bring chilled me.

As soon as he waved us off, Amu yelled about how crazy I was. "If you talk this way, you will end up killed by that scum right there!" He sighed deeply and unsuccessfully tried to even out his breaths.

It only took minutes for us to arrive in Ramallah, now that we were past the Qalandia checkpoint, where Amu and I were separated and I stood in a line of women and children waiting to have my body and bag searched. My legs and feet were so sore that they were almost as wide as my head, and the thought of having to step out of the car was painful.

My family didn't live in a camp anymore; they had been living in the poorer part of Ramallah the last few decades. It had decrepit buildings all around, some half bulldozed, graffiti appearing intermittently. Everyone stared at us, taking the last few minutes of fresh air before the curfew. Amu had the nicest car here, one of only a few cars around. It seemed like the resentment washed from their faces when they saw that we were Arabs. I didn't imagine there was much to do here; maybe this was the most interesting part of their month or even their year.

Amu muttered the whole time about how now he would have to stay here because he couldn't make it back to East Jerusalem before curfew, but I didn't care about Amu's discomfort or whatever he was feeling. I only cared that I was seeing the place where Baba came from for the first time.

When we arrived at Sitti's house, a large crowd was gathered in the front. Never before had I been so popular. Everyone gave me hugs and kisses as soon as I got out of the car and introduced themselves to me. Most were first cousins, some of them old enough to have little children of their own, but I still had a few who were not even in the double digits yet. There was only one girl around my age, Faten, and she was one year my senior. She spoke the best English and led me to meet my grandmother, who was sitting in a lawn chair and pulled me down for a hug and several kisses. "Anti jameela, jameela," was all I understood. You are beautiful.

Faten translated for me, asking about what happened to my mother, if I had seen my father at all. How could they have not known these things? Baba left me alone in that apartment four years ago. Mom died of cancer. I couldn't tell them anything else.

"She says that you look as your father," Faten said, elongating her vowels. Then Sitti said something that was almost as long as a speech, but Faten only said, "She is very sorry for what habbened," making her *p*'s into *b*'s like Baba did. His accent had been much thicker than Amu's. Someone came with a camera and had us huddle together to take a picture. Faten said "sheese" and laughed.

There were three houses I could have stayed at, but Sitti said I should stay at her house, which was also the home of Amu Musa, my oldest uncle. Faten lived there too, along with her four older brothers, two of whom already had wives and the oldest a child. Sitti said that because Faten was the only girl, we could be as akhawaat, sisters, for my time here. Faten had a small room that looked more like an office, and I kept my things in that room and shared the bed with her.

She went to school every day until noon except for Friday, and because everyone in the house got up early, I did too, so as not to be the lazy one in bed. Amtu Nada, Faten's mother, didn't want me to help her with the cooking or cleaning, so I just watched TV most of the time. There were news broadcasts, Egyptian and Syrian soap operas and movies, and American sitcoms dubbed in Arabic. I found those the funniest. Back at home I wouldn't have watched them, they were so vapid, but hearing voiceover exclamations like "Ya Allah!" or "Mabrook!" coming from those Waspy actors kept me laughing. I didn't understand much of the Arabic soap operas, but I would watch the ones with the handsome men who made passionate—and chaste, by my standards for TV—declarations to their loves, beautiful blondes and brunettes, all with light olive skin and makeup as thick as a mask, their emotions too hidden to be seen or so exaggerated that they didn't seem real.

When Faten was home, I helped her with her chores. She took care of Sitti and washed the clothes by hand, usually with Sitti nearby. My grandmother became more talkative when I was around. She seemed compelled to tell Faten to tell me every story she remembered of Baba. He was a good student and excelled in his studies just as Faten did, and he dreamed of moving to America or Europe for his education, so he could make a good life for himself and save his family from occupation, even if Falasteen was never liberated. He took it hard when his father was killed on the way to work, caught in a crossfire as bullets were fired through the car window.

"That's so terrible," I said. I was curious about how Sitti managed six kids with no husband, but no matter how many ways I phrased the question, I couldn't seem to make Faten understand me enough to translate it. I settled for wondering about it; Faten had pretty good English skills, much better than my stilted Arabic, but we both seemed aware of our limits when we had to communicate with each other. Still, I couldn't help wondering about my father's reaction to his own father's death. Did Baba cry then? Probably he would have to, just for the sake of the others, but did he mean it? Did he feel the searing pain of grief, did it pinch his heart unexpectedly, even now, wherever he was?

I refused to cry for Baba. What did he care for my pain?

Sitti said in English, "We live in Jerusalem, and lose everyzing. Your father lose everyzing."

Sitti usually took another nap before dinnertime, and that's when Faten and I would talk to each other. She assumed because I lived in California that I saw movie stars on the streets, and she asked me a few times if I had ever gotten an autograph or shaken a celebrity's hand. "No," I answered each time. "Where I live is far away from Hollywood. It's like—" I thought about how I could make her understand the distance using Middle Eastern geography "—at least as far away as Damascus." There weren't any roadblocks or checkpoints along the way to Los Angeles from Fresno, but it was still quite a drive.

"You lucky to live there," she said.

I nodded. It was one of the first times I felt that way.

While my family didn't like that I spoke little Arabic—especially Faten's oldest brother Hassan, who sometimes derided my imprecise pronunciation and my long pauses, struggling to find the words to express myself—there were other things about me that surprised them. Amtu Nada and Hassan nearly gaped at dinnertime when I ate the goat that had been slaughtered that morning at a family friend's house just outside of the camp and that I shared a twin-size bed with Faten with no complaints.

They expected me to be difficult and pouty. More American. I was from the United States and had had a white mother. I should have been the most spoiled, but I knew what it was like to have so little to eat that it didn't calm the hunger pangs, so I wasn't going to turn down a meal.

Sensing my boredom without Faten for most of the morning except for Fridays, Amtu Nada suggested that I go to school with her. "It will be very fun for you, habibti. You will meet other girls your age. Everyone want to see you." She grabbed my curly bun and jiggled it playfully like she was coaxing a five-year-old to start kindergarten.

I had already met quite a few people. A bunch of people had come to visit Sitti's house to see the Amreekiya in town and ask me about my life, the people I knew, if I had met any of their relatives in the States.

It was just a ploy to ease me into the new life I would have to start here, I was sure, but I went anyway. I couldn't sink into my new life. I had to make do. I didn't need Amu, no matter what he thought.

I caused a sensation the first day, taking up nearly all the instruction time. It was the same thing: questions about my life and where I lived and if I knew such-and-such a person. A lot of it I couldn't even understand. This would be my life. Me standing around in a crowd of people I could barely comprehend. What had changed? I didn't understand those spoiled rich kids I went to school with in the States.

The excitement died down as time passed. I sat next to Faten and listened to her teacher lecture about Arabic, English, mathematics, science. Also, the history the woman taught was like what I learned in the States, except they spent some time on the Middle East, which none of my American teachers ever mentioned. No one in my classes back home even knew what a Palestinian was, sometimes not even what an Arab was. But I wasn't expected to do the work or take the tests. I memorized a few poems that the teacher gave to me in Arabic, along with an English translation, something she thought would be good for an American girl. I forget most of them now except for two lines from Abu Salma's "We Will Return": "Kaifa ahyaa / Ba'eedan ayn suhoolikiwa al-hidaabi?" My English translation said it meant: "How do I live / Away from your plains and mounds?"

It had been four years since my mother's death, and those last days she had been lying in a hospice bed, pale and emaciated, having aged about forty years in the last two. This Abu Salma seemed sure we would return, but nothing was more final than loss.

I went to the living room late at night while everyone else was sleeping. It was one of the few moments I had to myself since the plane ride here. I found a small window to the right of the front door, way off in the corner. I imagined windows would be a hazard. I was shivering, but I had to stay up and look at the blue-black sky with no stars. I saw no one, heard nothing until the loud buzz of an Israeli army vehicle. I saw hard hats, but I couldn't tell how many there were or the gender of those who wore them.

The day before Amu Nasser's expected return, I stayed home from school and lay on Faten's bed, staring at the ceiling. Baba wanted to save his family from the Israelis, my ass. He couldn't even save me, and I was born in the States. He'd made no effort to communicate with his family in almost a decade.

Amu Nasser would not come back. I told Amtu Nada I needed to stay home to pack my things, and I waited for her to tell me that there was no need for that, I would be staying. She only nodded and said it would be fine if I stayed home. Sitti would probably want to spend more time with me anyway.

When Faten came home, I asked if her parents said anything about Amu Nasser coming to pick me up tomorrow. "Laa, they have said nothing to me," she said. She looked at me sympathetically, the spoiled American who could not stand a few weeks of the life she had been living for thirteen years. And I guess I was. I had to leave. It was too much; I couldn't handle hearing stories about this house being bulldozed, that relative being shot, and seeing the effects of it all the time. My pulse raced nearly all the time, my stomach always knotted with fear.

One day we had taken a bus trip to Jericho with Faten's second-oldest brother Muhammad and his wife, because she had some family there. The bus was stopped several times and inspected by Israeli soldiers, who came on to check everyone out. They even took one guy off the bus. There was something wrong with his identification, so they hauled him away.

Muhammad's wife turned around and told me, "They will take him to jail." I heard an older woman in the background sobbing and heard several other women making feeble attempts to comfort her. I couldn't bring myself to look. Muhammad's wife snorted in disgust.

Amu Nasser arrived after breakfast, the earliest he could make it. He had some coffee and pastries with Amu Musa and his two older sons while I spent more time with my female relatives. Amu Nasser wanted to get out as soon as possible, though, so he came into the kitchen where I was sitting and rushed me out. "I do not want to miss the flight. We must get through the checkpoints."

We said our goodbyes for at least half an hour, but once I was driving away in the car with Amu, my lips trembled and my eyes filled with tears. We spent nearly the whole day going through more checkpoints to get into Jordan. By the time we got there, I was already asleep, and I woke up in a pool of sweat. When we got into the airport, I guiltily basked in the air-conditioning and wondered what would become of my family.

CHAPTER ELEVEN

I got up early with Yusef the next morning and made eggs with tomatoes while he showered, observing all that was around in a new light. Everything was clean enough, but so much had to be changed. The refrigerator needed to be stocked, the couch deodorized, the kitchen floor mopped. Once Yusef left, I scoured the house for cleaning supplies—he only had bleach. I spent more than an hour going to stores to buy all I needed. At Amu's, I had usually cleaned with my mind in the clouds, fantasizing about living in a big house and having hired help to do such drudgery for me. Today, though, cleaning consumed me, so much so that it was close to noon when I stopped to look at the clock, and I barely had enough time to shower before work.

When I arrived five minutes late, the nurse smiled and said it was because I was a newlywed. Her eyes went starry as she handed me a patient's file. "So how's your husband? I didn't get to see him at the reception, but I remember when he came here." She smiled again. "You are a lucky girl."

I used to think the Arab girls and women swooned over him because of his green eyes, but his looks translated well to other women. "Yeah, I know."

"I married my high school sweetheart, too." She shook her head at the recollection. "Of course, we were a lot younger. Right out of high school, and he never brought flowers to my work." She went on about how he was threatened by her dedication to her education and the nursing program she was in; he'd decided to forgo college and worked in his father's construction company. He was convinced she was cheating on him all the time. "Just 'cause he was jealous of my education, you know. I ended it in about a year."

I nodded sympathetically. "That's too bad."

"So what does your husband do?"

"He's a researcher, and he teaches part-time. He still has a semester of graduate school left."

I had woken up in the middle of the night and found Yusef working on charts and graphs on his laptop. When I asked him if he had a deadline coming up soon, he said no and bored me with details of his thesis—a theory of what caused an increase in cancer cell growth. I came to the conclusion that I had too many connections to the medical profession: I worked at a doctor's office, Sana was a nurse, Yusef was constantly staring at disease through a microscope.

Sana first told me about this job a month into college, and the possibility horrified me, but the promise of my own money and a way to get out of the house spurred me to apply. That was around the time that Sana was officially accepted into the nursing program and decided that she would specialize in oncology. She told me it would be a good field; it had lots of openings.

Of course it did. Who could stand seeing the gaunt faces and shrunken bodies of cancer patients, see in their eyes the sorrow or anger about their fate, or worse, the resignation to suffering and death? But she felt certain that she could keep her distance and truly help them. "People get over cancer," she said. "There have been tons of advances in the field. Practically everyone gets it at some point in their life. It's the disease of our generation."

"It'll never be cured."

"Isra, you're such a pessimist."

But I realized early in this job where Sana came from. Yes, some people did survive severe diseases and illnesses—the ones who had money, like the rich clientele that frequented this office. Their biggest concern was if the air conditioning or the heat was turned too high or low, not whether they would live. That was a given.

I started dinner as soon as I got home, making stuffed grape leaves that Amtu said I could never make like her mother. She claimed mine had too much tomato and not enough lemon, like the ones from a cheap Mediterranean restaurant. She didn't like any of my food, but she still had me cook almost all the time and only decided what would be cooked.

The food was almost ready when Yusef came home with his huge backpack. He sniffed the air. "Smells good in here."

I nodded, my eyes still inspecting the grape leaves.

"It smells clean, too." In the living room he picked up the two candles I had set on the coffee table, sniffed them, and put them back down. Then he moved on to the kitchen and took note of the new silverware set I had bought, along with a few pots and pans. "It's nice. Looks like someone lives here."

I walked over to him and rested my face between his shoulder blades. I was relieved that he seemed pleased with the change.

"You didn't have to pay for all this, though. It must have been, what, a couple hundred dollars?"

I shrugged. "Almost, but it's not a big deal. Really." I had never spent that much in one day, or week, or even a month, unless I was ordering my textbooks or when I saved up enough to buy my car. But suddenly it wasn't anything to drop that kind of money on a new household; I was a woman now, and I had bigger expenses.

Yusef kept insisting he had to pay me for this.

"Yusi, it's all right. It's not like this is a monthly expense; it's a one-time thing."

He walked off to the bedroom and came out with a bunch of bills in his hands, $200 in twenties, tens, fives, and a fifty. He tried to shove it in my hand, but I walked to the stove because I had to check on the grape leaves. As I broke one open to see if the rice inside was done, he tried to nudge the money into my jeans pocket. "No, Yusef. I paid for the stuff, okay?"

He changed tactics and took my face in his hands and kissed me. He had a grain of rice on his lips from my lips. "Come on, just take the money." He put his hands on my hips and pressed my body up against his. "And then we can make love while the food cools down."

I pulled away and took out a plate for the grape leaves. I took the tongs and started pulling them out one by one. I thought: What's the big deal? Let him pay for it. But he was the one who made such a fuss about it in the first place.

He may not have been into me using my money to pay for things, but it didn't bother him to give me control over the finances. He made his bank account a joint one, put my name on the apartment lease, and had me pay the rent, electric and gas, and our cell phone bills. I did the grocery shopping, decided what our breakfast and dinner would be, and when we would eat it on the silverware I chose. I cut corners anywhere I could and started saving money for both of us. I had no goal in mind for the money—there wasn't a fortune left over—but having a little in the bank always made my heart beat steadier and calmed my thoughts.

Amu Nasser never let Amtu Samia control the finances. Amtu Samia was a bit extravagant—she needed to buy herself at least a couple new outfits every week, though she rarely visited anyone except Imm Samir for the last several years—but I had seen more excessive spending from other bored housewives, and Amu gave her a "spending money" allowance for that. If she went over her limit, he usually gave her the money with no argument. Amu claimed he was tired and overworked all the time, so why didn't he hand over the household expenses to Amtu? It made no difference to me, because when he gave her money for school shopping for us kids, she made sure to give me at most half of what each of her kids got, so if she paid the mortgage, the water, the electric, it would be a burden off his back with no negative consequences.

But he had to know about every dollar she was spending.

One thing way out of my control was Imm Yusef. My new family was a lot more social than my old one. Yusef's mother expected us to see company almost every night of the week. "Come to our house, Yusef habibi, I am making the fatayer you have such a love for," she would say. Then she'd say another day that one of Yusef's sisters missed him and wanted him over for dinner, though his sisters spent most of the time socializing with the other women they invited. Then it was come over to one of her friends' houses so they could see the newlywed couple; then it was see the friend of the friend of the friend of Yusef's parents.

Yusef was obliging. It even seemed that he liked going out to see his relatives and their friends and his friends and everybody. He wasn't picky about the company he kept, so I was the downer because I didn't like it. His sisters weren't bad, although they were nosy, especially the middle one, Fatima. Sometimes she would even ask what Yusef was eating, and if he ate enough (he ate plenty—I still cooked the same portions I did at

Amu's house when I cooked for four or five, and we had hardly any leftovers). Khadija, on the other hand, claimed that he had more color in his face and had gained weight since our marriage. It was good for him to be living with women, or a woman, again; she never understood why he moved out on his own. And Imm Yusef of course had her strong opinions about Yusef's health and looks, which varied each time I saw her.

Lubna was the only one of them who didn't idolize and baby Yusef. It might have had something to do with the fact that she worked part-time and had two children under the age of eight. She didn't go out for company quite as often, and when she was there, she was busy watching her own children, usually chastising them or giving the boy a spanking for running in the house.

On top of that, all the older women seemed to believe they were surrogate mothers to Yusef, since they were almost as curious about our marriage as anybody else.

I realized there might be other reasons. One woman, Imm Ali, mentioned casually that a couple years ago she thought Yusef would be perfect for her daughter.

He turned the offer down.

And clearly she believed he hadn't turned her daughter down for a better woman.

Once I closed my eyes, I felt Yusef rustling under the sheets. He sat up and picked up the new bag I had bought for him (with his money, of course). I grabbed his arm with both hands. "No, stay in bed, Yusef." Getting out of bed to do his work was becoming a nightly ritual, just like it was his nightly ritual to have me before he relaxed a while to get back to more important matters.

He half-lay on his side, still slightly propped up on his elbow, and kissed my forehead, my eyes, my nose, my cheeks, and my hair so intensely it was more like he was going away for a year rather than an hour. He gave me the usual excuse. "Isreenie, I've gotta get in at least some work. I'll be back in bed soon." He sat back up, yawned loudly, and stretched. "I'm gonna put my foot down. A body can only take so much." He leaned over for another kiss, but I turned away, hoping he would make good on his promise.

I stayed in bed nearly the entire morning, drifting in and out of sleep.

Around eleven I resolved to get up, but that took more than an hour for me to finally do. My stomach gurgled, and I leaned over onto my knees. I must have gotten food poisoning, I thought, or my period was coming. I heard the rustling of papers out in the living room and the incessant clack of laptop keys. I stood up and dressed slowly, closing my eyes hard every few seconds. Then I had to run to the bathroom; I puked in the toilet, my stomach contracting with each watery chunk that came up. I rested my cheek on the seat and took in deep breaths. It had been so long since I had been sick like this.

Yusef knocked on the bathroom door. "Isra, what's up?"

My eyes fluttered. Gathering the energy just to speak was a struggle. "Oh, I'm . . . I'm a little sick."

"Let me come in." He opened the door before I answered and helped me off the floor. He tried to take me to the sink to wipe off the vomit residue from the corners of my lips, but I insisted I do it myself; I was dizzy, not disabled. He put his arms around me and led me back to the bedroom, tucking me in bed. He suggested that I have some tea with maramiya, the sage leaves that his parents gave us from their store.

That was Baba's solution to any sort of stomach ailment. We never had it at Amu Nasser and Amtu Samia's. Amtu preferred Maalox.

Yusef kissed the corner of my forehead and brushed the hair out of my face, then left the bedroom to start the tea. Soon he came in with a steaming, fragrant cup, and I sat up to gulp it down. It was sweeter than my father's, and I thanked him for it.

He placed his hand on my forehead. "You don't have a fever. Still dizzy?"

"Not anymore. Just tired." I didn't like having him examine me so closely, moving his hands clinically from my face to my chest, squeezing my breasts, which he claimed were plumper than he remembered. "It's something I ate."

He moved his hand down to my stomach, which was still gurgling every few minutes. He grinned. "You're pregnant."

"I'm not!" I didn't think I had the energy to answer as ferociously as I did. "How would you be able to feel it this early? It's food poisoning." Maybe Imm Ali had done it to me for stealing Yusef from her daughter.

He chuckled. "Morning sickness, fatigue, wild mood swings. Pregnancy symptoms."

I guarded my stomach from him with both arms and glared.

"Damn, I thought my mother and sisters could give some killing looks, but you have them beat with that one." That didn't keep him from leaning in to kiss me, puke breath and all; the maramiya probably killed off some of the smell by now. At least he didn't put his tongue in my mouth. "Imagine us, Isreenie. Carrying the baby around, smelling its head, watching you breastfeed." He had thought this through pretty well. "Then when it's bad you can give it a look like you just gave me; we'll have the best-behaved kids ever." He squeezed the top of my arm.

"We don't even know if I'm pregnant," I said with less conviction than I previously had. I felt stupid that the thought hadn't even occurred to me. I had been having unprotected sex for almost a month. Even though I was inexperienced, I had attended enough sex education lectures in high school and college to know that once was enough.

He shrugged. "I know it's gonna come soon, hayati." He took my face in his hands, murmuring a new Arabic term of affection with each kiss, albi, helwati, making a song out of his feelings for me. "I wonder if our kids should call us Baba and Mama or Mom and Dad. My parents would hit the roof if we used the American ones, but then we're not old-school like them."

"I'm sure I'm not pregnant." It had to be impossible that I'd be feeling symptoms this early.

Yusef told me that I should take an at-home pregnancy test—just so we could plan ahead, not to get our hopes up.

But his hopes were already up from what he thought was "morning sickness."

That must have been why I wouldn't do the pregnancy test. Yusef even went to the trouble of picking it up for me the next day, Sunday, after I had another bout of vomiting and dizziness that lasted into the afternoon. I felt lethargic almost all day until sunset, when it cooled down. I didn't want to pee on a stick. I felt fine; I only had a bit of sickness, maybe the flu. It was nothing.

That started our second disagreement. It wasn't harsh enough to be an argument or a fight. He was condescending and pitying. "Isra, I study disease and illness for a living. I could tell if you had the flu. It doesn't pass in the evening and come back the next day." He pressed his hand on my belly. "You're pregnant."

"I don't feel like it. I feel like crap, and I've gotten so behind on the housework and everything else. I don't have time to do it."

"The test doesn't take that much time."

"Why does it matter if I put it off for a day or two?"

He shrugged. "Don't put it off too long."

Hanan called while I was making dinner, so I put her on speaker phone. I set the stew to simmer and started pulling apart shredded phyllo dough at the kitchen table. I was having an intense craving for anything sweet, and nothing would be more satisfying than a kunafa, a creamy cheese dessert—the only one I could ever master besides cake. Yusef wondered why I chose one of the hottest days to bake, but I just said it would be nice to have a good meal at home for once; if I told him about my craving, he'd add that to the long list of pregnancy symptoms he believed I was having. Another piece of evidence he didn't really know me. My craving was more a symptom of my fear of pregnancy than a symptom of pregnancy itself.

"Let me come over," Hanan said. "I want to eat kunafa." She lowered her voice. "I've been eating Mama's food for weeks, and it sucks."

Yusef chuckled as quietly as he could, but I could tell Hanan heard him from the uncomfortable silence.

I broke it. "How about you come over tomorrow before I go to work?"

Yusef put his arms around my shoulders and kissed my neck. "She can come over today. I'm sure we have enough food for one more person."

"But I have a lot to catch up on since I've been in bed all weekend, and we've practically been living at other people's houses for the last couple weeks, so I have so much to do afterwards that we won't be able to spend time together." Anyway, how could I vent my anger about Yusef to Hanan while he was still at home in this tiny apartment following me around, badgering me about the baby he felt certain was in my pudgy belly?

I got enough of it out right then to make Yusef walk off and mutter something about wild mood swings.

And it didn't do anything to ease the uncomfortable silence with Hanan. She said she'd call back tomorrow or stop by at ten or something. Even she ran away from our bickering.

The only sound being made at the dinner table was the clink of silverware on our plates. I couldn't wait until we were finished and Yusef went to work on his thesis so I could devour half of the kunafa. At Amu's, our dinners were just like this most of the time—Hanan and Amtu and me all sitting uncomfortably at a table. Sometimes Amtu might lecture us girls about something while we were eating, reminding both of us that we would get fat if we ate too much, but she got minimal response from us on those occasions. She ate faster than Hanan and me, and consumed much less, before she left to watch the Arabic channels on satellite TV. Then Hanan and I would start talking naturally, knowing that Amtu wasn't there waiting to insert some snide remark about what we were saying.

I considered apologizing, but I was convinced that this wasn't all my fault—Yusef was pressuring me too much to take the pregnancy test, and ignoring me and exhausting me with seeing some member of his family nearly every night. I didn't want to volunteer an apology; I hadn't apologized to anyone since grade school, and that was only when I was forced to do so. What if he didn't return it? Because he was wrong too, and I would be damned if I was going to take the fall for everything.

Still, I figured I could risk humiliation for a little bit of peace. "I'm sorry that I've been so bitchy lately. I've been really tired, and . . ." I ended it there, but I had plenty more to add: I didn't realize it would be such an adjustment having to live with you, especially after that first great week together. And I can't stand being compared to other women who you could have possibly married, my performance as a wife constantly being assessed by your mother and sisters. Who is there to assess or even care how you treat me? Maybe Hanan. And right when I've started having my doubts about marriage in general, I've probably already gotten myself pregnant.

I said it quietly, so I wasn't sure if his hesitancy was because he hadn't actually heard me. He sighed and tapped his fingers on the table, his lips pursed. "That's it?"

"Yes," I answered defensively. What did he expect me to do? Plead with him and kiss his feet? What I had been doing was not that horrible. He wasn't perfect either.

"Well, it seems like you've still got a chip on your shoulder. It's more than that you're feeling a little sick."

"Oh, sorry if I failed your expectations for a wife, but I was just irritated." I folded my arms. "I feel like you're setting your expectations too high for me being pregnant, and I haven't even taken a pregnancy test."

"You won't take a test, Isra."

Tears came to my eyes with no warning. I stood up from my seat and yelled. "You're insensitive, that's what it is! Of course, a baby's all fun for you because it's not going to be in your body, and you'll probably hardly take care of it!"

He said that was the problem: I wouldn't tell him anything. I retaliated by telling him that he wouldn't give me the space or the time to say something, with the way he carried on.

"What?" He stood up. "I'll give you your space. I'll get my keys, take a drive or something." He went from the table to the bedroom and back to the front door before I could consider trying to stop him.

I wouldn't have done it anyway. I had already apologized, and look what it got me.

Hours passed. I ate the entire kunafa and made sure every piece was soaked in my homemade syrup. I'd never eaten so much dessert at once before; I got a stomach ache from it, like when I was seven and ate too many chocolates at school on Valentine's Day or Halloween. The last thing I wanted to do was lie down and think about my stomach or Yusef while watching bad television. I opened the box and peed on the white stick and let it sit.

I was pregnant. The fear ran cold through my veins. The familiar fear, the one that I would end up alone with a child with no one to turn to. I chided myself for being hysterical. Yusef hadn't left for good, and I only found out I was pregnant alone because I wouldn't take the test while he was here.

I cleaned the kitchen and vacuumed. Free time was scarce these days. It took me time to remember my usual hobby: reading. I started on a long book, but everything reminded me of Yusef: the man on the cover with a smirk, the naïve child in the book. It was almost ten o'clock. I'd end this stalemate and call him to yell at him until my lungs were sore. Where could he be at this hour? Maybe out with a former girlfriend, or he could have found a brand-new one, one that would let him fuck her for as long as he wanted and would listen in sympathy when he vented about his crazy wife. Now, instead of being Mom, I would be Amtu Samia. He'd never leave me, but I would know every day that he wished he could. He would express his feelings by coming home late, hardly eating with the family, refusing to take vacations with me, and not even staying by my side while a parent was dying a slow death. Those thoughts winded me, and I lay down on the bed in defeat. I had to admit I enjoyed having the soft, comfortable bed to myself—the one at Amu's was as hard as wood, and it was a lot better than the lumpy full-size Yusef had in here before— but that was scant comfort to a woman facing a loveless marriage.

I threw the book at the wall. It only made me angrier, and my teeth were clenched so hard I thought they would fall out. I got a hold of myself and decided against calling him. Maybe I should just leave and tell him he wasn't about to trap me and treat me like shit. I'd rather be Mom than Amtu. I'd been the "less than" for the better part of my life; it would not be my permanent place. I wasn't playing second fiddle to some other woman, or women, who knows? If Amu—a man who had become increasingly fat, bald, and wrinkly—had the ability to play two women, at least two women, Yusef probably had an infinite number of opportunities.

Just as I opened the closet to find something decent to wear and start packing, I heard Yusef's key in the door. It would be better this way: I could tell him all those things to his face. He called my name as soon as he locked the door again. I met him in the hall, my hands on my hips. "Where have you been?"

He raised his hands in surrender. "Look, I'm tired, and I'm not in the mood to fight."

I stabbed his shoulder with my forefinger. "I didn't ask that. I asked where you were."

He gaped and raised his eyebrows, outraged, folding his arms. "I drove around for an hour or something and then stopped by my parents' house. What do you think I was doing?"

"Don't act like I'm crazy. You've been gone for like four hours, and it's almost eleven."

He took both of my hands in his. "I needed to blow off some steam. I don't want another fight."

I pulled away and smelled the cigarette smoke on him. "You could have called, and you didn't have to stay so late!" I continued to berate him, telling him if I had done the same, he'd be a thousand times more enraged than me. I stomped my foot down hard.

He threw his hands in the air. "Maybe I should have called. I wasn't thinking."

I went out into the living room and saw one of those grocery bags with red "Thank You" labels that his parents carried in their store. "That's some more maramiya that Mama gave me. She put some dessert and food on the plate." I sat down on the couch and opened the bag, which provided enough evidence to prove he had been at his parents' house. I wasn't sure if that was better than him being with another woman.

"What did you tell them? Did you tell them we were fighting?" I closed my eyes and covered my face with my hands.

"I said you were sick, and we were having some . . . issues." He wanted to know what was wrong with talking to his parents about the problems we were having. After all, they had been married for over forty years; we could stand to learn something from them. We had been arguing and snapping at each other for days, and he was confused about what to do. He didn't realize marriage was this hard. He only wanted us to be happy.

"What did she say?"

He shrugged. "Mama didn't say anything bad about you. I don't see why you're worried."

"Because she judges me. Her, your sisters, all of them."

"They mean well."

"They mean well for you, and I'm just the whore who lured you away from their bosoms."

Yusef sighed. "That's not true, Isra. They all wanted me to get married." He sat down beside me on the couch. "And they definitely don't think you're a whore."

He wanted to know how I felt, and when I told him he didn't listen. "I am pregnant. You were right about that."

He took me in his arms and nuzzled against my neck. "I've always wanted to be a father. I love babies."

Because he hadn't taken care of any.

We cuddled on the bed and talked about children. He wanted to make love at first, but I still felt all the kunafa in my stomach and wasn't in any mood to do anything that physical. It might make me puke all over him. "I guess I'll have to get used to this when we have the baby," he said, and laughed. Then he pulled me to him and asked me if I wanted a boy or girl.

"I want it to be healthy and good." I had a feeling that a boy would probably satisfy his mother and give me more of an upper hand in our relations with one another, but the thought of being one of those women who preferred a boy for the advantages it provides made my stomach turn again.

"Me too. I want it to look like you." He wrapped his fingers around one of my curls and smiled.

I looked at his face, the light brown skin that felt so smooth under my fingertips until I reached his stubble. "Your skin, though."

He shrugged. "Hmm. Definitely your nose." He ran his finger down the smooth edge. His had a small bump at the bridge, and it hooked a little at the bottom. He moved his finger down to trace my lips and kissed them softly.

"I don't think this is about the baby."

I turned over so he couldn't reach my lips.

He grabbed a hold of me and kissed the back of my neck and licked behind my ear, tickling me. "You can't blame me for trying." He continued with the soft, light kisses on my neck that felt more like a brushstroke, but he couldn't put me in the mood, couldn't take me all the way there, because I didn't want another thing inside me that night.

CHAPTER TWELVE

After I put the stuffed chicken in the oven, I cleaned up the mess I had made on the counters and the dishes I used to prepare the meal. By the time I was eleven, I had been cooking all the meals for over a year and a half, and I knew that since Arab food took forever to finish, I might as well get some cleaning done while I waited. The whole time I cleaned, Hanan would show off the new skills she had been learning in kindergarten: the alphabet, how to add and subtract. "I'm going to read soon, 'Sra!" At that age she still couldn't say Isra correctly.

She sprinted to the living room and came back with a pencil and paper and wrote out her name for me: Hanan Shadi. After I dumped the crumbs into the trash, I looked at the paper. "Oh, wow, that's really good," I said. Once I gave Hanan enough praise, she'd usually get out of my hair, so I pretended the littlest things were great.

"You know that's not how we say it, though?" I added, following her into the living room, where she now started coloring little hearts around her name on the coffee table while Rasheed watched TV. "It's al-Shadi. That's how you say it in Arabic."

Baba and Amu pronounced it "ash-Shadi." I wondered why both Baba and Amu had decided to leave the "al" off our last name for English-language documents. Until I was seven, I thought my last name actually was Shadi. Then Baba told me that it wasn't, talking to me like I was stupid. "Don't you know anything about where you came from?" he asked me. "Sometimes I cannot believe you are my child."

But I looked almost exactly like him.

"Why didn't you just put the 'al' in there anyway?" I asked.

"Don't ask dumb questions" was his best explanation.

Probably it made the name sound whiter. And Amu was a hypocrite for looking down on my whiteness when it always seemed like he was trying to be whiter himself. At least I wasn't pretending to be something I wasn't.

"Isra, when will the food be ready? Wallah I can't wait any longer. You should have got off your teez and started dinner earlier!" Amtu was yelling from upstairs, her congested voice breaking at the end.

"It's going to be a while," I answered. "I can make you a snack." I cringed at the offer I made, but it was better than having to hear her complain about me for hours and then pass those complaints on to Amu, who would get mad at me and criticize me some more. If I did something really bad, I knew he would hit me.

I couldn't hear Amtu's response clearly, so I had to walk to the stairs while Hanan followed me with questions about why we did not put the "al" in our name when we spelled it in English. I saw Amtu at the top, looking exhausted and huge and disheveled. She was in her seventh month of pregnancy, with another boy.

"What did you say?" I asked.

She opened her mouth to repeat herself, but nothing came out. At first it looked like she was rolling her eyes at me because she was so irritated by how deaf I was, but her eyes blinked over and over, and she held up both her arms, her hands balled into fists, her whole body shaking. Then she fell down the stairs. I reacted as fast as I could, but I only made it to the second stair before I caught her and stopped her from falling farther. There was blood dripping from the side of her mouth; she had bit her tongue. Hanan was screaming, and Rasheed got up from the couch and yelled "Mama! Mama!" He helped me move his mother to the flat carpet. Hanan was still screaming and crying. I was trembling, but I made feeble attempts at telling Hanan everything would be all right. I needed her to be quiet.

"I'll call Amu Nasser," I said to Rasheed. "Stay with your mom!"

I went to the kitchen to use the phone and saw Hanan with tears dripping from the bottom of her face. Her screechy little voice called out her for her mother just like Rasheed had been doing.

"Shut up, Hanan! I need to call your dad."

I had to call twice, and when he answered he called me a stupid himara for not calling 911. "She's pregnant, ya Allah, and she needs medical attention right now. I will be on my way." He muttered more things in Arabic, probably insulting me, but I hung up on him in the middle of it and called 911.

Amu got to the house a few minutes before the paramedics, but he didn't want to take the chance of hurting Amtu or the boy in her belly any more than they already had been, so he tried to comfort her on the floor while she and Hanan simultaneously cried out for their mothers. I led Hanan away and told her she had to leave her mother alone for now.

The paramedics were careful when they loaded her on the stretcher. The two of them asked for Amu's assistance so they could be extra careful with her. Once he saw she was safely loaded into the ambulance, he whirled around and yelled at me for not watching her close enough. "She is pregnant, ya hiwana! I cannot trust you to do anything." He made the spitting sound and motion, but nothing came out.

I knew it was my job to always babysit Hanan. I didn't know it was my job to watch his wife as well.

He took Hanan because he couldn't trust me to watch over his daughter, and Rasheed wanted to go to the hospital to see his mother.

I was all alone.

Amtu Samia stayed in the hospital for a couple of days. Her baby died, but since it had gotten so big already, they had to cut it out in a C-section, and the doctors told her that her seizures worsened during her pregnancy, so she couldn't get pregnant anymore. She had to go to the hospital a little later for another procedure. I knew that she came out sterile, so she must have had her tubes tied, though no one ever said that was what she was doing. If anyone asked, I would say it was a hysterectomy, because people would just assume she got cancer and had to take it out for that reason.

To me, Amu and Amtu were never in love, never seemed to like each other much, but they tolerated each other and must have slept together enough for her to get pregnant once in a while. Now they barely spoke to each other. Amu Nasser worked even more, spending twelve hours at his office on the weekdays, going in most Saturdays for several hours, even

Sundays a couple times a month. Amtu Samia didn't get up until noon most days and rarely ever got dressed unless she went to visit her new best friend, Imm Samir, or Imm Samir came to visit us. Since a visit to them was spending the entire day and evening together, either Amtu was gone when I got home from school and took Hanan with her, or Imm Samir and Amtu would be at the house together, gossiping and laughing their girlish, high-pitched laughs in a futile attempt to appear young. I knew most of the time they were talking about me: what a bad girl I was and my sharmoota for a mother, while I watched Hanan in the living room. They usually stayed in the dining room, basking in their superiority.

That's when I began to wish I'd pushed her off those stairs. Because she deserved the worst she could get, and I wanted to be the one to give it to her.

But it wasn't all bad for me. Even though Amtu Samia picked on me more, Amu Nasser wasn't as mean to me and rarely believed her accusations against me now. Amtu Samia would punish her own children on occasion, but not often, because Rasheed was a godsend and she was rarely alone with Hanan now that Hanan was in school almost as long as me. She would give me much worse than she gave them: slaps instead of ear tugs, punches instead of spankings. Besides that, she always wanted me to get more of the abuse from Amu Nasser; she only told Amu about her own children's bad behavior when it was terrible.

Amu Nasser grew impatient with having to do what he considered her job. "You sit at home all day, and you cannot control three children? I work my ass off to support this family and to make a good life for you in this country, and you want me to come home to tell Isra she should talk to you in a nicer tone? You're a sad excuse for a woman. My mother raised five children better than you can raise three."

Amtu claimed that she knew how to raise her children, good Palestinian kids, but she had never signed up to raise some bint min haraam, a bastard, with an Amreekiya mother, who didn't know manners, modesty, or respect. She'd like to see how his mother would deal with that.

"Ya Samia, she is not that bad. Her father is Falasteeni, she is Falasteeniya. My mother took in her dead sister's two children, and she never once complained."

I liked that she got a taste of her own medicine, got to feel what it was like to be treated like a good-for-nothing.

One evening Amu Nasser got home before five, which he never did on weekdays even before Amtu Samia fell down the stairs. Hanan was coloring at the dinner table while I was chopping meat and parsley at the counter, Rasheed was at a friend's house, and Amtu and Imm Samir were out somewhere. He looked surprised to see Hanan and me in the kitchen and asked me where his wife was.

"She's at Imm Samir's, I think." Not that she ever told me where she was going or even when she would be back.

He frowned and went to his office to put his things away, trailed by Hanan, who was trying to show him a picture she just finished coloring. "Yes, nice, habibti. Very nice. Baba needs to finish some work. Go show your cousin, okay?"

I could tell he was angry. Amu Nasser knew I did chores around the house and that I helped Amtu with the big weekend breakfasts we ate, but for some reason, him finding out I cooked dinner every day would set him off, and he and his wife would have a huge fight. I thought she deserved to be punished for the way she treated me, but I hated having to hear them fight all the time. With Mom, our home was so peaceful and serene unless Baba was around, but at Amu Nasser's it was fight after fight after fight, even though he was only around in the late evenings and nights. Sometimes I wondered why they didn't divorce, and why Amtu Samia would fear Amu Nasser divorcing her (something I picked up from her conversations in Arabic with Imm Samir). I knew if you were married to a man, you could get half of what he had; Baba didn't have anything, but Amtu Samia could have made a killing off divorcing Amu Nasser. He was a lawyer, though, so he would probably have everything tied up in court. They'd battle each other for years, destroying each other. The thought made me smile, though I'd be out of a place to live.

I was sitting on the couch when Amtu Samia and Imm Samir walked through the door, and they were laughing about something. Amu Nasser came out of his office right away, and Amtu Samia's smile dropped instantly. He greeted them and asked Imm Samir how she was holding up after her husband's recent death, and if she was lonely not living with any family. Amu Nasser made his questions much shorter than they would have normally been, and Imm Samir's responses were the same. She knew she had to get out; she could sense Amu's barely-concealed anger.

They went into his office to yell at each other, but it was pointless since we could still hear them. Rasheed came home in the middle of it and asked me what was going on, and I shrugged. "I guess they're mad at each other again," I said. Hanan was upset and cried at first. I would have taken her somewhere else in the house, but there wasn't anywhere where you couldn't hear them. All three of us waited in the living room, silent, stomachs empty. Dinner was ready and got cold. Eventually I couldn't take it anymore and made myself and Hanan two plates of food. Rasheed came in a few minutes later and got out a plate and ate at the dinner table with us.

"Do you think they'll be mad we ate without them?" Rasheed asked.

"When aren't they mad?" I didn't know why he was so concerned. If they were going to blame someone for being rude, it was going to be me. Not Rasheed. Not their golden boy.

"True," he said, and went to get seconds.

Amu Nasser's voice boomed. "I did not marry an eleven-year-old girl! She is the only one who cooks and does anything around the house. You run your mouth about her. You should thank me for getting her. I got you a maid and a babysitter all in one child!"

"No, you bring your cousin's bint min haraam for me to raise, and all I try to do is teach her how to be good woman!"

"You are a liar, Imm Rasheed." He called her "Imm Rasheed" when he was super pissed to remind her she wasn't living up to that name, the mother of his son, named after Amu's father. "How can you make her a good woman when you tell all around town that she is a bint min haraam? How will she ever find a good husband if everyone knows this? You want to keep her here forever, that is what you want! Lazy, lazy, lazy!" He kept on shouting that over and over; he didn't want to let her get in a word edgewise to defend herself. He reminded me of one of those kids that covered their ears and said "La, la, la" because they didn't want to hear what the other person had to say. I laughed.

"What's funny?" Hanan asked, her forehead wrinkled in confusion.

"Your mama and baba are stupid. They're like babies."

That made her laugh. "Babies?"

"It's just like how they fuss and cry when they have nothing to do. It means nothing. It's just noise."

But nothing changed. Amu Nasser threw his weight around, yelled, and criticized when he made an appearance, but that hardly mattered because he was never there, so less than a week after that argument I went back to making dinner every weeknight and cleaning the house and watching Hanan all the time.

Nothing would ever get better.

CHAPTER THIRTEEN

Just after eight in the morning, Yusef's cell rang and vibrated so furiously it nearly fell from the nightstand next to my side of the bed. I startled awake and accidentally elbowed Yusef's ribs when I reached for it. He whimpered and let out sigh-snore from his nose and mouth.

"Fuck whoever calls this early on a fuckin' Saturday," he said, and turned over on his other side, his back to me and his phone.

"It's your mother."

He turned back over and answered the phone.

I heard Imm Yusef's voice going on and on. I closed my eyes and lay back down on my side, but I couldn't tune it out completely. Yusef put in the occasional aiwa, yeah, to let her know he agreed and was listening. I opened my eyes when he stroked my belly, his eyes red and droopy but his lips smiling. I had told him not to announce it to anyone until I reached my second trimester.

He said I was morbid and negative, as usual, in a half-accusatory, half-playful way, but he agreed. We would keep this to ourselves for another two months, and then he would be given free rein to shout the news from the rooftops.

I hardly spoke Arabic, and my understanding of it was only a little better, so I was afraid that he would announce the news to his mother right in front of my face without me knowing, but Yusef was barely contributing anything to the conversation. Announcing a baby took more than two words at a time.

He hung up and lay back down. "My parents are coming over."

"Why?" I asked. Then, to seem less resentful, I added, "I'm so tired, I want to sleep more."

He groaned and rubbed his eyes. "She got a deal on two Laz-E-Boys, and she has to bring them over right now. She picked up one of Khadija's sons to help me lug the things up here. Baba can't be doing any heavy lifting."

I snuggled up to the pillow and savored rest for a couple minutes before I forced myself to get up and dress. It wasn't so bad to be up this early; at least there was another hour left of semi-cool air before the heat set in for real.

Yusef was still lying in bed in his boxers; by the beginning of June, he'd stopped wearing his pajamas to bed because it was too hot. He was a big boy. If he didn't want to get up to look decent in front of his parents and nephew, that was his problem.

While I brushed my hair, I remembered that I would have to at least make something to drink. As soon as I put the tea on to boil, I heard a knock. Abu Yusef's gravelly voice called from the stairhead, ordering Yusef to open the door. "Ya Yusef, ifta al-bab al-aan!"

I opened the door. "Sorry, I was putting the tea on the stove."

Abu Yusef shook his head, slightly embarrassed, but still smoking without interruption. His lungs had to be as black as charcoal. "I am very sorry, bintee Isra. I believed Yusef was keeping us waiting out here."

I showed them in and tried not to breathe the cigarette smoke. Abu Yusef made himself a place at the kitchen table with one of his ashtrays that we kept on the microwave. I followed Imm Yusef and her grandson back into our bedroom, where I wasn't surprised to find Yusef still lying on the bed in his underwear, snoring away.

She made a loud exclamation. "Yee!" I wondered if our downstairs neighbors heard all the commotion this early. " 'ayb, 'ayb, 'ayb," she kept saying. "Shame, shame, shame." She ordered him in Arabic to get up and dress, and some other things I didn't catch, but she looked to me. "Why does he wear these, these underwear that are as shorts? From when he is boy, I buy him briefs, but as soon as he leave high school, he is wearing these shorts."

Yusef got up and threw on some jeans and a T-shirt. "You know, Mama, you shouldn't be calling and waking us up so early. We need our rest, especially Isra, because she's pregnant."

Imm Yusef jumped up and down, something I would have never expected from a woman her age. She grabbed me and kissed me on both cheeks over and over. She gave me one of her bone-crushing hugs. "Already! God has smiled upon us."

She did the same to Yusef except she pulled him down to sit next to her on the bed and spoke to him in Arabic for almost fifteen minutes. His nephew Muhammad looked my way and congratulated me. I smiled, trying to look as happy as possible while I considered how I would punish Yusef.

She left, announcing the news to Abu Yusef. I shot Yusef a look, not caring that Muhammad was still in our bedroom. Muhammad took the hint and left. Yusef's bright smile deflated into petulant annoyance. "I don't see the problem in letting everyone know a little early," he said. "I don't like keeping secrets."

"It's not a secret. It's just keeping things private for a little while." I turned away. He could be so stupid and inconsiderate.

"Hey, look on the bright side: I bet she won't be calling here early anymore."

"She will be here more."

"Is Baba smoking out there?"

"What? Yeah, of course." That's all he ever did.

Yusef brushed past me. "He shouldn't be smoking in the house while you're pregnant," he said, closing the door. "I'll tell him to stop and air out the living room. See, this is why we should tell people."

So now I was quarantined. In about ten minutes, Imm Yusef came and said that the living room was now sufficiently smoke-free because they kept the door open. I got up, ready to leave, but she sat on the bed and motioned for me to take the seat next to her. "My son tells to me you want to keep pregnancy to yourself."

Yusef always knew how to make things worse. "I only wanted to keep it quiet for a little while in case something happens."

She closed her eyes gently as she nodded her head, though I knew she wasn't agreeing with me. "This I know. Do not be angry. We will not tell to anyone else. I have two miscarriages." She held up two fingers on one hand and then put them on her ample midsection. "One between Fatima and Lubna, and one between Lubna and Yusef. Still, I am very excited that this happens for you. Yusef ibnee waheed." Yusef is my only son. She put her hand on her heart, pledging herself to this child already.

She already had at least ten grandchildren—ten I could remember—

but I didn't think she'd gotten as choked up about them, even when they first got out of the womb, as she did about the one I had in my belly—not even a fully formed fetus, no eyes, no face, no gender yet. I couldn't help but be a little touched despite everything, though I couldn't let it make me forget what fueled her love. A penis made that much of a difference in how a mother would love her own children, even her children's children.

Imm Yusef wanted to have a celebration, which meant going to someone's house to eat a lot of food. It sounded good to me. I didn't get the chance to have breakfast. She was on the phone with someone in our living room. She was already spreading the news. I knew "walad" meant boy or just a generic child; why would she need to say it so much? I didn't know who she was talking to. I wouldn't sit by Yusef or even look at him. I kept myself busy making sure his father had his fill of tea, which the old man was inhaling like air now that he couldn't smoke. Imm Yusef's tea lay there half-finished, cold, while she went on and on to whomever she was talking to.

I went back to the bedroom and lay down on the bed, door ajar, not caring that Yusef's family was still here. I caressed my belly the way Yusef did, going up and down a few times and then making two circles at the same time. The door creaked, and he shut it and came over.

Normally I would have pulled away if I was angry at him, but I just lay there, still and slack, staring up at the ceiling. He placed kisses on my neck and went up to my ear. "Don't be mad, Isra. It's not good for the baby."

So now we came to the point where we were past apologies and arguments. We only had anger that we were too spent to acknowledge. His mother came to the door and announced that we would be going to Khadija's house for breakfast. I shrugged him off when I sat up and heard his nephew in the hall, giggling. "That's how he gave her a baby so fast."

Imm Yusef commented on how wobbly the apartment stairs were, especially when you had to walk down. "It is not good for older ones, and when Isra becomes bigger." She demonstrated my increasing size with one arm protruding from her belly. She rubbed her husband's back and made sure he was steady. She seemed to treat him like a very old man, and I realized that he was significantly older than her, somewhere from ten to fifteen years. Abu Yusef added something to Imm Yusef's comment in Arabic as Yusef gently escorted his father down the steps.

"He said one of our cousins says there's a nice house for a good price a little ways away, three bedroom," Muhammad volunteered.

I nodded, embarrassed at how he instantly knew that I didn't fully understand. "Oh, okay."

Imm Yusef turned around and told me that she had seen the house. It was only thirty miles from here. We should look at it sometime soon.

Muhammad's eyes lingered on me. I wasn't sure if it was my breasts or my belly he was looking at. He blushed and turned his face from mine. In a few seconds he looked back at me and asked me how old I was.

"Twenty-two."

"I'm going to be eighteen in January."

"That must be exciting."

"Habibi, don't ask a woman her age. That is shameful," Imm Yusef said while she took hesitant steps.

"But she's not old, Sitti."

When we were off the steps, she hit him upside the head and muttered 'ayb to him a couple times. Yusef laughed. "I guess you're not so good with the ladies. Better hurry up and learn. You're almost a man now."

We didn't come back until three in the afternoon. Yusef and I didn't speak the whole ride home, or at his sister's house for that matter. There was so much conversation and congratulations, no one seemed to notice the tension between us. For a brief moment of doubt, I asked myself why I wanted to keep this a secret. Everything was going well; people were happy for us, even if it was a sexist happiness. But just because things were going well for now didn't mean that it wouldn't blow up in our faces (and I suspected it would be more in mine than in his). Besides, if I asked him to keep it quiet for a couple of months, he should do as he promised me. I had told him not to say anything to anyone, even his mother, because telling her was the same as announcing it to his whole family.

I lay down on the bed once I got to the bedroom. If Yusef came and took this as a signal that I wanted him, I would yell at him to give me some peace.

I looked down at my stomach. It felt like I was growing a small pouch of fat there, but a bit had been there since I could remember. I imagined myself getting a big belly, waddling down the rickety stairs. The fear of falling down them suddenly became real. My heart raced; not only would I lose the baby, I might die, crack my skull open, or break both legs. With the indifferent people that lived here, I imagined most of them would walk past me, not even bothering to call an ambulance.

If I made it all the way to giving birth . . .

I couldn't imagine that pain. Having sex the first time was bad enough; at least it was relatively short. This would be hours, maybe an entire day, or days. I wouldn't let Yusef bring his mother into the hospital room. The last thing I needed was her jabbering on about how easy childbearing had been for her and her daughters, or looking down at my vagina for God knows how long.

If he violated that rule, I might kill him.

Because he wasn't going to make all his plans in life without me.

After dinner I went back to our bedroom and read while he watched TV and worked on his thesis. Three hours must have passed. I was nearly done with the novel I started in that sitting when he came in. He sat at the foot of the bed and rubbed my bare legs. His arm hair tickled, but I wouldn't look at him or laugh.

"I'm almost done with my thesis, at least for the summer. I'll have to make some revisions in the fall after I meet with my advisor, but I've got all the research and conclusions down on paper. That's the difficult part, really." He paused and looked down at my legs while his hand moved up to my thighs. He leaned over and kissed them.

"I'm not in the mood." I turned over on my back. I figured my thighs looked fatter from that angle; they would be less alluring to him.

"If you're angry, tell me. I'd rather have it out in the open than this."

"You know I'm angry," I said. "I'm tired of doing this with you, and it makes no difference at all." I still had my eyes on the book, but I'd lost my place.

"But I don't see why I've got to hide things from my family."

I bit my lip, resisted giving him my reasons.

"They're your family, too, Isra, now that we're married. My parents think of you as a daughter, my sisters as a sister."

I kept my peace on that, too.

He waited. I said nothing.

"Fine." He left the bedroom. A couple hours later, he came and got a pillow to sleep on the couch.

I didn't say a word then either.

We kept up the cold war for a week and a half. I cleaned, but I didn't cook. We went out to visit some people about every other day. He worked on his thesis; I thought about Sana, the way we'd vent about men and their idiocies and selfishness. She was busy now, working fifty-hour weeks and helping her older sister with her second child. I pictured myself in a place of my own, spacious and pristine, far out in the country, away from nosy mothers-in-law and disappointing husbands.

"Mama wanted to say congratulations on the baby," Hanan told me over the phone as I sat on the bed and organized my photo collection. I had just received our wedding pictures and dreaded making an album of them. Our marriage did turn out to be just like that day: long and exhausting with every action predetermined by someone else.

"You told her?"

"I didn't tell her. Imm Samir did. Everyone knows. I didn't talk about it with anyone except you."

"I know you didn't."

I wanted to break the silence with Yusef and scream my head off, but I wouldn't give him the satisfaction of knowing I would be the one who gave in.

"Are you still there?" Hanan asked.

I confirmed that I was and asked if Amtu Samia genuinely congratulated me.

"Oh . . . I think so."

"Tell me what she said."

"She said that you probably got pregnant so early because you guys had been trying before you were married." She paused, waiting for my reaction. "She was in a bad mood, Isra. I don't think she actually knows anything."

I woke up with sharp stomach cramps. When I was a preteen and first had them, they felt like knives penetrating my uterus with a steady force. The ones I had now were much worse. My crotch and bottom felt wet. I lifted the top sheet and saw the fresh, deep red stain on my pajama bottoms; there was a circle of blood on the sheet underneath me. Turning over made me nauseated and dizzy. I cried out and panted. I had to be dying. I had to be. This was it. I never thought I would die alone in my bed at twenty-two.

It took all I had to reach and grab my cell phone. I called out for Yusef several times, thinking he was still out on the couch where he slept the night before or drinking coffee in the kitchen. The time on my phone was well past nine in the morning. He'd been gone for over an hour.

I was surprised when some of the pain subsided. I could sit up with just a piercing, not a stab, of pain in my belly. I remembered Hanan had no key when I heard her banging on the door. "Are you all right, Isra?" she kept on asking while I walked, half-hunched, to the door. She gasped when she saw me. "Oh my God!"

She helped me stand straighter, and she looked at the bloodstain smeared on my pants. "Does it hurt really bad? I should get a pad or something."

She set me down on the couch and said she'd go in the bedroom to get me a change of pants and underwear before we went to the emergency room. "Find another pair of pants. Don't get me jeans." She was back fast, or I might have just been so out of it that I lost my sense of time, and she helped me into the loose-fitting track pants, asking if she needed to be gentler every time I winced in pain. "It's not anything you're doing," I said.

There was a hospital only two miles away. The hard part was getting down the steps and making it to Hanan's car. Each downhill step felt like a knife penetrating deeper into my uterus, the steps on flat ground only a little more bearable. Most of the time I had my eyes pressed shut, and Hanan kept her arms around my waist. Her breathing was uneven. I could feel her pulse beat against my back.

I lay down in the backseat, my eyelids fluttering, my head spinning. I wrapped my arms around my waist, wishing I could have some real rest.

"Isra, shouldn't we call Yusef or something?"

I groaned. "You can call him, but I don't want to speak to him."

She called him once they took me into the ER. While I was lying on the hospital bed, taking in drugs through the IV, she told me that he seemed upset. He thought there might be hope that I could still be pregnant. She picked dirt from under her fingernails. "I don't know, I thought if there was bleeding, that automatically meant a miscarriage," she said, looking at the curtain separating us from the other patient in the room. "Maybe he knows something we don't."

"It does mean a miscarriage." I rolled my eyes and shook my head at his naïveté.

Her shoulders tensed, and she looked back at the curtain. "He said he'll be here soon."

The pain subsided, and Hanan distracted me by talking, which she hadn't been able to do uninterrupted for weeks. Her mother was getting on her nerves, complaining about the house being a wreck. Hanan couldn't wait for her mother to leave for Imm Samir's most days. Rasheed had gotten serious and was taking summer school. He might graduate within a year. We chuckled.

"Rasheed might actually make something of himself," Hanan said.

I shrugged. I considered telling her that making something of yourself was a lot harder than it seems as a teenager, but I was too drugged and exhausted to make her understand. Yusef walked in, his eyes wide and filled with tears. He tried to thank Hanan for getting me here, but halfway through he choked and cried. She patted his back before she left to give us time alone.

He came over, pulled me in close to his chest, and kissed my forehead.

Though everything was all right except for the miscarriage, I wasn't discharged until after 6 p.m.—after spending more than eight hours sitting under fluorescent lighting and suffering intermittent exams from Yusef—with orders to meet with my gynecologist in a week. I still felt exhausted, but the cramps had lessened, and I could walk upright again. Yusef kept his arm around my waist in case I felt dizzy or anything.

Once we got home, I sat in one of our new chairs while Yusef changed our bedsheets. It seemed like an eternity. All I wanted was to sleep and for this day to be over, forget it ever happened, though I knew everyone would be talking about it and sending me condolences, reminding me over and over of what I had been through. If I had to have pain, I'd prefer it to be private, so it wouldn't be subject to the opinions of others.

"The bed's ready, Isreenie." I could get up myself, but he insisted on helping me, holding out his hand. "Yeah, I didn't know where the sheets were. I guess that makes me a pretty bad husband." He laughed a few short bursts.

I lay down on my back, and he slipped the heating pad up my shirt and pressed it against my belly. "Is that how you want it?"

"I just want to sleep." I was awake the whole time in the hospital. The only thing that terrified me more than going to a hospital was falling asleep in one, making myself a home there.

"Well, Isreenie, I have to call my mother and tell her we won't be coming over tonight, but I won't say anything about today."

How could I have forgotten about visiting his family? I closed my eyes hard. "Look, tell her the truth. We're going to have to get it out there sooner or later, 'cause everyone's expecting a baby. Please ask her not to come over, not tonight at least. Please. I know she's family and whatever . . ." My voice broke and tears ran down my cheeks. "I want to be alone, for right now, because I don't want everyone seeing me like this, and I always feel like I have to impress her or she'll judge me. I can't take that right now, okay? She can come over tomorrow, but I need to be alone now."

He wiped the tears from my cheeks and promised he would ask her to leave me alone, let me rest. It was no problem. "I can stay home with you tomorrow. She can come over and help, because you can see I'm kind of domestically retarded." He attempted to chuckle.

"No, you don't have to miss work. I'll ask Hanan. She's still on summer vacation."

"It's no problem, Isra. I want to be here, and I'm pretty sure that my mother would be okay with helping out."

"I'm more comfortable with Hanan doing it." I took a breath and pressed the heating pad against my belly harder. "She needs an excuse to get away from her mother anyway."

He squeezed my hand and kissed each fingertip. "Let me know if anything goes wrong. If things are going well, I want to know, too. Hanan can call, you can call. I want to know what's going on."

"I'll be fine."

He sniffled again. "I'm so sorry. I'd heard about these things before. I think Lubna had one, but, you know, I found out about those after it happened, after all this worry and grief and everything. I'm a dumbass, and now I'm crying like a fuckin' wimp every five seconds."

It would be cruel to agree with him. I told him to come and lie down next to me. The whites of his eyes were veined red, the tears making them a darker green. He did come to lie behind me. He reached over to hold my hand, and I felt his spurts of breath on my neck.

My boss gave me a week off from work, and I spent most of it watching TV, reading, and eating big bars of dark chocolate Hanan brought to the apartment. She spent the entire day with me. When evening came, I would put something frozen in the oven for dinner. She ate with me and Yusef and went home. Imm Yusef didn't come over much in the middle of the day; she hardly ever left the store or her house now that Abu Yusef's health was deteriorating, but she came over during dinnertime and kept on insisting that she could make something instead of us having to eat frozen American food.

I stepped on the scale before I left for work. My pants felt a little snug. I had gained seven pounds in addition to the five I put on during my short pregnancy. Twelve pounds heavier. Soon I would be a whale and have no children to blame it on.

I wouldn't let myself stop by the store to pick up chocolate, and I made dinner that day instead of warming it up. My meals didn't have as many carbs and calories as the frozen ones. I used chicken breast instead of cubed beef in the bamiya stew I made; I cooked brown rice instead of white to go along with it. The brown had no flavor, no matter how much salt, cumin, and olive oil I put on it. Yusef said he liked it, but I noticed him mostly eating the bamiya from the top of his rice instead of eating the rice itself.

I cleaned up the kitchen and let the food settle in my stomach. Yusef filled the coffee table with his thick textbooks, his laptop, and a hard copy of his thesis. I changed into a T-shirt and leggings in the bedroom. "I'm going to take a walk, Yusef," I said on my way out.. "I'll be back in half an hour or so."

He looked up and frowned. "Really? It's almost seven."

"It'll be light out for another hour."

"I'll go with you."

We ended up walking on the track field across from the apartment, hand in hand, silent. I looked up at the pink light coming out and felt certain that Yusef must be pondering my failings as a cook and as a wife. Maybe he would consider moving back in with his parents so he could have a good meal if he was not going to have a child. He might as well return to his own childhood. I rolled my eyes and bit the inside of my lip hard enough to draw a little blood.

He interrupted my thoughts and my walking to kiss my forehead, my nose, and my lips. I giggled and hugged him, getting a faint whiff of his musk. I pulled away. I needed to actually do some walking. He caught up to me and wrapped his arm around my waist. "How're you feeling? What'd your doctor say?" he asked.

I stared down at my worn tennis shoes and the white chalk marks on the grass. "She said everything's fine. I haven't been bleeding."

"That's good." He pulled me closer. "So why'd you start the walking?"

My cheeks got warm. "Because I'm getting fat," I said.

He laughed. "That's why you're eating that brown rice bullshit?"

I playfully slapped his chest and grinned. "I knew you didn't like the brown rice!"

"You can't blame me. I got taste buds."

I gave up the brown rice, but I made myself exercise a few times a week, wore makeup every day, and had my hair cut and straightened. I liked my hair curly and felt more like myself with it, but I looked too young and informal. I had not only let my weight creep up since my teens, but I had let womanhood creep up on me at the same time. I shouldn't dress like a nonchalant teenager anymore. I was a college graduate and married. I had almost become a mother.

I spent the entire day filling out job applications and emailing resumes to any print or online publication. I figured that was better than working as a part-time receptionist at a doctor's office and especially better than being unemployed, only a wife and maybe potentially a mother. I had worked my ass off finding ways to pay for my education so as not to become that, getting scholarships because Amu wasn't going to pay to educate his not-daughter. I liked working at the office, but I was meant for more than answering phones and sending out appointment reminders to rich people. I needed to move on and become a real woman with career prospects.

Sana had been calling once in a while for the past few months, but we hadn't had much time to talk. We talked for an hour and a half this time. I invited her over for lunch that weekend. Seeing someone without having to cook a big meal or worrying about their judgment, proving my worth or qualifications, was an enormous relief. Hanan was only an intermittent guest, because her mother had decided that since the miscarriage was now in the past, there was no reason for her to be over here so much.

She came over soon after Yusef went to see his parents. Abu Yusef was feeling lightheaded and was bedridden. I felt cruel, but I didn't offer to come with him. I didn't want to see Imm Yusef or his sisters, hear their condolences, or answer their questions.

I gave Sana a condensed explanation of where Yusef went while we were sitting on the balcony, drinking soda and eating chips. "Is there something wrong? Well, besides . . ."

I shrugged, watching the bubbles dissipate in my drink.

"Most guys are vultures. They use you and leave you."

I covered my face with my hands. "It's just pressure, pressure, pressure. When I lived with Amu and Amtu, I hated them; they made my life hell, but I didn't give a shit about what they thought, just as long as they wouldn't kick me out. Now I've always got to worry about what his mother and sisters think of me, and all the other women. Nobody thinks I'm good enough for him. He's perfect, and I don't know how to be a 'good woman.'"

She snorted. "Yusef is a nice guy, but you are good to him. Look at how you fixed up this dump he lived in. Look at him now."

I laughed, something I hadn't done for a while. I shook my head. "Things are getting better between us, but it's been bad for a little while."

Yusef came back while Sana and I were still out on the balcony. He stopped by to say hi to Sana and give me a kiss. "I'm just going to work on my thesis or take a nap or something," he said. He went back inside and headed for the refrigerator. I couldn't believe Yusef came from his parents' house hungry. Abu Yusef must have been worse than I thought.

Sana mouthed "Should I go?" I nodded. He seemed upset. I saw Sana out and went to Yusef and rubbed his back. I should have gone to his parents' house with him. "I can make dinner early if you want."

I moved away when he closed the refrigerator and grabbed a bag of chips from the cupboard. "So how are your parents?"

His shoulders sunk, and he leaned over on the counter. "Baba's been in bed for days. The doctors don't know what's wrong with him. Well, he does have heart disease, and he still smokes. The only reason he hasn't these few days is because he can't get away from Mama to hide his smoking from her."

"How old is he now?"

He sighed. "Seventy-one. It's old, but I wish that he had more time. Good time."

I pulled him in for a hug.

"I just wish he wanted to be around for longer," he managed to say before his tears spilled from his eyes.

I weighed myself before I went to bed: I had lost five pounds! I kept the news from Yusef. The last thing he needed to hear about was weight loss when he was worrying about his father. I felt ashamed for caring so much about something like this at such a time.

But Yusef must have noticed. He practically pounced on me when I got into bed, burying his face in my breasts and telling me how much he missed my body. "This isn't too soon, is it? Your doctor said everything's all right?"

I pulled his face up and my shirt down. "Um, she said we should wait three months before I try to get pregnant. Only four weeks have passed." It had been over five, pushing six weeks.

He cupped my breast and caressed my covered nipple with his forefinger. "I could get condoms at the store. This would be purely for pleasure."

I hesitated and looked away.

"You're not ready?" he asked, pained.

"Just a little while longer." I turned over on my stomach and closed my legs as tight as I could, and he cupped my butt the same way he did my breast, his fingers kneading the fat. "I can think of other ways to make love without running the risk of pregnancy," he said.

I skipped a few breaths when I realized what he wanted me to do with him. "That's so disgusting, Yusef!" I got off the bed so fast that I almost tripped and banged my arm against the side of the doorway.

Eventually he convinced me to come back to bed. He claimed I was over-reacting, that he was not going to do it if I didn't want to. I only came back because I didn't know how to argue with him; I didn't know what to say at all.

But I couldn't sleep. I thought about when one of my friends in my junior year of high school told us she had anal sex with her boyfriend because he said he was bored in bed and could find a million other girls to do it for him. My other friend and I were horrified, me especially. I thought anal was something only gay men did. Both my friends were sur-prised at my innocence: everyone my age knew that straight men liked anal. But now I learned that women knew straight men liked anal—and straight men liking it was okay—but only the sluts would give them the pleasure. No one said the last part, but I could tell by my non-sodom-ized friend's reaction that that was what she thought about my sodomized friend. The sodomized one seemed to feel my judgment more, though, and told me, "Not everyone can string a guy along for a year without even kissing him like you did, Isra."

Because Sana was in college and knew a lot more about sex than me but didn't look down on me for my ignorance, I took the information to her in the most inappropriate place: the outdoor celebration of Eid while we were sitting on a bench, watching some kids hit a piñata. Sana was as disgusted as me but not surprised. "If a man wants to do that to you, he should have you put on a strap-on and let you do it to him." She made the humping motion with her hips and arms before I told her to stop, that we'd be in deep shit if we got caught talking about this, here of all places.

"You know, I have a theory." That didn't surprise me. Sana always had theories about those kinds of things. She liked to say that she'd grow up and write a book titled *Sana's Laws of Sexuality*. She'd be on the cover in a stylish pants suit with a knowing smile, and the book would cause a sensation in America and the Middle East. Her parents would probably disown her and even change their names, but who cared what old people thought? Besides, they let her brothers run around and stay out all night like sharmootas. "So this is my theory: straight guys like anal because it's sort of gay but not quite if you do it with a girl."

From the corner of my eye, I saw her father marching toward us, his face scrunched in anger. He could spot Sana's unladylike behavior a mile away. When she saw him, her slight smile vanished. He barked her name. "Sana, what is this you are doing?"

The color drained from her face in an instant, and she incriminated us more when she tried to explain. I felt sick to my stomach when she used the word anal in front of her father, and she said we were only discussing a movie we both saw. It angered him more that we were watching filth, and he didn't seem to believe her. He stormed off, and I felt relieved that we'd gotten off easy; he didn't threaten to tell Amu or punish Sana.

But Sana was only more freaked out. "God, Isra, he's going to get my mom! I know he is. If he's really mad, he always brings her in on the punishment so they can gang up on me." She tried to breathe evenly but was unsuccessful. "Damn it, you're always getting me in trouble."

"Shut up! You didn't have to sodomize the air and talk so loudly." We saw Sana's father heading back not with her mother but with Amu, and both walked with an angry, self-righteous confidence. Amu instantly berated me for talking about shameful things, and once he was done verbally abusing me, I told him Sana and I were discussing a former friend I had at school and how outraged I was by her behavior. I needed a girl my age to sympathize with that outrage, so I went to Sana. Who else was there who would agree with my views? I wouldn't talk about such things with Hanan. She was too young.

Sana's father's face softened, and he praised me for being a good girl. "You must not be taken in by these bad women," he said. "America is full of them, and you should not emulate their ways."

Amu was more hesitant in his acceptance of my explanation, but he only said, "You must never see this girl again. If you hang around such girls, people will think you are like her. I forbid you from ever seeing her."

Now I wanted to be that Isra again, the Isra who only heard about men's strange desires that weren't so strange and didn't have to worry about them, didn't feel compared to all the invisible other women in her husband's past, didn't feel boring and inadequate.

Though we missed our opportunity for the three-bedroom Abu Yusef told us about, one of Yusef's cousins who was in real estate let us know a two-bedroom house in town was available. It was late in the semester, and

Yusef was teaching three classes and researching and finishing his thesis. He had little time to check it out, so Amer, the cousin, dropped the key off with me. "Only bring back to me if you don't like," he said. "If you like, you can keep. I have copy."

Yusef had Saturday night free to look at the house. He drove us there in his car, and the heater couldn't warm the car up enough, so I ended up cuddling with the passenger door for warmth. "I need to replace this piece of junk, too," he said.

He was always tired and cranky now. He was gone all the time or grading tests or putting the finishing touches on his beloved thesis, but I suppose his paychecks and recognition were worth it: he made almost double what he was making in the summer, and some of his findings might be featured at a conference in the spring.

The house was almost as cold as the car, but it had a good-size kitchen with lots of counter space and even a real area to put a dinner table. While Yusef went off to look at the bedrooms, I checked the cupboards. There was a big hall closet where we could put the spare bedsheets and towels. All this space. I missed living in a house.

"The master bedroom's big."

I passed by him to verify and noticed the window that looked out into the backyard. "I like this house. If it's a good price, I don't see why not." I smiled and put a lock of hair behind my ear.

He smiled back. "It's about nine a month. Pretty good for a house." He took my hand and led me through the hall to the patio.

He slid the door open, the wind cold enough to make me fold my arms. "Let's check it out later," I said.

He kept on insisting, and anyway he had the door open still, so there was no avoiding it. We walked out, huddled together, and he pointed at a rosebush against the window of the master bedroom. "Look, there's still a couple of roses," he said, and walked over to the bush. He took his keys out and used the Swiss Army knife he had on the chain to cut one off and shave the thorns, pricking himself every now and then.

He brought it to me with a proud smile. Now that it was in the light, I saw that it was pink. I pulled my hands from my pockets and took it. "Thanks." I hugged him and gave him a peck on the mouth, but he pulled me in for more and put his tongue in my mouth and tasted my lips.

I pulled away and put my hand to his mouth; he kissed the fingertips.

"Let's make love here," he said, then laughed. "Well, inside. I don't think my dick could handle this cold."

"Not now."

He bit down on his lip hard. "When's it going to be, Isra? It's been four months, and yes, I've been counting." He looked to the side and stepped back up on the porch. His lips turned paler in the cold. "Is it about that thing I asked you about? If it is, I didn't mean to scare you. I was curious, that's all."

"It's not about that." Though it still made me cringe when I thought about it. "I'm . . . I was thinking that I've been going on all these interviews and trying to make a career for myself, so it wouldn't make sense for me to get pregnant."

He tucked in his bottom lip. "So what's that mean? We'll have a sexless marriage?"

What right did he have to take that tone with me? "No, I was thinking we should use protection." He should know about that. That's probably what kept him from knocking up any of his girlfriends. Unless he was fucking them the way you didn't have to worry about pregnancy.

He stormed back into the house and sat down on the hardwood floor. Right when I came inside he lashed out at me. "I want to be a father. I want a baby, and I thought you wanted the same, and . . . you just change that on me because of one loss. You don't let me touch you at all—"

"You don't touch me because you can't fuck me, and I'm just saying that I don't want to have a child right now! I want to build something for myself. You do it, and I never have a problem. I never say anything about how you're gone all the time. I let you have your life, and a baby will get in the way of my life now."

He shook his head. "What I do is for us. I share everything I have with you."

"But it's always yours. It's always what you want! And it is such a lie that I'll have it, because if you're gone, it won't be mine. It'll be all yours, and I'll be the idiot who gave everything I had to a man."

His expression was hard and cold, but his whole mouth shook. "Let's go home." He picked himself up. He wasn't finished, though. "You never told me any of this before. I've been working hard for us to have that life." He turned his back to me and blew air from his mouth.

"I didn't think you were so backward that you would have such a problem."

He whirled around. "If I were backward, maybe I'd at least be getting laid."

I refused to go home with him. I told him to leave without me, I would figure out where I'd be staying and how I'd get there. He relented and admitted he went a little too far with the last comment. "You cut me deep, though, Isra, with all this backward business and not wanting children."

"It is too soon for us, Yusef. Look at what happened when I got pregnant last time. We can't agree on anything. You really want to bring a child into this?"

"Yes." He folded his arms. "We'll never be perfect. We won't be able to do anything if you wait for that."

"That's easy for you to say." I balled up my fists and shrieked. I slid down the wall to the floor and sobbed in my fists. "You do whatever you want, and no one thinks worse of you for it, but—"

"You think worse of me for it. God, I made a mistake, and it's so hard for you to forgive anything."

I stood back up. I said we should just go home, that I didn't know it was so much to ask for him just to listen to me. What did I expect, though? All he ever cared about was his own needs and wants. That's all that ever mattered.

I walked past him and went out the front door, waiting for him to follow. It took a minute, but eventually he came as I wiped the last of my tears from my face.

CHAPTER FOURTEEN

Amu Nasser and Amtu Samia never announced Amtu Samia's pregnancy, at least not to us kids. She just started showing fast. She hadn't gained much weight, but she had been so thin before that her protruding belly stood in great contrast to her skinny arms and legs. As she entered her second trimester, she looked better than she had before; her body and face were filling out, her straight chestnut hair came in thicker, her skin showed some color.

It was the first time I noticed in over three years of living with her that Hanan looked a lot like Amtu Samia. Before I only noticed the early lines that framed Amtu's mouth and her sallow skin.

I didn't think it was possible, but she became even lazier when pregnant. I used to only clean and cook, but now I had to bring wet washcloths for her to put on her forehead and bring food up to her bedroom when she was feeling too tired to get up.

"I want to have a little sister so I can be like Isra to her," Hanan said one day while she rested her head on her mother's belly, watching an Abdel Halim Hafez movie. Amtu Samia's pregnancy hormones made one of her few consolations watching all the Hafez movies she owned and having her relatives in Jordan send her more nearly every month.

"No, a son will be better," Amtu told her daughter. "There's too many women in this house already." She looked over at me with her eyes narrowed.

Amtu got her wish. She was having a boy.

And that's when Amu Nasser's interest in the baby awakened. He spoke about his plans for this son to go to an Ivy League school, which Amu had dreamed of for himself since his childhood in Jerusalem, but he ended up "only" going to Berkeley. He said that this boy would follow in his older brother's footsteps, though he didn't seem to believe that part of it. Rasheed was just about to start eighth grade, but he had been getting into a lot of trouble, and his grades were dismal.

Amu hadn't yet resigned himself to having a loser for a son, an oldest son no less. He would lecture Rasheed about how he would soon be a man and had to act like one. Amu Nasser would look at his son's quarterly report cards and sigh and fuss about them, but he wouldn't yell or name-call the way he did with me. "Do you want your little brother to see you this way, see you with these bad grades going to a community college?" he would say to Rasheed.

Rasheed would shrug and say, "He won't even know anything when he's born. What's he gonna care about my grades?"

Amu gave him countless lectures about how he had risen from a poor family in Jerusalem and worked his way to Berkeley, where he got his law degree. "I had no money, no nothing. I never slept more than three hours every night. I studied five hours each day and attended class and worked." He would continue by bragging about his job and his salary and his two houses (he didn't have the third until I was in high school). "This is what hard work brings you. I can only carry you so far. If you are lazy, you will end up like Isra's father. He was my cousin, so I got him a job here, but what does he do? He uses drugs, and he gets fired and runs around." Whenever he saw a loser on TV or spoke to us about one of his clients who was unsuccessful, he made sure that Rasheed knew he could not follow in that man's footsteps.

But, true to form, Amu did not enforce his rules. When his son got terrible grades, he never took away video games or banned the use of the TV or the computer. He might give him an ear pull or criticize him, but he never gave him any idea of what it was like to be a poor loser: no video games, no spending money, no new gadgets that Rasheed seemed to get all the time. Because Amu couldn't bear to make his oldest son, his father's namesake, the continuation of his branch of the al-Shadi family, suffer for poor performance.

Even if it would have turned him into a better man.

Everyone was excited about this new baby. Relatives called on the phone, people came over to give their congratulations, and Amtu Samia walked around with her back straighter despite a lot weighing her down in the front. I couldn't believe that the flurry of attention had been greater when Amtu Samia was pregnant with Rasheed. Back then Amu Nasser and Amtu Samia had been a young couple and felt blessed that they had a boy the first time around. Nothing could match that, Amtu assured Rasheed, but this was a great excitement to have the second time around. Another boy to be Rasheed's companion and make him feel more a part of this home.

Hanan was left out of all the celebration and not given any reassurance, though I thought she needed it more. She had been the baby of the family, had grown used to her father coming home and blowing raspberries on her belly and giving her extra candy on the weekends. That abruptly stopped when everyone found out her mother was having a boy. Her parents became busy talking about the boy, buying things for the boy, and discussing what they were going to name the boy. The boy, the boy, the boy. Al walad, al walad, al walad. That's how they always referred to the baby. Hanan became convinced that when her parents had this baby, they would forget all about her and even leave her behind in a grocery store, like her friend's mother did one time. She would have to always make sure her parents didn't forget her.

I found Hanan's complaints irritating and tried to come up with ways to get her to shut up, but there was no way to stop her whining and tears. I was the only one who listened to her at all.

Still, I realized that Hanan's concerns were more than the woes of a spoiled little girl. We had something in common now: we were both treated like we were invisible. The only difference was that I suddenly morphed into visibility when something went wrong, and Hanan just remained invisible. I had an ally. A very little, young, and naïve one, but I had to take what I could get.

Sometimes I read Hanan a picture book from the big collection that was handed down from Rasheed. Her parents added to it once in a while, buying her a book to go along with her birthday present or for Eid or some other holiday. She barely knew how to sound out words, and her parents rarely ever read them to her or helped her get through them. These books usually made Hanan fall asleep faster, so I read to her, but the only ones I thought were half decent were the educational ones and the ones about animals. The other ones were always about some problem that a "normal" kid had, like getting in trouble at school or feeling jealous that a new baby was coming along. No one worried about where the next meal would come from, if Daddy would come back home, if Mommy and Daddy would have a huge fight that day and call each other horrible names.

I made up stories myself to tell her. We lay side by side while I told her about a girl who was trapped in a land of snails, toads, and rats—Hanan hated slimy things, and rats terrified me, so it seemed fitting—and the only way she could get out of this land was to kill the monster that lived in the enormous ocean that separated her from the rest of the world. The monster regularly fed off the land's inhabitants, but still, if this girl tried to kill the monster, all those snails, toads, and rats would try to attack her because they believed the monster was what kept them safe from the rest of the world.

"Oh, no! Is the monster a boy?"

"No, he's a man."

Her eyes widened and her mouth turned into an oval. "What's the girl's name?"

"Noor. Because she has to get up in the morning at first light before the monster wakes up, so that's her name. Light. Noor." Now that I had her name settled, I had to figure out a way she could conquer this monster. "So Noor gets up early in the morning, before all the light is out, and she goes into the water—it's clean, so she can see through it—and she sees the monster sleeping. He snores really loud."

She giggled. "Like Baba."

I nodded. "He makes the water bubble up a lot with his snoring, so she has to go in there and take out her sword. She stabs the monster in the head, but he makes a loud scream." I did a muffled scream to illustrate what I meant as best as I could, but I couldn't be too loud or I'd get in trouble.

Hanan gasped, her eyes riveted on my face. It occurred to me that this might be a bit violent for a child's bedtime story, but I liked it too much to stop. "Then all the snails, toads, and rats in the land wake up because they hear the monster screaming, and they want to stop Noor from killing it. They all run in the water—they're bigger than regular snails, toads, and rats—and they have swords."

"Are they going to hurt her?"

"Well, they try. They run into the water and try to beat her up, but she throws"—I didn't know the name of much weaponry, and I had to think fast—"she throws arrows at them. It's not enough, but it gives Noor time to call for her cousin, a girl who—"

"What's her name?"

"Um, it's . . . Zaynab." I didn't know the meaning of that name, but I figured I might as well give all the characters Arab names.

"Is she big like you?"

I raised my eyebrows and widened my eyes. "Bigger, and she has magic powers to stop all those gross things and the big monster." Why didn't Zaynab come at the beginning and save Noor all that trouble? But I figured Hanan was five, so I didn't need to iron out that plot inconsistency. Besides, help always took its time getting to anyone. "So Zaynab shoots the magic out from her mouth, and the monster explodes. She picks Noor up and brings her over to where she lives, an enchanted forest. None of the snails, toads, or rats know where Noor is."

"What happens to Noor and Zaynab?"

"Well, you have to wait until tomorrow night." I was out of ideas.

"No, 'Sra, I can't wait!" She pouted.

"See, it's way better than that shit that's in your books."

"Ooo-whoo! You said a bad word."

"You know where they tell you you can't say bad words? In the land guarded by the monster. Because if you don't have bad words, you can't say bad things about them."

"Saying bad things isn't nice."

"Yeah, but sometimes you need to say bad things."

"Oh," she said, but I could tell she was confused. She had a deep wrinkle between her dark eyebrows.

By the time I turned out the lights, I regretted telling Hanan that story. Hanan was very sociable, and she volunteered a lot of information. I was relieved when the next day she didn't mention anything to her parents about Zaynab and Noor and a monster that snored loudly like her baba.

I continued the story every night, keeping her up past her bedtime on the nights when I felt most creative. My stories didn't have much of a point, or an ending; they were just scenes in the life of Noor and Zaynab. Sometimes a few snails, toads, and rats would break through the enchanted forest Noor and Zaynab now lived in, and they tried to steal the magic that the two girls shared. Noor and Zaynab had to find a way to fight off those creatures. They would create new weapons, hide in trees, or simply step on one of the creatures to kill it. If I was in a better mood, Noor and Zaynab might just sing songs like the ones Hanan saw on *Barney*, sometimes even the Arabic ones she saw on satellite television. She kept on insisting that they sing "Baba Fen?" (Where's Daddy?) because she liked seeing all those Egyptian kids dancing in the video and getting on and off the phone to sing, but I said no, it was a stupid song, and why would two girls who escaped from the monster be singing about where their babas were?

"Because they love their babas."

"Well, Zaynab doesn't love her baba because he was really mean to her, so she doesn't like to sing that song, and it would be mean of Noor to sing that song in front of her."

"Okay."

As her mother's belly grew bigger, Hanan wanted to know more about why the snails, toads, and rats believed they needed the monster. I had no explanation. I told her it was part of the mystery, and probably those creatures were just too stupid to think about what the monster really was. She wanted to know more about how the monster looked.

"It's sort of like a crocodile, but it has bigger eyes and smooth blue skin. That helps the monster blend in with the water better. The water's a clear blue, too; it's not full of junk like the lakes here."

"We should go and visit Noor and Zaynab."

I laughed, picturing the two of us running hand in hand, wheezing and red-faced, to visit the girls while on a high-speed chase from big snails, toads, and rats. Maybe the monster would even find a way into the forest to kill off the visitors. If we did manage to make it through and meet Noor and Zaynab, I imagined us in a shack deep in a sort of forest/jungle (I hadn't quite decided what Noor and Zaynab's land looked like) that was always damp and smelled like mold and mud. Hanan would probably cry nonstop, having to sleep in such a place. I didn't tell her these things. I said I didn't know how to get there, and if we found it, Noor and Zaynab would most likely run from us. After all, they didn't know what sort of trouble we would cause them.

Hanan lay in my bed that night and pestered me past midnight with schemes she came up with for finding Noor and Zaynab's enchanted land without them being afraid. She suggested that we walk everywhere on earth until we found them, and when we did, we could tell them that we were nice and could help out with the snails, toads, and rats. I told her this was impossible: no one could walk everywhere on earth and make it out alive. My eyelids were so heavy that I couldn't keep them open any longer.

She sat up and shook my arm. "Do you think my little brother will be mean?"

I shrugged. It was likely, considering the kind of parents and brother he was going to have. "We can help make him not mean," I said.

But we never got the chance to try.

CHAPTER FIFTEEN

I managed to find a job as a part-time contributor to the local newspaper. Basically, every week I had to cover three or four events they told me about, and send in my articles that day. It was a start, I consoled myself, a start at a career. I tried to keep my job at the doctor's office until I found something full-time, but the events I had to cover tended to take place in the afternoon, and I couldn't do both. I put in my two weeks' notice, but they arranged to have the doctor's niece come in after a week to take over my job. On my last day, the nurse gave me a hug. "I'll miss you," she said. "The new girl is sixteen."

I laughed. "I was only eighteen when I started. The new girl might not be so bad."

"Isra, that was four years ago. The girl is half my age. And a young sixteen, too."

As we hugged, my stomach was folding inside itself. I was sure I had made the wrong decision.

When it came to Yusef, I wasn't sure about anything. The tension had cooled between us; we didn't fight, we didn't fuck. We didn't anything. On the way home from looking at the house, Yusef told me I projected everything Amu and Baba did onto him, and it just wasn't fair that he had to make up for the sins of others. I could barely look at him after what he said. I could just as easily have told him: I'm not your mother. I won't worship the ground you walk on. I'm my own person. He was so conceited.

I woke up early the next morning to go to a regional spelling bee. I sat in the sparsely populated audience and took note of how many were competing, who won the thing. My butt fell asleep in the stiff metal chair, and I adjusted myself every few minutes, trying not to look too antsy or make the chair squeak. I spent the rest of the time thinking of clever ways to describe the facial expressions of the contestants and the audience's reactions to the children without exaggerating. Everyone looked as uninterested as me.

Jaseel al-Jundi ended up beating out all her competitors. She had to be Middle Eastern. Her mother went up there to give a congratulatory hug. She was white, I was sure, not just a light Arab woman. I wouldn't have guessed Jaseel was a half-breed like me. She had straight black hair and dark brown skin. She smiled, showing her white teeth to a couple of photographers. My chest fluttered, seeing those two together.

I went up to interview the girl and introduced myself to her and her mother.

"I'm smarter than all my brothers," Jaseel announced to me.

Her mother and I laughed. "Well, I'll put that down in my notes." I asked her the mundane questions about how she prepared and how much she studied. Then I moved on to her mother and asked if she was proud.

"Of course, I'm very proud. You know Jaseel could say the alphabet when she was a year old."

"Impressive." I smiled down at the little girl. Her mother's hands were on her shoulders, and the child was looking away, tapping her foot on the stage's wood floor. She was already bored with this interview.

Her mother hesitated. "Are you Arabic?"

I nodded. "Yes, Palestinian. And white, too, on my mother's side."

She was sure that she had seen me somewhere before. It turned out she frequently went to Yusef's parents' store.

"He's one of their sons, right?"

"He's the only son. The other ones are their grandchildren."

"The older one? He's a very sweet boy." She laughed. "Doesn't give me too much trouble when I say the names of things wrong." I imagined Imm Yusef would. One time during our engagement, she went on for nearly half an hour about how much she hated when people called hummus "hum-is" instead of "hoom-moos." (She also hated being called Arabic instead of Arab.) I found it disturbing because I felt the same before our conversation. "You two look too young to be married."

"Oh, we're old enough. I'm twenty-two; he's twenty-five. It's only been—" I paused to count the months on my fingers. "Almost seven months." And I hadn't been sleeping with him for over four of them.

I stopped by the mall on the way home and went to the perfume store toward the entrance. I wore jasmine on rare occasions, but I was starting to run low on the two bottles I had bought at the end of high school. This store had only the designer scents, which all smelled the same to me, flowery and strong, and I got a headache soon after I arrived. I didn't find the kiosk that used to be there, the one with a rack of perfumes that I liked, so I went into a lingerie shop. I could only find a couple bras that were in my cup size, 38D. I wandered over to a display of silky and lacy underwear. Pretty, and not too pricy.

I didn't see the point, though. I wasn't having sex, and I doubted if I ever would again. The first couple of months I assumed Yusef enjoyed the sex we had together. He initiated it most of the time, so he must have liked it, right? But maybe I was just who was available, enough satisfaction to keep him from being too horny. What he really wanted was a woman who wore lingerie and let him put his penis wherever he wanted. For a short second I considered being more open, letting him do more to me, but I couldn't make myself something I wasn't. People had been trying to force me to do that ever since I could remember, and it hadn't worked yet.

Still, I bought a couple of pairs of underwear and a lacy bra that almost fit.

Yusef came home while I was chopping onions. He didn't make eye contact and barely acknowledged my greeting before he walked to the bedroom. I waited for him to come out as I started frying the onions and put the rice and lentils on low heat on the stove. I didn't hear any noises, and it was at least ten to fifteen minutes since he had gotten home. He never took that long to undress and put his things away, but still he didn't come out to see me.

My breaths quickened when I reached our bedroom door. I hesitated a minute, standing in the doorway. He sat on the bed with his hands dangling between his legs. "I miss you," I said, forgetting all the things I planned to say to him.

"I'm here."

"Well . . ." I looked up at the cracked ceiling and sighed. "I still think we should wait to have a baby."

"I figured that much." He turned his face to the wall.

I folded my arms and glared. I wasn't sure whether I should cry or scream at him. I left, not wanting the onions to fry into charcoal.

By the time the food was done, I was close to tears, but they wouldn't drop from my eyes. I bit my lip and wondered why I even tried, why Yusef had the nerve to act so high and mighty. It's not like he knew anything about being a mother, or even about being a father, but that never occurred to him.

And it's not like he was some saint. He had committed his fair share of sins—sins he wouldn't be able to deal with if I had been the one to commit them.

I heard the bedroom door squeak open. Yusef came out to the kitchen and pulled me closer to his chest, burying his face in my neck and sucking my skin. He reached for my breasts, and goose pimples pricked up all over my body; my breath reverberated in my chest. I turned around and wrapped my arms around his waist.

I pressed my body against his and felt the sharp, wet pain between my legs.

We moved out of the apartment and into the house his cousin set us up with. Yusef enlisted the help of two of his nephews to move the furniture and the heavier boxes. Not Muhammad, though, because he needed assistance, not someone to ogle his wife, he told Khadija when he spoke to her on the phone. I talked Yusef into getting rid of the old couch, saying the black corduroy and the smell would make our house look run down and ugly. I could find something decent for a good price. He pulled me to his chest and said, "Whatever you want, whatever you want."

His nephews exchanged amused glances. Though his back was to them, Yusef sensed it and turned around and ordered them in Arabic to lock up the U-Haul. Once they left, we kissed on the floor in our empty living room for a while. "I've got to check on them," he said. "I'll find some place to get rid of the couch, and I'll come pick you up after I get rid of them."

"Okay," I said, kissing the day's stubble he had on his chin and cheeks.

"I should grow a full beard for you."

"No! I shave mine for you, you should do the same for me."

He stroked my chin, jaw, and neck, soft and smooth. "You do keep up with it better than me." He leaned in for one last kiss. "But a beard is the mark of a true man."

"You're not even thirty. I don't want you to look like an old man."

I saw Yusef walk into the driveway as soon as I turned the corner; he was back from dropping his nephews off. He looked distracted. When I parked my car next to his and took my old duffel bag out of the passenger seat, he walked to me. "I can't get the heat to work in the house."

"Really?" It was so cold outside, and the house was worse. I wrapped myself up in a blanket and sat in one of the Laz-E-Boys and flipped through the channels on TV.

Yusef joined me after he came back from picking up our fast food dinner. "You know how long it took me to find a place that's open on Christmas Day?"

I surveyed the pile of boxes stacked around me. We didn't have many: a couple of suitcases of clothes, some boxes of kitchen utensils, my personal box with some books, journals, letters, and pictures, and Yusef's heavy box of textbooks and a bound, pristine copy of his thesis. It was too cold to do any unpacking, though. I didn't want to move.

During our dinner Yusef went to the hall every few minutes and messed with the thermostat, cursing under his breath. "I'm going to call Amer. He should have told us this before we moved in," he said, picking his phone off the top of the TV. "He better come here and fix this tonight."

I wrapped the blanket tighter around me. "How is he going to have it fixed? It's a holiday. Everything's closed."

"He can fix it himself or he can find a way to get someone."

He had a long argument with Amer, peppered with curses. "My wife is freezing! I want us to be alive in the morning." He hung up the phone and sat on the arm of my chair. "You know what he told me? 'I sheck the heat yesterday and is fine.'" He pointed toward the hall. "I checked the heat, and it's not fine. I can't believe I agreed to have this *sharmoot* as a landlord."

I told him to sit with me and keep me warm. He splayed himself from the leg rest all the way to my chest. I massaged his shoulders and the top of his chest. He was still going on about his cousin. "He'd better be here soon."

"Yusef, at least we have room and privacy here."

"Yeah. The apartment was almost like living with family, everyone all in our business." He laughed. "And we have space for kids to run around. Someday at least."

We both had time off for Christmas, and we spent most mornings on our frameless mattress, making love or cuddling or discussing our plans for the new house. It took us a few afternoons of unpacking to make the house look decent enough for visitors, who were eager to see the place and congratulate Yusef on his master's degree. Imm Yusef was elated that her son had become so successful, though he hadn't pursued medicine like she wanted. She was itching for a grandchild, though. At least one. "Habibi, your father is getting so old and sick now. I want him to know the grandchildren from his only son."

The day she said that, I expected there to be an argument, or at least a snide comment, about how I was taking birth control and keeping him from what he wanted. He only told his mother that we would have a child when the time was right. "When God wills it, right, Mama?" he said with a sad smile.

We even had sex that night.

When I called Sana the next day, she said she believed I had him so "in check" because I had withheld sex from him for such a long time. "Nothing matters more to a man."

"If he has that much of a problem with it, he can go and find another wife. Probably there'll be a lot lined up to snag him. I haven't come this far to let some man's desires dictate my life." I sighed. "I never kept him from anything. He wanted to wait seven years before he came back to me and committed to me. He wanted to sow his wild oats"—and sodomize other women—"and I gave him that. He can't give me this? We're both young; we have plenty of time."

Things improved once Yusef went back to work full-time. He was teaching four classes, all meeting once a week at night. He still did some part-time research, but that was in the late afternoon right before his classes, and any interview or event I had to attend for my job was usually later in the afternoon or very early in the morning, so we had most mornings and afternoons to ourselves. He started a workout regimen, waking up every day at seven to run five miles. He bought a weight set, and he used that in addition to the weights he had before to build his muscle tone. He ate even more ravenously than before and said he wanted to gain twenty to thirty pounds of muscle. The refrigerator was stocked with things like Muscle Milk and other muscle-building products. He had a shelf in the pantry filled with his protein shake powders and bars. Even in mid-January he walked around the house shirtless, claiming that the extra layer of muscle he was acquiring made him warmer.

He did have something to be proud of. I couldn't stop looking at him, his developing pecs and his strong arms, when he loafed around the house and oohed and aahed over dinner while I made it, stealing bites from it every other minute, or worked out in our office/gym.

"So where do you run exactly?" I asked while I lay on the sweaty weight bench he'd just finished using. He was lifting thirty-pound dumbbells.

"You know. Around." He paused and panted. He gathered his strength and did more reps. "Sometimes I go to the drugstore, or if I go the other way I'll make it to the high school. You should come sometime. It makes you feel great."

Instinctively I pressed my hands against my belly to see how much fat I had there.

"No, I'm not saying you're fat, Isreenie." He took a few steps closer to look down at me, the weights still in his hands. "Why do you always have it in your head that you're big? I love that your body is soft." He flexed his arms. "Your amtu's just jealous."

I sat up and watched him wince with the effort of lifting the dumbbells. "You know about that?"

"Mama told me how she was acting at the dress fitting, and I figured anyway." He finished his reps and set the weights down, drawing a deep breath. "I mean, you've never even been fat, not since I've known you. When we were younger, I remember you were really developed, not fat," he said, smiling, staring in the distance.

"You're fantasizing about a girl who's barely a teenager."

He nodded. "I was thinking how I felt that first day I saw you. You and Sana were talking or something in the dining room. You were so beautiful when you were looking at those magazines. I couldn't think about anything else. I almost lost to Bassam that day."

I drew my knees up under my chin, not sure if I was touched or horny or what. I felt the same for him right then: the sweat dripping down his pecs, the light hitting his eyes at the right intensity to make them a warmer green, his skin a perfect, even brown.

"I'm going to take a shower," he said.

I joined him.

At first I felt lonely in the evenings, but Hanan came over once in a while and helped me make dinner like old times, except Amtu wasn't hovering over us. Now that we lived here, her parents didn't have as much of a problem with her coming over. If Sana was off that night, she visited sometimes. The first couple of evenings, her mother came with her, because her parents suspected she might be going out to see male friends.

I had other guests who were less welcome, though I couldn't show that. Abu and Imm Yusef stopped by, supposedly for dinner, a couple times a week. I always made enough for them, because they never called before they came, and made a pot of tea for Abu Yusef, his only comfort since he was forced to quit smoking. The tea was wasted when they didn't arrive, but Yusef usually ate the leftovers the next morning for breakfast or that night in addition to the plate I saved for him. I knew his mother was checking on us, and now that she had such a heavy workload with her husband's care and their store, this was the only time she could find to make sure she knew what we were doing.

One evening Imm Yusef picked up a folded note I had left for Yusef; I had forgotten it on the coffee table. "Don't read it!" I said, my cheeks already warm and probably blood red. Of course, she read it anyway, sounding out the letters slowly without her reading glasses.

She set it back down, her shoulders stiff. "It is nice that you have a love for my son," she said, her eyes moving everywhere but my face.

I was pissed, but relieved that it was one of the cleaner notes I wrote him.

Another night she stayed after Hanan left and cornered me in the kitchen while her husband was in the living room drinking tea on the couch. She patted my back like she was congratulating me on something. "Ya Isra, I think it is very good for you to have your cousin over here," she said. "She is very nice girl, but Sana . . ." She tightened her mouth in disgust. "Sana not very good girl. She acts bad." She moved her open hands up and down to explain the state of Sana's mind. "I believe she bad influence. You are good girl, but whenever thing go wrong before you marry my son, she is always involved. I have known her since she was very young, and I see that she is bad, and I do not want her to make you bad."

"She's not bad. She's only a little loud. Nothing dangerous."

She shook her head and clicked her tongue. "No, I see always something cooking in her mind, and is bad. Very bad. Yusef is very nice man, and he does not want to say anything, and he is like you, he believes the best in beoble, but I am old, and I see these things." She pointed to her head while she said it.

I leaned against the counter. "Really, Sana's good. We've never gotten into trouble."

She shook her head. "I know you were in fights at the Sunday school. I know at Eid she said some nasty things to you about men. I have heard these things when I asked around about you. I do this when Yusef tell me he want to marry you."

"Those were nothing," I said. "We were just curious kids."

She shrugged. "Sana is not the worst. I have seen much worse, but she is not good." She put her hand on my shoulder and looked me in the eye. "With Yusef gone for night, is this why you have not become pregnant?"

She threw me with her change of subject. He wasn't gone that late, always home before ten. We weren't so old that we couldn't have sex after that hour. "No, no, no. I don't know why. I'm just not pregnant yet. Sometimes it takes time. When you try, it doesn't happen. When you don't, it happens like that." I snapped my fingers and shrugged.

"Inshallah it will be soon."

"Yeah."

"I must take my husband home. He needs rest. He is so sick these days."

I nodded somberly. "I know. I'm so sorry about that."

I saw them out, helping Imm Yusef help Abu Yusef into the passenger seat of the car. He looked so sickly, pale and skinny, with paper-thin skin that seemed to show almost every vein in his arms and face. I thought about repeating the request that Yusef had been making to her recently: to close the store and move in with us. Though she was significantly younger than her husband, she was old herself, and she'd only be breaking her body down more caring for Abu Yusef and taking care of the store. Khadija's older sons came to the store regularly to help, especially with the heavy lifting, but she had a lot to deal with still. She didn't want to give it up, though.

Anyway, I couldn't bear the thought of having to live with her. She'd be nosy, find out about my birth control pills or that we had sex in the shower. It would be almost as bad as living with Amtu Samia again, except with more to hide, more for her to find.

"I never knew Mama didn't like Sana," Yusef replied dutifully as he stretched his body on the bed, his muscles popping.

"Do you think the same thing about her?" I asked.

He cracked his knuckles. "I don't know. I never thought much about her. I remember her being a real pain in the ass when we were younger." He chuckled. "My cousin Amer was thinking about talking to her father about marrying her. Can you imagine those two together? Her with such a boater?"

"He's still thinking about it?"

"I don't know. He wanted to a while ago, but then it never happened." He laughed and closed his eyes as he set his head back down on the pillow.

I rested my head on his chest and put my arm across his torso. "She also asked if we were having sex since you've been working nights."

He scoffed, his chest vibrating underneath my cheek. "Mama cuts right to the chase, doesn't she?" When I said nothing in response, he said impatiently, "You know she doesn't believe in privacy. I don't know an Arab parent who does."

"In some cases, they do believe in privacy. When do you ever hear about all the shit their sons are doing? Hardly. A girl has one misstep, and everyone remembers forever." Though I didn't consider beating up Motabel or talking to Sana about sodomy missteps. They were just part of defending myself and growing up.

"What do you mean by that?"

"You know better than me."

We were both silent for a few minutes.

"Maybe we should think about trying again," Yusef said. "We wouldn't have to lie, and people would think we might be having sex."

"Wow, that's a fantastic idea." I lifted my head and moved over to my side of the bed. "Let's have a baby because that's what your parents want. Are they going to raise it for us, too?"

He sat up and folded his arms. "What's wrong with having a baby? We're adults. My father is sick, and she's just thinking about if he'll be able to see our child while he's still alive."

"Yusef, I know it's hard that your father is having all these troubles, and he's suffering so much. I get that. And I want to help them. I'm fine with them moving in here. I'm fine with visiting them. I'm fine with them coming over here almost every evening and spying on me. I'm fine with that, but we can't have a child for them."

He threw his arms in the air. "I want children for us. It would be good."

Now I sat up and turned my face to his. "Us or your mother? It's not even about your father. He's never come and breathed down our necks about having a child. Never. Your father has lived to see ten of his grand-children, and those don't matter because his daughters had them?"

I couldn't help but recall that I saw Mom suffer for two years with illness; she was barely in her thirties, and she didn't even live to see me make it into the double digits.

Our argument blew over in a day, but less than three weeks later, when I finished my pink pills and started the brown placebos, my period didn't come.

Sana couldn't believe it, couldn't believe that I was taking actual birth control pills correctly and conceived a child. She came over to look at my compact; I still had a month's worth of pills. We took them to the kitchen. "Do you mind if I take one out?" she asked.

I sighed. "Sure. It's not like I'm taking them anymore."

She sniffed the tiny pill and examined it studiously. She sighed and shook her head, her eyes wide, still in awe. "I can't believe it. This soon. How many times were you going at it in a day? I wonder if it is scientif-ically possible that you had so much of Yusef's sperm in you that all the estrogen couldn't fight it off."

I pulled a chair out at the dinner table and sat down. "We should have just kept on using condoms. At least I would have known that his sperm was not getting into my uterus at all."

She shook her head, her mouth open in disbelief. "No, no. The condom's too much responsibility on the guy. They want to get laid, and they don't care about putting it on right." She walked over to the table to sit with me.

"Did you use condoms or the pill when you started having sex?"

"Condoms. They're easier to get when you're a teenager. The last time I did it with my high school boyfriend, that dumbass didn't put the condom on right. It slipped."

I felt her past fear in my stomach right at that moment.

She nodded. "I know. I had to talk my older sister into getting me that morning-after pill because she was nineteen, and I was only sixteen. That was the first time she found out I was doing it with someone, and she was such a bitch about it, told me I was a whore and going to hell." She glared at the wall like it was her sister.

"I thought the morning-after pill was hell, though. I was so friggin' sick my mom tried to have me hospitalized. I kept on telling her I was fine, and then I'd go puke all my stomach acid out—I couldn't stand eating. That made both my parents concerned. But at the hospital, they'd be able to find out what I did and tell my parents."

"God." I couldn't believe she had never told me all this.

"I broke up with that asshole after that. It was too much drama. I thought the whole point of having a boyfriend was so you could have fun with a guy and not have to be all serious and everything—but he was such a prick. He started seeing another girl a week later." Now the wall became that ex-boyfriend, and she shot hate darts at him with her eyes. "And believe me, the sex wasn't so good that he made me want it every day."

Mom must have considered adoption or abortion with me. She was almost twenty-four when she got pregnant, significantly older than Sana then, but was unmarried, with few marketable skills. If I ever thought about Mom considering getting rid of me like Baba did, I might have hated her for it. Now I felt a mix of empathy and resentment.

Sana leaned over to reach my eye level; I was slouched and looking down at the table. "You're married. He wants it. He'll be a good dad. He's nice, and he's got good jobs and all that stuff."

"God, Sana, it's not that simple! He wants a kid because he doesn't know what it's like to be a dad. He's never even babysat for anyone."

She dismissed that with a wave of her hand. "He'll learn."

"It's not just about if it's good for us now. I have to think about the future." I sank into my chair and folded my arms in front of my stomach. "What if something happens to one of us?"

"You guys are young. Relax."

"What if something happens to me? He can't raise a child on his own. He doesn't even know how to fold sheets! I don't think he would leave, for right now I'm pretty sure about that, but I know he would need a lot of help if he was alone for some reason. Who would he get it from?"

"His mom probably. His mother would worship the kid, especially if it's a boy."

"She's almost sixty. He would remarry, and I don't want some step-mother treating my child like shit. What if something happened to him? What would I do? I barely make enough to support myself in some one-bedroom shithole in the ghetto. How would I support a kid, too?"

She sighed. "Take a breath. You know you have me. I'd help out, and you'll eventually find a good job. It took me a year to get a full-time one, and I went into nursing." She laughed. "Or you could remarry. There'd be lots of guys interested. Maybe that little nephew of his, get yourself some young meat for your second marriage."

I cringed and rolled my eyes. "The only thing worse than a step-mother is a stepfather, Sana. Especially if I have a daughter." I sat up straight, the adrenaline bursting through my veins. "He doesn't think about any of these things. They never enter his mind at all."

"If everyone thought of all that, no one would procreate. The human race would be extinct."

CHAPTER SIXTEEN

After we came back from Mom's memorial service, Baba was mad. He couldn't believe Mom's family had snubbed us, me especially. "Are you not her daughter, and they turn away from you as such?" We were walking up the staircase on the way to the apartment, and I was a couple of steps behind him, unable to keep up with his long strides. He muttered to himself in Arabic and shook his head while he ran his hand through his curly black hair. "What kind of family does this? Acts in such a way?" he asked for the third time, struggling to unlock the front door.

Once Baba got the door open, I went back to bed and stared at the ceiling, not wanting to be around him. I was sentenced to live a life with him now, at least until I was eighteen, which was ten years away. I needed to learn how to avoid him right away. What would happen? Grandma claimed he would lock me in the house until I married or send me off to his country, but that didn't seem likely. Mostly I would have to live out my days in his apartment that was below freezing, go to a school where I was teased for being white but not white enough for Mom's family, and spend all my time by myself.

In the middle of my self-pity, Baba came into the bedroom and told me he had errands to run. He gathered some things from his closet and told me not to let any strangers in, or let anyone know I was here alone.

Mom would never have left me home alone. No one ever said it, but I knew Baba was kind of dumb and didn't know anything about taking care of kids.

Hours passed. I didn't go to sleep. I just cried and thought about how

I used to sleep in a bed with Mom all the time. My stomach growled; I got up to make myself some food. I wasn't very good at it, but since Baba either made me wait forever for him to get around to making me something or refused to do it all, I had learned how to prepare my own food.

The refrigerator was empty except for some old cheese slices and mustard. At Mom's, we almost never had home-cooked food. Our diet was pretty monotonous, sandwiches or some boxed food, but at least there was something to eat.

I took out a cheese slice and tasted a small pinch of it; it still tasted good. I put some mustard on top of it and folded it in half. I did this with a few slices until my stomach stopped hurting. I turned on the TV, but nothing good was on. I watched the news and saw that a murder had occurred that day less than a mile from Baba's apartment. That didn't surprise me anymore. Some major crime happened at least once a month for the past seven months I had lived here. Sometimes it was a drive-by, sometimes a domestic dispute, and sometimes there was no apparent motive at all. I was certain that this was a death apartment, a death neighborhood; just a year before, I hardly ever heard about death, but now death penetrated almost every thought I had.

I went to the window to see if there were any cop cars passing, headed toward the crime scene. I saw none. The cops didn't do anything around here; they came to the schools and warned kids not to get involved in gangs or else they would end up in jail or rotting in this ghetto for the rest of their lives. They would come around to clean up their guts but not to prevent them spilling in the first place. Mom told me so, and she told Baba even more than me.

That would be me. This wasn't a temporary situation. I would live here, go to the school where the kids called me names like ghost or gringa, and either run with gangs or get involved with drugs. Drugs more likely. What gang would take me? When I explained to them what my actual ethnicity was, made them understand what an Arab was, they would be even more horrified. Say I was a terrorist or something and tell me to go back to "my country" and join up with a terrorist group.

I wondered why Baba lived here, why he wouldn't find someplace better, where people didn't break into the apartment just to steal women's or girl's clothes and then leave. I knew Baba had a job, but I didn't know what it was or where he worked. Maybe he didn't make enough money. Maybe they didn't like him enough to pay him well.

Or maybe he was a drug dealer. I had picked up hints from Mom's conversations with her friends that Baba was involved with drugs. Taking them, not dealing them. At school some of the boys said they knew drug dealers. One boy told me that his older brother dealt drugs. He said he talked to some of his brother's clients, stupid crackheads who didn't want to pay, and he'd threaten to bust a cap in their asses. They listened to him and paid up right away. He was only my age and shorter than me, so I knew he was lying. I was afraid he would tease me or beat me up if I said so, though, so I said nothing.

"You can come by my house, and you can be my girlfriend."

"My dad won't let me go to a boy's house."

"That's cool. You can stay at my place." He claimed to have had sixteen girlfriends, but none as pretty as me.

I declined the offer multiple times. I hated Baba for living here, for leaving me here.

I noticed that the box with Mom's ashes was gone. That didn't alarm me, because Baba took that everywhere with us since we had gotten it a couple of days ago. He was worried that burglars might steal it, thinking it was something valuable they could sell on the streets. This place was filled with scum, he swore. But he wouldn't move.

I started to worry when the sun went down. I thought I had conquered my fear of the dark, but being alone brought it back. I heard noises outside, people arguing, yelling. I smelled the now familiar scent of sour weed. I was calling Baba a good-for-nothing and a deadbeat and an idiot just like Mom used to. A disappointment in every way.

I went back to bed, knowing I wouldn't sleep, but I cuddled up with one of my big bears and figured that if I was in the bedroom, it would be easier for me to hide from burglars because I could just crawl under the bed when I heard someone trying to break in. Unless they tried to steal the bed! Then they'd find me under there, and I didn't know what they would do, but it made my stomach churn to think about it.

I was hungry again, too. I had already eaten all the cheese in the house, and I tried eating some mustard by itself, but it tasted sour and went down my throat like acid. My stomach still rumbled as I walked back to the bed.

I fell asleep on top of my stuffed bear late that night with the light still on. I woke up to daylight, and someone knocking at the front door. Baba probably. He was always misplacing his keys; Mom said he had enough new sets for the next five tenants. I wondered what he did all last night, why it was so important he couldn't come back before morning. I wasn't sure if I should open the door. Baba said not to unless I knew the person, and I wasn't quite tall enough to reach the peephole yet. Who cared what he said, though? He wasn't here.

I opened the door and saw a man who was light brown with thick straight black hair and a mustache. His eyes widened at me. "Are you Isra?" He said my name the way Baba said it. Is-ra.

I nodded.

"Allah! How old are you?"

This man was a nosy stranger. "Eight."

"Wallah? You are so tall. I have a son who is two years older, and he is not so tall."

I believed him. I was taller than every boy in my class and all the girls except for one. I was even taller than the teacher.

"Well, I am your amu. Your father is my cousin. I got him a job." He explained how Baba had lost that job by never being there on time and sometimes not showing up. He hadn't seen Baba in a few years. "This you must not do, Isra. You must always be hardworking."

He wasn't even inside yet, and he was already giving me a lecture. I didn't even know why he was here in the first place. I let him in eventually. He might be a serial killer who wanted to murder me by pretending to be my father's cousin, but he did know my name. "I have come to take you to live with me," he said. "I have a nice place for you to sleep, and I have one son and a little daughter and a wife."

I had nothing to say. I sat there on the couch and stared at him as he told me the news. His eyes examined the apartment, as if he was looking for something to indicate why I didn't say anything back. "Do you want to live in my house?"

I hesitated, but then I nodded. "Sure."

"I will help you pack your stuff up. It does not look like there is much to take." He looked around, and I saw his lips pucker in disgust under his mustache.

I took my few pairs of clothes, the photo album that Amu had to look through to make sure all the pictures were appropriate, and a few things of Mom's: her keys, her purse, her makeup bag. Amu snatched the bag from me. "Why do you need this?" he asked.

"It's Mom's."

"A little girl doesn't need makeup." He slammed the bag down on the dresser.

"Why does Baba not want me to live with him?"

Amu looked down at me, and his brown eyes softened. He sighed. "Your father has gone the wrong way. He cannot raise a child. Look at the mess he has made of his life, having babies when he is not married with kafir women."

"What's kafir?"

He chuckled and told me I said it wrong. Not "ka-fear" but "kaa-fer." He made me say it over, and I got it right. "You have it in you to be a Falasteeniya."

"But what is kafir?"

"It is those that go the wrong way."

"But Mom didn't." I hated how everyone always said that. I heard a few people at her memorial service say that she had been a "good girl," just a little chubby and antisocial, and then she met Baba. Her fall from almost-perfect grace.

He snorted. "Your mother has a child, and she is not married. You need to have a husband to have children with."

I looked up at him, bewildered. No wonder he wanted to get out of this place so bad. A few of the kids at my old elementary school didn't have married parents, but here it was the norm to have parents that were broken up and/or never married.

"It is good you are young. You must not live this way. Look what it brings you." He surveyed the bedroom again.

He took me down the stairs and helped me with the two bags we'd packed. He had parked his car across the street, and he made sure to keep looking at his surroundings, but it was morning, maybe ten o'clock, so nothing bad went down. Crime rarely occurred between the hours of five in the morning and noon.

He had a button to unlock his car, and when he turned the engine on, the seat warmed up. I had never been in a car so nice.

And I cried because I wanted to share this with Mom.

"Eh, what is it, habibti?" he asked. "What are these tears? Your cousins and your auntie want to see you. They already love you."

"I want Mommy," I whined like a baby. I hadn't called Mom "Mommy" for a couple of years now, but it came out automatically.

He leaned over and hugged me. No one in Mom's family cared about my tears. I wasn't really Mom's daughter. I looked nothing like her. I had no right to grieve for her. "It is okay. Don't worry. She is with God now."

I heard about God around school, especially at Christmas time, which was supposed to be God's son's birthday, and sometimes I saw televangelists on TV ranting and raving about God, but my parents never mentioned Him. I didn't know God took the dead to be with Him. It wasn't a comfort to me. I hated God for taking my mother away from me. If God had so much power and had so many things, why did He have to take my mother away? I was only a little girl who was now forced to get in a car with a stranger—something I had been warned against ever since I could remember—because I had no choice. I was going to starve in Baba's apartment, or get killed.

Amu was more patient than Baba and withstood my crying without yelling at me. He assured me I would feel better once I got to his house, where his wife had food and a warm welcome waiting for me.

I wasn't sure if I believed him.

But I had to take him at his word. The bitter taste lingered in my mouth.

Amu half lied. His house was warm enough, and his wife did make a small lunch of cucumber salad and labna, which I wanted to wolf down, but I kept my composure and took polite bites. My kafir mother had taught me manners, after all.

But it didn't feel like everyone loved me already. Rasheed seemed annoyed by my presence and had to be forced by his father to acknowledge me. Amtu Samia was mad, her jaw set tight, her demeanor as aloof as her son's. Hanan, though, looked at me with her light brown eyes, inherited from her father, lit up when she met me. She led me into her bedroom and told me all the names she had given her baby dolls.

CHAPTER SEVENTEEN

I was flipping through the channels and settled on a non-cartoon version of *The Secret Garden*, one of the few movies I liked as a child, despite Mary Lennox being a spoiled brat with a nanny or an ayah. Yusef came home soon after it started. I was applying moisturizer to my skin, and using a special cocoa butter oil for my belly because I heard it was good for preventing stretch marks.

He brought his food out into the living room to eat at the coffee table and sit by me. He had never seen the movie, so I spent a couple of minutes explaining the plot. I finished at the same time Mary was telling Dickon that the children on the boat taunted her by singing "Mary, Mary, Quite Contrary."

"Do you ever think about where your father is?" he asked.

I stopped rubbing the lotion on my skin for a minute. "Rarely," I said nonchalantly. I had told Yusef about Baba during our engagement because I figured he would find out anyway, no matter how Amu Nasser and Amtu Samia tried to spin my family history to Yusef and his family. "Only when people ask." I was barely five when Mom kicked him out for good, but he'd always gone back and forth, promising to stay and be stable and lots of other things he never delivered. Growing up, hardly any of the children I was around had fathers who lived with them or were present in any real way; when handing out permission slips or report cards, the teachers asked for our "mother's signature," not a "parent's signature." Poor kids don't have fathers.

I noticed him closely observing my movements, seeing if my face or body language would betray any hidden emotion. "I didn't think fathers were important," I added. "A man's love for his child is directly related to his love for its mother, so it's more tenuous."

He chewed his food slowly and stared at me, his eyebrows raised. "That's a big, hateful word to say to an expectant father," he said. "'Tenuous.' I'd love my child through anything. But then, you know, I can't imagine ever falling out of love with you, so maybe we won't get to test the theory."

I didn't argue. I was right. I'd seen how Hanan and Rasheed had fallen from Amu's favor as his marriage conflicts grew, especially how Hanan had lost his deep affection. A daughter had more to lose from her father in those cases.

Setting his empty plate aside, Yusef put my oily foot in his hand and rubbed the toes. "What about your mother's family, do you ever think about them?"

I didn't, not anymore. I kind of knew my mother's mother, spent time with her on a few occasions. She barely noticed my existence until close to the end of Mom's life. "No, they've had plenty of time to start a relationship with me," I said. He thought I saw myself as Mary, a girl unloved by her now-dead parents who then tries to solicit love and approval from her extended family. But I wasn't about to beg for anything, not from Mom's family, not from Amu Nasser, not from Baba.

"If I went into porn, that'd be my name: Dickon," he said, and laughed.

The role would fit perfectly for him: the slightly older, poorer boy who fell for me, a sour-faced girl, who fell for him in return. Instead of singing, "Mary, Mary, quite contrary / How does your garden grow?" he would sing, "Isreenie, my little meanie / Where did your family go?"

"There's cousin love," he said when we got to the part where her cousin Colin reveals that he wants to marry Mary when they grow up. "If they went to an Arab country, their parents would already have the two of them set up to marry each other." He laughed so hard that his whole body shook, and mine too, so that I spilled a bit of the cocoa butter oil on the couch, the first stain.

I picked up the remote and changed the channel. "This movie is stupid anyway."

My pregnancy brought a light to Imm Yusef's life. Abu Yusef was intermittently bedridden and becoming less able to do basic things for himself. She had to put on his shoes because he couldn't bend over. He didn't like going out much, so she invited us over to their house for tea and dinner and sweets and anything she could think of. Abu Yusef didn't come out of his bedroom most of the time, but Yusef went in to see his father while Imm Yusef kept me in the living room, taking in all the information about my pregnancy. She listened to me with as much intensity as she had when Yusef and I were engaged. Now she was trying to gauge what kind of mother I would be, if I would raise her grandchild the way she wanted, the way she raised her kids.

"I hope to God very much that you have a boy," she said, her hand on her heart. "Waiting for a boy is too hard."

"There's more to life than men," I said. "Where would they be without women?" She should have known that. Abu Yusef would have been a bum begging on the streets if he came to America without Imm Yusef, and now he would have been in a nursing home. What did he ever do for her but saddle her with more mouths to feed?

"Yes, but is easier for mother to have boys. With my daughters, always we have problems. With Yusef, laa, everything is fine."

Amu Nasser and Amtu Samia said the same thing to Hanan and me up until Rasheed's fifth year in college. Then Amu got fed up with Rasheed's slacking and refused to acknowledge any of his son's good points. Before that, though, Hanan and I were the bad ones. We always had to be punished for not following the rules; we always talked back; we always did our chores poorly. But Rasheed was a good boy who never did any of those things. I told Amu that Rasheed never broke the rules because he hardly had any; he didn't talk back because his parents never scolded or even lectured him; and he didn't do his chores poorly because he had none to do in the first place.

Amu told me that my response just proved that I could never stop talking back, could never take what was given to me with any sort of appreciation.

"What if we have a daughter?" I asked Yusef in the car, picking at my nails.

"I would throw her in a Dumpster," he said promptly, "or feed her to wolves." Then he paused. "C'mon, I would love my daughter. I want daughters, you know. I love women. I love you, I love my mom, I love my sisters." He made a cautious and slow right turn. He was already driving like an old man because I was pregnant. "I don't want some madhouse like Khadija's with five sons. They all got black eyes and bruises all the time, and my sister and her husband have a bunch of gray hairs in their early forties. Even Mama says Khadija has got too much of a good thing."

I sighed, exasperated. "I know you would love our daughter, but I don't want you to be some patriarch that just wants her to stay inside and clean all the time."

He glanced over at me for a second and turned back to the road. "Okay, I'm not going to be like my father and go through my daughter's stuff and interrogate her every time she goes to a friend's house to make sure she isn't out screwing. I would trust her, but I don't want her to have boyfriends or anything." He cringed, but then smiled. "I want her to be smart like her mother, her head always in a book, ignoring all the guys and breaking their hearts."

I gave him the most searing glare I could manage. "That's so hypocritical! What do you think about me having you in my life when we were teenagers? You were practically my boyfriend. We spent lunch together almost every day; you walked me to the school bus every day; I was in your car alone with you." Not to mention all the other women he had been with, the ones he whored around with, doing all sorts of things to.

"Isra, that was different. I was the perfect gentleman. I didn't have my hands all over you until we were engaged, and we were in love. It wasn't just about hormones."

"You were not the perfect gentleman. Remember when you tried to kiss me in the car? And then you tried to kiss me the next day when you were 'apologizing' for trying to kiss me."

He nodded dutifully. "Shoot me for slipping. It wasn't like I grabbed your breasts or anything, though I thought about those kinds of things a lot, and I had to take care of those feelings myself. I know men, Isra. Most of them don't control themselves, and they're not going to be pawing my daughter." He gripped the wheel harder with his right hand. "I know you have good intentions, too, but if you knew the things men think when they see a beautiful woman—and our daughter is definitely going to be one of the most beautiful—you would be so disgusted that you wouldn't even want her to get married."

I was fuming. He wasn't going to have his way on this one. "So our son can go out and have girlfriends?"

He shrugged. "I don't want him to be a sex maniac, but I don't think it's bad if he has a few."

I couldn't let him finish. "You. Are. Such. A. Sexist!" I took a breath, told myself yelling wouldn't do anything for me but make me angrier. "Yusef, you don't know what it's like being a girl. Yeah, yeah, I know you grew up with three sisters and your mom, but you don't get it." They would never tell you the truth; you never told gods the ugly truth. "I don't want our daughter idealizing how fun it is to be around boys. I want her to know. I don't want her to be thrown into marriage, not knowing anything about how things work."

He tapped his fingers hard against the steering wheel. "It's harder for a man to control those urges, and they don't suffer as much in those situations," he said grudgingly.

I put my hand up to shut him up. "Wait, wait. You're saying that women can either be good girls or whores, but men can whore around and be a good man? And what about those women our son whores around with? What about them? They can be used and discarded? Is that what you did with your girlfriends?"

That broke his cool, though he still tried to keep himself under control. "I didn't use and discard women. I was always open with them. I didn't lie to them. None of them thought it would lead to marriage, and that's the way they wanted it, too."

"How are you so sure? Because the girls who give it up to the guys don't want to be loved and married?"

He pulled into the driveway and turned off the car. "I don't think those women are whores. I know that, but I want . . . Well, I don't want her to go through all that pain and trouble. I want to find a good man for her, or, you know, she can find a man and let me check him out. I don't want her getting hurt. But I want to know the man she's with is decent."

I folded my arms and shook my head. I couldn't look at him. "She's going to be a person, Yusef. Her own person. And women are a lot stronger than you think."

Ten minutes after my scheduled time, we were still in the waiting room. I had drunk a lot of water for the ultrasound, and my bladder was about to burst. I held onto Yusef's hand like a death grip, figuring if I peed on myself, it would be some comfort. I didn't want to miss this ultrasound; I was already well into my second trimester and had missed my first-trimester one. "What's the point of making an appointment if she's not going to stick to it?" I sighed and pouted. "It might as well be walk-in if I have to wait like this. I don't even think I'm going to make it." The ultimate humiliation: peeing on myself at the doctor's office.

"Just hold on a little longer. I'll go see what the holdup is," Yusef said, squeezing my hand. He went to the window and did as he said he would, but when the receptionist took an impatient tone with him and answered that the "technician is busy," his shoulders stiffened. "This appointment's for fifteen minutes ago, and this technician should know that she's dealing with a pregnant woman who was advised to drink a lot of water. Can you please check and ask her if she's going be able to see us today?"

The receptionist nodded while she glared. "Okay, sir. I'll see what's going on."

"Wow," I said when he sat back down.

"No one's keeping me from seeing my baby in the womb, and no one's making you piss on a chair." He took my hand again and kissed it.

The technician was out in a few minutes. My bladder was heavy, and I struggled to stand up straight. Lying down made it easier to control my bladder, but the cold gel that she spread on my round stomach didn't help. Yusef held my hand the entire time, but he had his eyes riveted on the screen as soon as my womb went live.

Almost immediately the technician gasped: she had found two fetuses.

"Two?" Yusef said, and got up and leaned over my head to get a better look. "Really?"

The technician gestured. "This one's a boy." She moved her pad more. "Let's see . . ." Yusef squeezed my hand hard, still standing. "Yes, that's a girl. Fraternal twins." She beamed at both of us.

I closed my legs tight and smiled, but there was no holding my pee inside any longer. Yusef turned to me and grinned. "We're gonna have two!"

"I need to go."

He nodded and helped me off the table. I pulled his arm hard enough that I heard a soft popping sound. He waited outside the bathroom door, talking the whole time, while I kept myself from gasping too loudly from the relief of emptying my bladder. "Twins. I don't even think twins run in my family. It must have come from yours."

I finally managed to heave myself off the toilet and wash my hands. As soon as I was out, I told him while I pointed my forefinger in his face that he couldn't be restrictive with our daughter or I'd kill him. He put his arm around my shoulders as we walked out. "And our son has to do housework, too," I said.

"As long as I don't have to do any."

"I'm not crazy about cuss words, but I especially don't want them to hear words like whore or slut or sharmoota."

I had to make the best of this situation, no matter how much my pulse raced or how hard my heart was pounding in my chest.

We avoided one argument just to get in another less than an hour later. Yusef suggested we stop by a baby store where we could look at cribs, strollers, and toys before he went to work, but I was wiped out from the effort to hold in my pee and said I wanted to go home and take a nap. I didn't know I was giving him the bait for his next request.

"Isra, I was thinking that you should take some time off work, especially since we're having twins. Well, until the kids are in school, you can stay at home and care for them. I don't want you to exhaust yourself, and then we'd have to think of who's going to watch them and blah, blah, blah. I'm sure Mama and my sisters'll help out, but as far as permanent, everyday care for the kids, you know, I think it would be best if you stay home."

I leaned against the car window, staring ahead at the road, so enraged I couldn't speak.

"Isra, it's a good idea. Works for both of us."

I balled both my hands into fists and hit my thighs. "It works for you because you get all the security, while I'm left staying at home with a load of kids, pulling my hair out! You get to have something else in your life. Your life doesn't revolve around me and kids, but mine completely will. Sure. Anything to make my husband happy."

He shook his head. "God, not this again."

I put my finger in his face for the second time that day. "Yes, this again. 'Oh, I'm not going to be a patriarch with my daughter, but I don't want her to have anything to do with boys 'cause she'll get hurt.' Like a woman doesn't get hurt in marriage. What kind of example will I set for her if I just do whatever you want me to do?"

He looked to the side to face me and scoffed. "You do whatever I want? That's a riot. You fight with me about everything, and I want what's good for us. What will be good for our kids."

"'Us' is you. I get maternity leave for a couple of months, but I don't think I should stay out of the workforce for five years, or God knows how long because I'll just keep popping out kids. That'll be my whole life!" Already I was sniffling and hiding my face against the window. This is what pregnancy reduced me to: I could no longer hold my tears in until the fight was over and Yusef was out of sight.

"Don't cry, Isra." He put a hand on my shoulder. He gave me his usual—this is not the end of the world; it's not as bad as you imagine it to be—until he stopped the car. I got out as fast as possible so I could rush into the house without having to say another word to him. He made it around to the passenger door before I was even out, though. He reached for my hand, but I pulled away. "Don't touch me."

"Why is everything so hard with you?" he asked as he followed me.

I searched for the keys in my purse and kept my back to him. Once I had a free hand, I wiped the tears from my face.

"We've got to think of these things before the babies come."

I had trouble keeping my hand steady enough to unlock the front door.

"I'll get it." He reached for my hand again, but I got the key in and turned the lock, pushing his hand away.

He went on talking. I considered locking myself in the bedroom, but I was too hungry. I opened the refrigerator and looked to see if we had anything quick to eat. We didn't. I didn't like ready-made snacks and never bought them. Now I regretted it. I reached up into a cabinet and got out a small pot.

He wrapped his arms around my shoulders and rested his warm cheek against my hair. "Look, sweetie, just sit, and I'll get you whatever you need."

I shrugged him off and slammed the pot down on the stove. "You can't make me anything!" That was enough to get me crying so pathetically that my tears dripped into the pot. "I don't even see why we argue about these things—" I made a sound that was like a high-pitched gasp and hiccup combined. "Because you always get your way, no matter what!" A lock of hair fell to the side of my face.

He took me to our bed, and he sat down beside me, thumbing the tears from my face before he set his hand down on my belly. I sniffled for a couple more minutes, and when I composed myself, he said with his calm, serious face, "Why is this upsetting you so much? I just want to let you know that I will take care of you and provide for you and our babies."

I lay down on my side and brushed the hair from my face. "I don't see why there's such a problem with me working. Even Lubna works, and she has two kids."

"The youngest is in preschool, and before that . . . Isra, her husband's a deadbeat who can't get his shit together. I don't know what my parents were thinking when they set them up. Believe me, I'd never stick our daughter with a guy like that."

"So that's what this is about, your manhood? How it looks to everyone? You can make enough money that your wife can stay at home after she has babies. Yusef, I don't even have to go out that much for my job! I do most of the writing here."

He groaned. "I don't give a shit about what people think. This is what's best."

"Fine, I'll think about it." Who was going to watch them all day? Even if Imm Yusef would do it, I wouldn't like it. I knew better than to let anyone else, especially someone who didn't think highly of me, raise my child.

He smiled. That seemed to be enough for him. He knew he was going to get what he wanted in the end. "You know everything I have is yours. I don't get it. You don't spend a lot of money, and you don't even like your job that much. You say all those community events are boring."

"I like having something of my own. I didn't realize it was such a crime."

"It isn't." He pulled my shirt up and kissed my big, warm belly. "You know, Isra, I think you are an intelligent woman, but being a mom isn't like you're not using that. It's not a cop-out."

I stared at him, my eyes narrowed. "If you treat our daughter like shit, I'll cut off your balls and force-feed them to you," I said.

He looked up at me, his lips still on my belly, and laughed his short, nervous laugh. "I'll have to guard them at all times," he said. He straightened up and covered my belly. "Well, Isra, you love our daughter more than our son. You. Are. Such. A. Sexist!"

"No, you have to fight more on the girl's behalf. The world is more against her."

He nudged my chin up. "I'll protect both of my girls from anything, and I won't die or think our daughter is a whore for having hormones." He took my hand in his. "What do you want me to get you?"

"I'm not hungry anymore."

"C'mon, Isreenie, I don't want you to starve. You have to eat for three."

"Everything we have has to be cooked, Yusef. You can't cook."

"I can drive. I can go and pick something up." He squeezed my hand between both of his. "Let me do this for you."

When I heard the door unlock, my eyelids were so heavy that I felt like I had been sleeping for hours, but it was only a little past eleven in the morning. My ultrasound appointment was at nine, so we hadn't even been home for very long.

Yusef was on his phone when he brought the food into our bedroom. "Ithnayn owlad, Mama. Wahid walad, wahid bint." Two children, Mama. One boy, one girl. He sat down beside me. I heard her squeal and yell on the phone. He laughed. He gave me a quick kiss on the cheek and rested his hand at the top of my belly while I took my food out of the bag. I heard him tell his mother about how the technician was taking forever to see me and my bladder was about to burst.

He kissed me again when he got off the phone and pulled out his container.

I did feel more calm and relaxed, but I was uncomfortably hot. The heat was starting to set in; I drank half of my 20-ounce water bottle in one long swallow and lay back down. Yusef turned the fan on for me and kissed me when he was back on the bed. "You have garlic breath."

"So do you."

"I like it, though. It's an aphrodisiac." He edged his nose into my mouth to sniff my breath, but I bit down gently. He held my face in his hands and laughed when he broke away. "You know what? I got a few hours left before I go to work. I can run you a cool bath if you want." He was gone before I had time to respond. I was more in the mood to lie down, bathing in my own sweat. Getting up seemed like too much effort. And I knew what he was getting at: he not only wanted me to accept his terrible idea, he also wanted sex. I needed sleep.

I heaved myself off the bed dutifully and waddled to the bathroom in the hall. The tub was almost full, and he was sitting on top of the toilet, watching. He looked up when I came in. "I thought I was gonna have to go in there and carry you off the bed."

I leaned on the counter, holding my belly, waiting for him to leave.

"You don't mind if I join you?" he asked, grinning mischievously like he hadn't seen me naked countless times.

I blushed. "I doubt if I can fit in that tub by myself."

"I think we both can," he said, already unbuttoning his shirt. "It's a lot bigger than the one we had at the apartment. Don't be embarrassed. I'm your husband and your baby daddy."

I slowly undressed, my limbs sluggish.

"See, I'm even putting my unprotected balls out there for you," he said, holding his scrotum with both hands. "But I'm not letting you near any knives."

I chuckled.

He helped me into the bath, saying he didn't want to take the chance of me falling. "Being pregnant with twins, too, that's increased risk for complications. Not much, but you can never be too safe when it comes to children."

We barely fit into the bath together. His arms and legs, pressed against mine, were a little darker, tanner, and hairier. My legs were almost as long as his and still skinnier; his had always been short and strong, even when he was a thin teenager. His torso was much longer than mine. I made up for it in width. My belly almost touched each side of the tub.

He didn't try to get laid. I suppose my body in daylight repulsed him. While he wet my hair and face, he told me he was so excited to see our babies. He did relax me, going on in his calm voice, resting the side of my face against his wet, hairy chest. "Your skin is so warm," he said. "No wonder you're sweating like this."

"I can't wait till winter."

He sighed. "You never liked the cold before."

"I was never this huge before, and I have my own internal space heater now." I put my arms over his, right between my belly and breasts. "What made you want kids, anyway?"

He adjusted himself in the tub, holding on to my waist. "Hmm. Never thought about that. Kids are so sweet and funny. Everything's not so serious with them." He sighed. "It must have been when I first became an uncle, Khadija kept on having sons, and I was like a big brother to them—I was always the baby before. When I got older, my other sisters had kids, nieces and nephews, and I just enjoyed being around them."

I gasped when I felt one of the babies kick. It had been happening intermittently for the past week and a half. Yusef was concerned at the gasp and then disappointed when he found out what it was for. He had missed all the babies' kicks.

"I was thinking that if they get a tenure-track position at a community college, I won't always have to teach these night classes, especially when they're older and in school. I don't want to be going to work right when the kids get home." He set his hand on my belly. "I should keep my hand on your belly all day, and then I'll get to feel one of the kicks. Take you to work with me."

"It'll happen, if you're patient."

"I know you'll be a great mother, Isra. Look at how much Hanan loves you, and you're not even her mother."

My lip trembled. "I didn't have a lot of competition, with the parents she had."

"You'd think they could have done better. They only got two."

I bit my lip to stop the trembling. "Nobody wants it to be that way. Things happen, and then just . . ." My eyes were full, and I started sniffling again.

He massaged his fingers into my belly. "Isra, don't worry so much. It's not good for you. What we can help, we'll help. Whatever comes up, we'll deal, okay? It hurts me to see you like this."

I knew I was being a little dramatic. Our children didn't have as much working against them as I did. First, Yusef and I were married, so they were legitimate, non-haraam children. Second, they were basically just Arab. His parents and his sisters would not treat these children like shit. Amu Nasser and Amtu Samia would have nothing to do with them, though. And that would be for the better.

"You worry almost as much as Mama." When I didn't say anything and clenched my teeth, he added, "I guess it's just part of being a mother." He held me tighter. "Have you been thinking about baby names?"

I hadn't. "Well, I think your parents will want the boy to be Musa." Taking Yusef's father's name, following tradition.

"Sure, but I was thinking for the girl, we could name her after your mother."

I skipped a few breaths. I hadn't thought about it. I was depressing myself over all the bad things that would happen; I hadn't even thought to name my daughter after my mother. "What about your mother? Wouldn't she be offended if we didn't give her her name?"

"Nah, I don't think so. It would be weird to have twins with my parents' names, like they're a married couple or something. What's your mother's name anyway?"

"Carol." I smiled, hearing her strong, warm voice in my mind. "She hated the name. She thought it made her sound like an old woman." Only she didn't live to be one.

"It's not bad. It's a name my parents can pronounce, or bronounce. I'm glad to see that you're not 'so sour' anymore." He said the last part with his awful British accent. He had been making references to *The Secret Garden* ever since he saw it on TV with me, calling me "contrary" and "sour" in that accent.

"Don't ruin it."

He teased me about being contrary a little longer. "Maybe we should do one of those water births," he said. "Then we can record it, and I'll be sitting in the tub naked with you while you're holding the baby. Well, I guess we'd each be holding a baby."

I thought those water births were a load of bull. I saw Sana's sister after she had her first child, and it looked like she just had a stroke, half her face drooping lower than the other.

"So that's a no?"

But I didn't think about giving birth. "I want you," I said, grabbing hold of his arm, kissing the stubble on his cheek, feeling pathetic the moment the words came out of my mouth. I never would have had to ask him to sleep with me before; then, I thought my body was flabby and less than desirable, but I didn't know what I had until I lost it. If he said no, I thought, I could cry more and eat a big bar of chocolate when he left.

But he jumped at the opportunity, kissing my heavy breasts and belly, even the stretch marks. "I do always get what I want in the end."

Just before my baby shower, Yusef received a call from his mother; his father had been taken to the hospital. Sana and her mother were preparing the house, so he told me in our bedroom. I offered to go with him, but he shook his head and squeezed my hands. "I'm sure Baba will be fine," he said. "And it's best if you relax."

I knew what he meant: It's best if you don't miscarry. But now wasn't the best time to snap at him. "I should be there for you."

He hugged me hard, and we walked out of the bedroom to the kitchen hand in hand. Sana and her mother, still preparing the small buffet, were suddenly silent.

"Thank you for making all the food and everything," I said. Yusef echoed my sentiment before he left, forcing a smile on his face.

Sana's mother dismissed her efforts with a wave of her hand. "Sana helped. I tell her all the time she needs to learn these things for her husband and children."

Sana had invited everyone we knew to my baby shower, and even though we weren't friends with most of them, she invited a lot of the girls we had first met at Sunday school, along with their mothers. She handed out crossword puzzles and gave out prizes for the winners of her scavenger hunt. I opened gifts. I got a lot of toys, pacifiers, and even one of those things to keep your baby harnessed to you in front. "I got a solid blue," one of the girls said. "Men usually use those baby carriers."

After a few hours everyone cleared out except for Sana, who said she would stay with me until Yusef came back.

"You don't have to," I said.

"Yusef asked me to."

"I need to call him," I said. "It's been, like, what, four hours since he left?" I grabbed the phone from my pocket. I got his voicemail.

"Hospitals have terrible cell reception," Sana reminded me. She went into the living room and turned the TV on.

I sat down next to her and felt tears come to my eyes. I was feeling sorrow for Yusef's pain, and the memories of seeing my mother with all the life drained from her body wouldn't stop coming. "I should just go to the hospital and check on him."

Sana smiled indulgently. "Isra, it's sweet how much you love him, but he did say he wanted you to stay home. Hospitals are full of drama and stress. You don't need that in your third trimester with twins."

"It's not like I'm on bed rest."

Sana and I spent another couple of hours together, and she told me about how her parents were getting desperate for her to marry now that she was close to twenty-five. "They even want to take me to Lebanon to find a man. Seriously, Lebanon. Right now. They are willing to endanger their lives and mine to find me a man." We both laughed when she said that her parents thought she was so pathetic that she had to cross three continents to get a husband. "One of my distant cousins is interested in me. He's like almost forty. Way past his prime. I'm gonna say I can't get the time off work. I should just go to med school, then my parents would get off my back about getting married."

I forced a chuckle and set my hand on my belly.

After Abu Yusef stabilized, Yusef and I became consumed with preparing the house for the babies. We bought clothes, cribs, and bassinets, and put them together in our bedroom.

Yusef took me in his arms while I was putting a purple fitted sheet in one of the cribs. I set the tiny bed pad and giggled when he nuzzled my neck. "I have to get this sheet on," I said as I turned back to the crib. He rested his face against my hair. "You're always interrupting my work," I said with mock exasperation.

"I can't help it if I can't get enough of you." He let go of me. "Our kids should learn Arabic."

I shrugged. "I guess so."

He hesitated. "I thought you might not like it if you didn't understand what I was saying to the kids. You might think I was talking shit or something."

I hadn't thought of that. Besides, all my years of overhearing Amtu and her friends gossip about me gave me a good ear for deciphering the more hateful Arabic terms. I concentrated on smoothing the edges of the sheet.

"You know I wouldn't do that, right?"

But his mother might.

"Yeah, I know. I always wanted to learn Arabic, but it never happened." My range in Arabic had increased considerably in the last year because of all the time I spent around Yusef's family, but it sounded so odd to hear Arabic in my voice. And I hated to see others' harsh judgment of my Arabic.

"Well, you'll probably learn more with time." He leaned on the end of the crib to be more eye level with me. "Why didn't your amu and amtu teach you guys how to speak it?"

"I don't know." They weren't going to advertise their Palestinian-ness too openly. They wouldn't be caught speaking a strange language outside or put a sticker of the Palestinian flag on their door right underneath one that said "In the Name of God, The Most Merciful, Most Compassionate" in Arabic calligraphy the way Yusef's parents did.

"Hey, when I go to Falasteen, they laugh at my Arabic, even Khadija and Fatima's, and they were born there."

I lifted the side of the crib to make sure it worked.

"When you were in Falasteen, what'd they say about you not speaking Arabic?"

I placed the matching blanket on top. "They tried to teach me Arabic words and work with me in English, you know. I went to school with one of my cousins." I still felt a pang in my heart whenever I thought of Faten. I had received a congratulatory private message on Facebook about my pregnancy before I even told anyone or posted anything.

"I went a couple of times," Yusef said, "but I just sat in the back and shot the shit."

"Oh, I didn't learn much. Some poems. I forgot most of them."

"C'mon, you must have remembered something. I want to hear it." He sighed. "I don't know any poetry."

In English or Arabic. He didn't have to tell me that.

"You're going to laugh at me."

"I won't, habibti," he said, reaching over to squeeze my hand.

"Kaifa ahyaa / Ba'eedan ayn suhooliki wa al-hidaabi?" I thought of looking out the window at Sitti's house at night, unable to see the hills and mounds in the dark.

He chuckled. "Kaifa ahyaa mish anti?" How do I live without you? I knew that much Arabic. "But you've got to cool it with the revolutionary poetry, Isra. We don't want to be thrown in jail before you have the kids."

A week later I couldn't sleep or satisfy my hunger. I was up at one in the morning, eating thick yogurt out of the container at the dinner table. Yusef was up with me, but I didn't care how much of a pig I looked like in front of him, so I stuck my tongue inside and licked all around the container. When I was done, I had some of the yogurt on my nose. He thumbed it away. "Let's go back to bed, and you can do that to me."

I rolled my eyes. He already tried to get some that night while I was still in bed, adjusting myself to different sleeping positions, none of which made me comfortable. We had spooned a couple of times lately, but I didn't like how much it made me feel like an enormous water buffalo that he was struggling to keep hold of. My belly was too big for him to get on top of me, so he suggested that I get on top of him. I laughed. I had been on top before, but not when I was this pregnant. I was forty pounds heavier, probably about thirty in my stomach alone. That was a lot of densely packed weight to put on him. I was sure I would break his legs.

"You won't," he said. "I have thighs of steel. I can handle a pregnant woman on them."

But he wasn't going to convince me to break his legs. If he couldn't drive, who was going to get me to the hospital when I went into labor? It would happen any day now.

We settled for some foreplay on the couch. While I was kissing his chest, he said, "I love how you don't care about all this chest hair." I took one of the longer ones between my finger and thumb and gently pulled on it, and we laughed. He put his arms around my upper body and brushed his lips against the bottom of my chin and my neck, giving me little nibbles after every soft kiss. "Oh, you're making me ready to crush you," I breathed.

"That's my goal."

I screamed. A fierce pain shot through my belly, much different from the kicks that I felt around the clock now.

"What's wrong? Did I hurt you?"

"No, it's . . . inside." I cried out. "It hurts so much."

It was like my uterus had ripped open from the front, and my heartbeat reverberated in my chest and my skull.

Then we were in the ER, waiting for answers. I was lying on a hospital bed, half asleep and half panicked. The doctor quickly determined that I wasn't in labor, but I kept on insisting that I felt strong pains for nearly an hour. Now there was nothing, no kicking, no pain. Sana said doctors and nurses hated when patients tried to diagnose themselves, but I hated it when they tried to convince me something that I knew was real was just my hormones or my babies being active and then going to sleep for the night.

So they ordered an ultrasound. Not long after the technician had my womb on the screen, his eyes widened and his back straightened. "I'm going to have call the doctor."

While we waited, Yusef and I didn't say a word. I was paralyzed in the hospital bed, forgetting my full bladder and drowning out the sound of Yusef's tapping feet. I closed my eyes to relieve some of the pain that had been building up in my head.

It didn't feel like I had gone to sleep, but I startled when I felt someone— it must have been Yusef—nudge me awake. The doctor stood still before us.

"I'm afraid it appears that your twins are stillborn," the doctor said. "The placentas have ruptured."

I couldn't speak, and my body tingled from my chest to my bladder.

"Both are stillborn?" Yusef asked, his voice breaking at the end.

"There is no fetal heartbeat in either one. We will need to induce labor or possibly do a cesarean section." He went on to explain the benefits and risks of both options while I stared at the empty wall ahead of me and felt the warm release of my bladder between my thighs.

CHAPTER EIGHTEEN

What struck me most about Mom's family was how their pictures looked so different from what Mom told me they were actually like. They looked so put together and all-American, untouched by any troubles. Just two white married parents and one cute kid that always stood in front of them in pictures with a big smile and her arms open, embracing the world and the photo that would capture that emotion forever.

In reality, though, Mom's parents were divorced, and Mom said Grandma's main concern was finding her next boyfriend or husband, while Grandpa's was the new family he inherited by marrying his second wife soon after he divorced Grandma.

Grandma looked sweet and virginal, with blond hair and light brown eyes, but she had had countless affairs since Mom could remember.

Grandpa looked kind, with dark blue eyes, thin brown hair, and a soft manly smile, but Mom told me he would become irritable and beat her for the smallest mistake when he was angry with Grandma. Mom had a collection of scars on her arms and back that she showed me to prove it. He would let plenty of things slide if things were going well with Grandma, but that was rare. He was easier to be around once they divorced during Mom's early teens, but then he never wanted to be around her anymore, either. Mom was part of his past life, the one he claimed was driven by anger. He needed to minimize contact with that as much as possible.

But then Mom had a child out of wedlock with a Palestinian and reawakened Grandpa's latent anger. He called her a shameful slut and washed his hands of her and was unwilling to meet me, his olive-skinned granddaughter with a weird name like Isra.

Grandma came to visit on rare occasions; the first time I remember was when I was five. She too was upset that Mom had a child out of wedlock, but she was more forgiving. She was between marriages, and Mom had just kicked Baba out for good. Mom would complain to Grandma about what a deadbeat Baba was.

"Honestly, Carol, I've always told you if you just lost fifteen or twenty pounds, you could get yourself a decent man," Grandma told Mom.

She visited once or twice a year, usually during the holidays. She would bring me a new Barbie or something, then ignore me and vent her frustrations with the world and the men in her life to Mom.

But now, three years later, Mom had cancer, and Grandma went back and forth on whether she would take me after Mom passed away. Sometimes she said it would be nice to have someone to live with, someone to help out and spend time with her, but then she would say the last thing she needed was take in an eight-year-old at her age, especially one with a father like mine.

Mom didn't trust her. "She'll want you when she's alone, and as soon as she gets a man, Grandma'll find a way to get rid of you."

Mom told more positive stories about her family when she put together the photo album for me, her hands newly thin and lined with pale blue veins. She didn't have energy to put it together before, and once in a while she said there was no point in it because what did all those pictures mean? Most of the people in them I had never met and probably never would.

Still, we sat in the full-size bed where we slept at Baba's place while she put it together. Mom explained who and what was in each picture before she pressed it down on the sticky surface. "Well, hopefully, Isra, your grandma will visit when you live only with Baba," she said. "Maybe this will make her turn around."

Mom went into hospice the next day, and Baba picked me up after school every day so we could go there and see her. Sometimes Baba would be in the room alone with her, but usually they kept me there to alleviate the tension between them. We had been living at Baba's, but I was sure my parents weren't together, and they wouldn't even have spoken to each other if Mom wasn't dying.

Every time Mom said she was tired and needed to rest, I was sure she was going to die then, and I would cry inconsolably, even though Mom assured me she wasn't leaving yet. Baba would take me out of the room and try to comfort me for a little bit, but he would soon become angry and tell me to be strong. Plenty of people had gone through much worse back home in Palestine, so my pain now didn't matter.

Grandma came soon after Mom went into hospice. She would take me to see Mom for the week or so that she was still awake and not drugged beyond comprehension.

And suddenly I wasn't invisible to Grandma anymore.

She now picked me to vent her frustrations about the man she was in the process of divorcing, and Grandpa as well. "I talked to Carol's father, and you know what he told me? He can't get the time off work! Can you believe that?" She sighed and clenched her teeth together. "'This is your child,' I said to him. 'Can you just pull your dick out of your wife's pussy for two seconds and remember you have a daughter?' You know those kids his wife has aren't his. She had them with the guy before. I don't see what's so great about her. She's as plain as wood."

Grandma took me out for ice cream once Mom slipped from consciousness. She said she couldn't stand to see her daughter suffering to death and that her granddaughter didn't need to see it either, so Baba let her.

Though I loved ice cream, I wasn't excited about getting some that day. Most of it melted on the back of my hand and dripped on the table, and Grandma had to take me to the bathroom to clean up. I could tell she was irritated; I saw her roll her eyes in the mirror, and she told me that I had to eat like a civilized girl.

We went to the hotel she was staying in—she would spend the night at Mom's apartment whenever she came before, but she hated Baba and wouldn't set foot in his apartment—and she put cartoons on the TV for me while she criticized all the men she had had in her life, reserving the worst for Grandpa. "I swear once I married that guy he became such a drag," she said. "We were so young, and all he wanted to do was stay in and drink beer. Even convincing him to go out to the movies was like asking him to drink cyanide." Grandma shuddered at the thought of him. She moved on to her three other husbands: the second was too mean; the third had affairs; the fourth, the one she was in the middle of divorcing, was a drag like Grandpa, but it was more understandable because he was almost a senior citizen.

I didn't say anything. My lack of response must have been made her sad; Mom always had some kind of commentary for Grandma, even if it was negative like telling her she should grow up or learn what monogamy was all about. "I'm not even sixty years old, and my daughter is dying. You're not supposed to bury your child; it's the other way around. Of course, it's no picnic to lose your mother at your age." She wiped a couple of tears that came from her overfilled brown eyes. "You know things are going to be different, right?"

Everyone used that phrase—"things are going to be different"— though they already were different. I hated spending time with Baba, asking him questions. He never knew the answers, and he would get irritated. "Don't ask dumb questions," he always said to me.

Baba was scary, too. Most nights I could hear him crying out in his sleep. When Mom was there, she told me that it was just because Baba had been through some terrible things since he was even younger than me, and he remembered them in his dreams, but I was sure that he was possessed. It was worse without Mom there to tell me to go back to sleep, to comfort me while I tried to keep my breaths even.

I had to live without my mother.

At school everyone I knew had a mother. A few lived with their grandmothers or someone else, but they at least visited their mothers sometimes. And their grandmothers liked them a lot more than Grandma liked me. They didn't talk about men all the time, and they didn't tell their daughters that if they lost weight, they could find a decent man.

But I had a feeling that Grandma was feeling sorrier for herself. She was losing her daughter, the one she could turn to between men. She also started to put on a little bit of weight, especially in the middle. She probably would never be able to find another husband, at least not a decent one.

Though it was almost my bedtime, Grandma had no plans to take me back to Baba's or call him to ask if I could spend the night with her. "Who cares what he thinks?" she told me when I asked if I was allowed to stay. "He isn't worth a shit anyway." She took me to the store and bought me some pajamas and a night light, though I had stopped using one the year before. "What about a toy or something?"

"No, I don't want to play."

"You sure are a mellow child."

After I took a bath and changed into the new pajamas, Grandma talked more about how the man she was currently divorcing was trying to hide his assets and get out of paying her as much alimony. "It's not like I'll be getting much. We were only married for a year and a half," she said. "Couldn't stand him any longer than that."

Baba pounded on Grandma's hotel door so hard I thought he must have bruised his knuckles, shouting at Grandma to open the door or he'd call the police.

Grandma didn't hold out for long, but she wouldn't let me go without letting Baba know that she thought he was a worthless Arab.

"You don't deserve a say in the matter!" Grandma said. "You haven't been there for most of her life, and all you'll do is lock her in the house until she gets married!"

Baba told her at least I wouldn't learn to be a whore like she was. He charged past her and pulled me by the arm. "My daughter comes home with me!" he yelled as he brushed her aside.

Back at his apartment, he left me in the pajamas Grandma got me, and he talked to me for a solid hour, which he never had done before. "She is a sharmoota, a slut. Do not act as she does, Isra. You do not want to live as her." He told me that he couldn't believe that a woman could act that way. His mother, my sitti, he said, would never have spoken to a son-in-law the way she had. Well, he wasn't actually a son-in-law. He never married Mom, but it should be the same thing to these Americans because they didn't believe in marriage the way Palestinians did, so Grandma should think of him as her son-in-law. And Sitti wouldn't have carried on that way, marrying all kinds of men for money or whatever the hell she believed she would get.

Baba woke me up in the middle of the night and told me to put my shoes on. Mom had died, and we were going to see her one last time before she went to the crematorium. I was still tired, but my heart was thundering in my chest, so it was easy for me to stay awake.

Grandma was at the hospice before we were, her face red and streaked with tears. Mom lay on the bed, no oxygen tube connected to her, pale and gaunt, her hair a darker brown than what it was before, her lips still red. I cried, and my chest now felt so light that I wondered if the center of my body was still there. For over a week Mom had been nearly unconscious, and the only way I could tell she was still alive was that she sometimes made a soft grunt when she was in pain. Then a nurse came in and gave her some more drugs to keep her quiet and comfortable.

Baba picked me up and carried me out of the room. People hadn't picked me up on a regular basis up for years, and by then I was only five or six inches shorter than him, but I guess he still thought I was four. He said we should go back home and let them take Mom away.

Grandma held the memorial service at a small banquet hall. I spent most of the time sitting at one of the middle tables next to my father, chewing on one of the black cloth napkins, my dripping saliva warming the back of my hand. I watched my mother's relatives, trying to see if I could remember them from the photos, and if I could recall their names or if Mom had ever spoken of them. But I couldn't place most of them, and they were just as distant from me in real life as they were in the pictures. They seemed uncomfortable around me and my father, and gave us short, awkward condolences. They spoke among themselves, telling their stories about Mom, what she was like as a child and a teenager.

That day, they had all had a close relationship with her when she was alive.

I slipped out and sat under a tree in the picnic area, crushing some of the dried leaves, mildly enjoying the slight pricks in my palm. Grandma found me out there and kneeled as far as she could to speak to me. She was reconciling with her husband. "I might as well," she said, tearing up. She always wiped her tears daintily. "Who else will have me at my age? And I can't live off alimony. I should just pack it in and face reality." She wished me luck with my father, though she doubted he would be a good one. "I hope he doesn't send you back to his country, but what can you do?"

CHAPTER NINETEEN

They kept me in the hospital for another day for observation and told me what I had heard before: they didn't know what had caused the two placental sacs to erupt, though having multiple babies at once can increase the chances. The doctor recommended regular visits to my obstetrician to study our case more closely. There were lots of fertility problems that they hadn't been able to pinpoint or treat yet.

Yusef drove us back to the house. We didn't say anything the entire time. We had spent enough time sharing our feelings about our loss.

Our bedroom wasn't the same as we had left it. Khadija had come and put the cribs away for us; she even made the bed for us.

"We're doing this again," he said, and sighed deeply.

He went to all my doctor's appointments with me. They did every possible test on me, ones to check for diabetes, high blood pressure, sexually transmitted diseases. My doctor questioned me minutely about whether I had been using tobacco or alcohol or drugs during my pregnancy. She even ordered an X-ray on my lungs to make sure I was not lying about smoking.

That seemed to be a possibility that she couldn't rule out, no matter how many times I denied it: I must have been smoking or drinking or using drugs. She asked me that same question in a thousand different ways. One of the times, she asked Yusef to step out of the room. She wheeled her chair close to me on the exam table and spoke softly. "I know maybe if you slipped, you wouldn't want your husband to know. You're young. Twenty-three. We all make mistakes."

"No, I didn't."

She took a breath. "Has your husband ever hit you, even early on in your pregnancy?"

"No."

"Never, not even before your pregnancy?"

"No."

She gave me a visual scan and found two old scars on my back, so yellowed you could barely see them. She asked me where they came from. The oldest was from Amu, one of the times he was punishing me, I couldn't remember when. The other was from Motabel, who dropped a desk on my back when I yanked his balls to the floor. I blamed them both on Amu, though. It was easier.

"Your father's cousin didn't hit you when you were pregnant?" she asked.

"No."

When Yusef drove us back home from that appointment, he asked me what she wanted to know that she didn't want him to know. "She asked me if I ever did drugs or drank during the pregnancy," I said.

His grip on the wheel was so tight his knuckles turned beige, and he shook his head slowly and scornfully. "She asked you four times before that. You know what, I'm not going to let that quack treat you like you're some crack whore who does that shit while you know you're pregnant."

So we went to another obstetrician for a second opinion. She said the same thing: all the correct tests had been done to identify the cause for the stillbirths of our children, and nothing indicated a reason for that event. She reminded us that multiple births often caused complications like this. "I see from your medical records that you were on birth control at the time you got pregnant," she said.

I nodded, a cold wind hitting my body.

"Do you two plan to try again, or do you want a renewal of the prescription? I would not recommend trying so soon after a stillbirth."

Relieved, I realized we hadn't talked about it. I didn't think about it. We weren't having sex. I was still bleeding so heavily that I would have dyed our sheets red if I lay down on them bottomless. Anyway, it felt like a truck had just come out of my vagina.

Yusef had thought of it, though. "Is there any other method that's more effective than the pill?" he asked. He looked over at me. "Just until you recover from this more, and we have more of an idea of why this happened so we don't have to go through it again."

She lectured us about how we might never find the cause and how there was a statistically low chance of having another stillbirth, though that chance was higher for people like us than those that hadn't experienced a stillbirth. She took a very condescending tone, and I could tell she was put off by Yusef's presence.

Yusef wasn't any happier about hers. He sat back in the chair, impassively listening to her. "There is a statistically low chance of a healthy man and woman in their twenties having a miscarriage and a stillbirth in two years, but it happened to us, and if there's any chance we can find out why this happened, we will look for the answers."

Her lips were pinched, and she pushed her glasses up. "Well, the pill is effective, but I suppose you could try and pair it with the use of condoms to have more security."

He had taken a week off from work, but he had to go back because finals were approaching. Though going to see doctors twice in that one week was depressing, it might have been the highlight. We stayed in bed late and rarely talked, and when we did, somehow it always reminded us of the twins, and one or both of us ended up crying. For two weeks I had to key myself up to get out of bed, drag myself to appointments with Yusef, and do the housework. I would wake up crying most days, the quiet, heart-pinching tears I wouldn't let him see. After those first couple of weeks, I did my best to keep myself busy. I cleaned the garage, rearranged the hall closet, and shampooed the carpets. I needed to find some work, not just to occupy my time but for the money. My medical bills were getting hefty. I had quit my job to stay home with the babies, figuring I could at least give them a couple of years. Even Mom stayed home until I was two; she and Baba were still together. Look what it got her. Look what it got me.

Yusef took it more stoically, but he concentrated on preparing for the end of the semester and keeping himself busy in any way he could. "I need to find a tenure-track position," he said. "Enough of this slaving away for these fucking places." He was also on a mission to find the cause of the stillbirth and miscarriage before he would take another chance on my womb. He talked to colleagues, old professors, doctors he knew. No one had any answers.

Hanan and Sana visited often, and Yusef's family came by almost every day with food, so I was expecting one of them when the doorbell rang in the middle of the day.

But it was Amu. He hadn't visited me since I married Yusef. He was wearing his long black overcoat that he had made me press meticulously for years. Like a spot of sunlight in the middle of my sorrow, I thought about how glad I was that I didn't still have to live with him.

I reluctantly invited him in. He went right to one of our chairs and made himself comfortable. "I'm so very sorry for what you and your husband have lost," he said. "Is Yusef home?"

I shook my head. "He's working." I took a seat on the couch, close enough to him but still keeping my distance.

"You must have many troubles in your life right now," he said. He reached into his big pocket and took out his checkbook and filled out a check.

I couldn't think of anything to say. He handed me the check: $3,000. "You and Yusef are a young couple, and I know this must be a great blow for your expenses as well as your hearts," he said. "Take it. Even if Yusef does not want to take it, I want you to keep it and use it for whatever you need." If Amtu Samia's father had tried to pull this—giving her money, trying to suggest that Amu couldn't handle their expenses—he would have hit the roof. I handed it back.

"No, thanks," I said. "We're fine." I had to use some of the money I had earned from working before, the money Yusef didn't want me using, but I didn't want us to be in debt forever.

"Don't be ashamed. You are like a daughter to me. You helped Samia with her responsibilities and cared for Hanan. You have done much for me. Take this."

I was more baffled by what he said than the money he was trying to give me. A daughter. I had never been a daughter to a man, and I hadn't been a daughter to a woman in a decade and a half. But it was too late to make much of a difference. He never said those things while I lived with him. I supposed this year and a half without me showed even him all that I'd been doing for his family with no thanks.

I took the check.

Because of Abu Yusef's health problems, Imm Yusef cooked steamed vegetables and poached chicken breast when she had us over for dinner. Though it was bland, she kept trying to spoon more food on our plates, especially Yusef's. He knew what kind of food she had to make now, and he always ate before he left our house. "No, Mama, I'm fine. I don't have a big appetite."

She tilted her head in concern. "Habibi, you are becoming so very skinny now," she said. "Wallah there is nothing more sad than the death of children, but you must survive." She turned to me and asked me about our eating habits. She noticed that I was losing weight as well, very rapidly. Yusef ate enough, from what I saw. He ate breakfast with me, and he ate the plate I saved him from dinner. He stopped working out, though, and seemed to be losing all the muscle mass he'd worked months to gain. I had lost fifteen pounds in the five weeks since I was discharged from the hospital, the first time I had ever lost a significant amount of weight without trying. My gynecologist said it was probably because the weight I had gained was for my pregnancy, and now that I didn't need it, my body knew to shed it. I thought it was more likely that most of the time I would be so absorbed in cleaning something or reading that I would notice at seven in the evening that I hadn't eaten since breakfast, and I would prepare a late dinner for Yusef before I went to bed. This was unfathomable for me before, the idea of starving myself by choice, but it didn't feel that way. I didn't feel hunger pangs.

Abu Yusef was the one whose appearance was alarming. He was paler and more haggard than when I had seen him a week ago, and halfway through dinner he was exhausted and wanted to lie down. Imm Yusef took him to bed and talked to him for a while before she came back out to tell us, "You both are young. You will have many children. Do not be too much sad for what has happened."

"We're not having children soon," Yusef said calmly. "We're waiting, trying to see if we can find out what's wrong."

She nearly collapsed into her chair, her hand on her heart. "What, Yusef? This makes me almost as sad as when you lose your children."

"This is what's best for us now, and Isra agrees with me, so that's what we're doing," he told her.

"Isra, you want this, too? This is crazy. You cannot do this."

"I can't stand to lose any more children, Mama!"

We left early that night. Another first. The whole car ride back he ranted about his mother. "You know why I told her? Why? Because I know that she'll be fucking relentless until you get pregnant again, and I want her to know I don't want it to happen. Not now, but she wants it right away." His eyes had a strange intensity that made them a paler green these days.

He had more to say when we got home and were getting ready for bed. When I lay down, I wanted to tell him to come to bed and cut his mother some slack, but it was better to let him blow off steam. He was so irate that he went on while he was undressing. "She's done this my whole life, put all these expectations on me. 'Yusef habibi, I want you to be doctor or engineer, we come to this country for that.' 'Ibnee, I want you to marry and have many sons to make your father and I habby.'" That last one really set him off. He pulled up his pajama bottoms. "I don't know why that burden's gotta be so heavy on my shoulders. Maybe I'm not able to do it. I'm not man enough for it." I heard his voice break. "Look at my sisters' husbands: they're doing plenty good having children, even Lubna's shitty husband. Maybe they're better than me."

He was crying at the foot of the bed. I put my arms around his waist. "You're a way better man than those guys," I said. "It doesn't say anything about how good a man you are, having a child." Just look at my father. He had at least one surviving child. "Anyway, it could be me, too. It's likely it was me."

"Baba's going to die, Isra. I know it." He sniffled and sat up straight. "I spent my whole life not wanting to be like my father. I was going to have more than a shitty store my wife practically ran by herself. The whole time I just put him down in my mind, and now I don't know what I'll do if he dies. That's what I get for being such an ungrateful son. I won't get to one-up my father. I won't even get to *be* a father." His eyes now dark, distant.

I was at a loss for words. "Yusi, your mother thinks it's the end of the world if we don't try now, but she's too . . . She doesn't get it, I know, but she cares."

His eyes were so blank I wasn't even sure he was listening to me, just looking past me. His full lower lip trembled. "But I want to be a father,

Isra. I want to be one right now," he said quietly. "I don't know how our grandparents could stand to see their own children die and suffer, but I . . . I can't do it. I can't lose one more thing. I loved them so much, and I didn't even get to hold them until they were dead."

I told him we needed time to get through this, and there was nothing wrong with taking that time, if that's what we needed right now. But I was speaking like a detached third party, and I didn't believe the words that came from my mouth.

I slept more than six hours that night, the most I had in one interval since we lost the babies. Yusef was snoring on top of my breasts, holding on to my belly when I woke up. I gently nudged him off me and went to the kitchen. The rest must have made me hungry, because my stomach was growling right from when I woke up, so I decided to start breakfast. I took out three pots and boiled a couple of potatoes and fava beans while I washed up and kept myself from crying. I had to get over this. I couldn't wallow in it.

He woke up while I was mixing tahini into the fava beans. "The noise woke you?" I was trying to be quiet. He needed to catch up on his sleep.

"The smell did." He walked over to the bowl and tasted some ful from his finger. He kissed my cheek and said I spoiled him. "I guess you're feeling better today." Lately he'd been telling me just to stay in bed for breakfast and relax while he made bowls of cereal for us.

"Yeah. I am."

We ate quietly. He kept his arm on the back of my chair once he was finished eating. He took a long gulp of guava juice from the bottle, finishing it off. "Is this our last bottle?"

I nodded. "I should stop by your parents' store and get some today." We still called it his parents' store, though Khadija had basically taken it over and had her older sons doing most of the labor.

He stared at the wall. "You drank it so much when you were pregnant," he said with a sad smile.

I squeezed his hand and sighed. He leaned closer and kissed me hard. I tasted the guava on his lips and his mouth. His back was warm and strong, and he held me tight. We both could barely catch our breath, but breathing didn't seem important at that moment. I was already wet, and I put my legs in his lap, used them as leverage to push myself up on top of him. He was hard. I wasn't on contraceptives yet. We might have had some old condoms in our bedroom.

He pulled away from me, panting. He moved me back to my chair and held my face in his hands. "Isreenie, you don't know how much I want this, but . . ."

I stopped by his parents' store after he went to work. His nephew Muhammad was stocking one of the refrigerators right in front of the door. He looked up and smiled at me. "Isra!" He stood, his arms full of cheese and yogurt containers. A couple of them spilled over onto the floor, and he put the rest of them down in the box to pick up his mess.

Khadija came from the storeroom, tying her hijab in the front. "'Isra'? This is your uncle's wife, and she is older than you, show some respect. 'Khaltu Isra,' at least. Auntie Isra." She stopped glaring when she gave me a hug. "How are you feeling?" She looked up at me with pity in her eyes.

I shrugged. "I'm fine. We're fine."

"Is there something you need?"

"I just came to pick up some of the guava juice."

She nodded. "Today we just got a lot of cases. Take a case."

"We only need a few bottles."

She brushed that off with the wave of her hand. "It's no problem. You can have a year's supply if you want, and it won't go bad in the cupboard."

"I can take the box out to your car," Muhammad offered. "It's heavy."

Khadija shot another suspicious look at her son. "Be polite," she said. Everyone could tell he had a crush on me. Sana heard through the grapevine that Yusef's middle sister Fatima attributed it to how provocatively I dressed. "She's just way uglier, so she thinks that makes her more modest," Sana said. "Her ass is huge, and not in the attractive 'Bubble Butt' way." If Yusef's crush was embarrassing back when I was a teenager, Muhammad's was painfully so. My being married made it much juicier for people to talk about.

I was surprised he was still interested. I was still ten pounds heavier, with a stretched-out stomach that would never snap back, frizzy hair I didn't care to fix, and dark circles under my eyes. "I can take it out," I said.

Khadija waved her hand again. "No, let him. He will be a good boy. I'll get you a bag of some other things to take home." She took me aside.

"You know how teenage boys are. His father and I have talked to him a thousand times. It is . . . innocent, I think."

He followed me out to my car with the heavy box. I kept a bit ahead of him. "My uncle is a lucky man," he said.

I sighed. This was the last thing I needed today. "Yeah, it doesn't seem like he's been that lucky recently." I'd thought the same thing about him before. An only son with two parents and three loving sisters. He seemed to have it all. Until he married me.

He folded his arms and shuffled his feet nervously. "I'm sorry, but, in other ways, he's been lucky, you know."

I unlocked my trunk. "Just lay off, okay? I'm your aunt." Identifying myself that way still seemed weird, especially to a boy not even five years my junior.

He pouted and looked down, his dark eyes lowered in shame. I felt cruel, and I thought that if our son had lived, he would have grown up to look similar to Muhammad. "I'm sure you'll find someone else," I said, though I knew that one person could never actually replace another. I might be the older-woman crush he would hold on to with fervor. Older woman. When had this happened?

"Yeah, sure I will," he said petulantly, and turned his back to me.

I went back into the store and picked up the bag Khadija insisted I take. "Where's Muhammad?" she asked.

I shrugged.

"I swear it's always something with these boys," she said.

She followed me out to order him back inside. As I eased my car away from the curb, she yelled at him about the cheese and yogurt getting warm sitting on the floor of the store.

Once I got home, I couldn't make myself get out of the car. I couldn't go back in our house. I sat there for a few minutes telling myself this was where I lived, to just go inside and do something to occupy myself, but I pulled out of the driveway instead. I stopped, my car halfway in the road, and ran to the front door, key in hand. I went to the bedroom and found the photo album Mom had made me, the letters from Falasteen, the receipts for the money I had been wiring. While I was digging for that stuff, I found the shoebox where Yusef kept my notes. I couldn't look at them. I hadn't thought to write him one since we lost the babies.

I drove around for a couple of hours. The traffic got heavier. Suddenly it felt like the car was slowly shrinking, and I was sure it would squeeze me to death. I parked at a motel, went to the office, and got myself a room for the night. I thought about Yusef the whole time. I didn't feel like I was that woman, the one who married Yusef and slept next to him every night, the woman he had stood by for fifteen hours of labor to deliver two dead children; I wasn't even the girl he noticed at Sana's house, who almost made him lose to Bassam at a video game. Yusef wasn't real; he was just a sweet dream that had gone horribly wrong. I was only a grown-up orphan and Amu and Amtu's burden who had managed to finally escape their house.

I was at ease when I lay down on the queen-size bed, my stuff thrown on the floor. I needed to confirm that I was still alive. I called Sana, put the phone on speaker, and set it down on the bed.

"I can't go home, Sana."

"What? What happened? Did you and Yusef have a fight or something?"

"No, he's at work. I can't go back."

"Wait. Why?" She kept on talking when I didn't answer. "Is something going on?"

"No. I can't be a wife. I can't go back."

"Look, Isra, I know you've been really depressed about your babies, and I understand, believe me, that must be so hard."

I closed my eyes, my stomach closing in on itself so hard I felt it in my chest.

"I don't think you should leave him."

I didn't say anything.

"Isra? Are you there? Tell me where you are, and I can come and talk to you and everything. I think you're just feeling really down today, and you need someone, so let me see you—"

I hung up and went to sleep.

She called me back several times and left messages, but they didn't disturb my sleep. I calmly listened to them when I woke up. "Isra, seriously, call me back and tell me where you are. I'm about to have a nervous breakdown over this."

Later Yusef started calling, just after nine o'clock when he got home and didn't find me anywhere. "Hey, Isra, just wanted to know where you are." He took a much different tone with me in the second message. "I was worried shitless about you, and I just called Sana's house, and she told me about your call earlier. I don't know what's going on with you, but call me back." He had to record the rest of his thoughts on another message. "I'm your husband, how can you treat me like this? Everything was . . . well, it wasn't all right, but it was better. At least call me and talk to me if you won't tell me where you are." He called and called well past midnight. After an hour of silence, at 1:44 a.m., he left one final message. I heard the tears in his voice, his words slightly slurred. "How am I supposed to sleep when I don't know where you are? Call me. Sana won't even tell me where you are. I know she knows. I don't know what I did to become the bad guy. I didn't do anything to deserve this."

I called Hanan; she picked up after two rings.

"I left Yusef."

She yawned and spoke in a groggy voice. "Right now?"

"No, it was earlier, but my phone line has been tied up."

Hanan asked where I was staying, and when I said I was at a motel, she hesitantly asked, "What happened?"

"I just . . . I can't do it anymore. I don't know what I was thinking when I married him. It's too much. I can't do it. Sana thinks I should go back, but—"

"If you don't want to stay, I don't see why you have to. She's not the one who's married to him."

It was such a relief to hear Hanan's agreement. I slid down the wall to the floor.

"I can come over tomorrow."

"Don't tell your parents where you're going."

"Oh, yeah. Of course. Just give me the address, and I'll tell them I'm going to a friend's house. Baba usually works a lot on Saturdays anyway, so he won't ask questions."

Out screwing another woman, I thought. That's what he's doing on Saturdays. Amu Nasser and Amtu Samia stayed together, with two surviving children, a boy and a girl, and yet Yusef and I were separated and childless.

I thought of the last time Yusef and I saw each other in high school. *You can call me. I'll pick you up, and we can go somewhere to be alone.* He promised me he wouldn't try to kiss me or do anything I didn't want him to do. *I just want to see you.* But of course, the only number he had to give me was his home phone number, and the only one I could give him was Amu and Amtu's landline, and I'd heard from Sana that Imm Yusef was unusually fanatical about her son's behavior. She told Sana's mother any Amreekiya or any other kind of kafir woman that would try to steal him away had to do it over her dead body. He would marry a Palestinian Muslim woman, one who would know how to take care of him and give him sons.

"Do you think she would consider me too kafir?" I asked Sana. I wouldn't be surprised if she did. Nearly all the older Arab women who met me didn't like me from the start, except for blood relatives and Sana's mother.

Sana shrugged. "I don't know, but you don't want to get your ass mixed up in that. His mom's bat-shit insane. Yusef's cute and all, but you've got to think that through."

The next day he called around nine-thirty, when I would usually finish breakfast on a Saturday, before our children died. I usually made a small one, some eggs and labna, not a feast like Amtu's or what I made him the day before, and we either talked or made love after. He left a short message this time, the exhaustion evident in his voice: "Call me, Isra. I need to know you're okay."

Hanan came over in the early afternoon. She gave me a hug and said she was sorry for everything.

I shrugged. "I should never have gotten married."

She nodded her head vigorously. "Yes. Okay, I'm not saying Yusef was a bad guy or anything, but who are the people who live the longest, especially the women who live the longest? The ones who never marry. Marriage is fatal."

I chuckled halfheartedly.

"And, you know, your kids, too. I know you took that really hard."

I sighed, suddenly feeling exhausted. "Yeah. I mean, you just never think of babies dying, but . . ." I lay down on the bed, my hands over my soft belly.

"We should go do something. Get your mind off everything. You've been in the house way too much these days."

But we didn't know where to go. We drove around in my car, going over possibilities. Mostly Hanan would suggest things, and I'd grunt in agreement, which she didn't consider enough enthusiasm to go forward with the plan. My mind was more focused on Yusef at the wheel of his car, except it wasn't him now but him at seventeen, in the car he had then when he took me home from Sana's house, or from school, or to the restaurant where he told me he liked me and thought I was beautiful.

Listening to the radio didn't help. Hanan sang along with all the pop songs, reveling in the sexually suggestive lyrics and giggling. To me, though, it seemed like every song mentioned love or lust, which made me think of Yusef. I don't know why, because our relationship was nothing like what was in those songs. He never told me to leave my man for him, I never said I could do more for him than the other girls (I couldn't anyway). We had a secret relationship for a year, then he came back after seven years to ask my father's cousin for my hand in marriage, and I made him wait for my answer just to see if he would. We argued, cried, lost babies. Romance gone awry. More tragic than Amtu Samia's soap operas. I switched to the heavy metal station, figured if any of those songs were about love, I wouldn't know it anyway. I couldn't understand their screaming, and it was a comfort to know I wasn't the only one who felt like that.

Hanan whined at the change. "Ew! God, you are white, listening to this!" She imitated the singer and made it sound like a throaty scream and a dog's bark put together.

I leaned against the window and stared ahead blankly.

After Hanan left, I found an unopened pack of cigarettes and a half-used box of matches in the nightstand in my motel room. Slowly I peeled off the red plastic strip on the cigarette box. I took one out and smelled the end with the tobacco. It didn't smell good or bad, but it drew me in. Lighting it, I inhaled and coughed so hard I nearly choked, but I took another stab at it. The cigarette left a burnt taste in my mouth and made me feel so relaxed. I understood why the men in Falasteen smoked them so much out on the porch: it was calming and shortened your misery. One of my first cousins had become such an expert at exhaling smoke that he could make an infinity sign. I tried to do the same, but it came out as a flood of white air.

I smoked a couple and read Yusef's texts. He was practically carrying on conversations with himself. "Maybe you're upset about me not being able to do that that one morning but don't be. Call me." He was more pissed off a few hours later. "You're acting like a selfish bitch! I've never done anything this bad to you." The next one came a few minutes later. "You make everything so hard."

I even got a voicemail from Sana's mother. "Isra, Sana has told me what happened. You must go back to your husband. He is a good man. Sana will not tell anyone where you are. You must call your husband."

A text message came from Sana a minute later: "I didn't tell my mom, but Yusef's practically been stalking me so she found out. Just deal with him."

Now everyone knew that I had left Yusef. Imm Yusef would be irate: the half-breed girl who couldn't even bring children to full term had the gall to leave her perfect son, the one who was conceived because of America's waters. She would quickly look into divorce and search for another wife. After all, she needed a grandchild from her only son.

"I think he's a dick," Hanan said as she unpacked the fast food she bought on her way over to the motel. "That's a totally messed-up thing to say, that it's all your fault."

We ate our hamburgers on the bed. The meat was chewy. I hated cheap fast food. "Well, I haven't even talked to him yet, so I can understand why he's mad," I said.

Hanan wolfed down her burger. "Yeah, you should call him, when you have divorce papers." She had thought this out more thoroughly than I had. "You are going to divorce him?"

"I don't see how we could come back from this, so I guess that's where we're headed."

"Come on, have more conviction than that!"

"I can't, Hanan! It's not that easy! We've had children together. I can't just forget him like that." That must have been why it took Mom so long to finally sever ties with Baba. Look at how worked up I was getting just now, and our children weren't even alive.

I lay down and cried, letting my half-eaten burger fall off the bed. "I miss him so much. It would hurt to see him, but I want to so badly. If I see him now, I know I'll go back to him." If he would even take me back.

"Why? You don't need him."

I was sure of that. I had lived all these years without my mother. I could go without Yusef. But Mom was dead. There was no way I could go back to her. With Yusef, I'd know he was out there, just a few miles away, and the temptation would be too much for me.

"I can't explain it. I don't need him, but I don't want to kick him out of my life. These things are complicated, Hanan."

"Really, Isra, I think if you wanted him in your life, you wouldn't have left, but you knew he wasn't good for you. Okay, he's not a terrible guy, but he's so self-involved and cocky, and marriage just kills you anyway. It'll probably be better for both of you guys."

I looked up at the ceiling and stared at a brown stain. "It would have been easier if I hadn't fallen for an only son," I said. "I should have married some guy who was the middle son or something in a family of all boys."

"I know. Look at Rasheed."

"No, what Yusef's family thinks of him is like what your parents thought of Rasheed on steroids. He was the baby, and he came after his parents were married fifteen years. You don't cherish anything more than when you had to wait for it." I sighed. "Besides, he's not a loser like Rasheed, and he's better looking."

She scoffed. "Yusef's not that good looking. Arabs will fall all over you if you got light eyes."

"It's not only that. It's his skin, his hair, his hands." His chest, his arms, his everything.

Hanan frowned, steadfastly unimpressed.

We took another drive, hoping that it would make me feel better, singing along to the radio and laughing at our awful voices. I smoked a couple of cigarettes. It was awkward at first because I needed my right hand to drive, but that was also how I smoked. In about an hour I had mastered smoking with my left hand.

"How do you know where everything is?" Hanan asked.

I had lived in most of the areas of the city, counting all the apartments Mom and I lived in, then Baba's apartment, then Amu's house far out into the suburbs. Not to mention living by the university with Yusef and now over on the northwest side of town. We were driving far from there and heading toward the ghetto, where Mom and I lived with Baba and where

I went to high school, where most of my teenage relationship with Yusef was carried out.

Hanan got quiet as we started to pass more decrepit buildings, dingy churches, and barking guard dogs. "Don't you think we should get out of here?"

"No, I want to see something." In my sophomore year of high school, I walked the mile and a half from school to Baba's old apartment complex, but right before I got there, I was stopped by a man who thought I was a prostitute. That sent me running the other way.

That didn't matter now. I parked at the curb in front of the apartments.

"Are you sure you want to leave the car here?" Hanan's eyes were wide.

"This is where I lived with my mom and dad," I said.

She unbuckled her seat belt and got out with me. They had closed the complex down a while ago, but one of the security gates was wide open, and I found the apartment in no time, 216B. I tried the lock on the door.

"You're just gonna go in?"

"Nobody lives here."

"Isra, I'm getting scared. What if your car gets stolen or the cops catch us doing this?"

"Believe me, all the cops do around here is call the clean-up crew for the dead bodies."

"That makes me feel so much better!"

I threw my shoulder into the door, and it opened easily. I smelled rat shit and saw alcohol bottles and dirty blankets scattered around the floor. "Hobos live here," I said. I went to the window I used to look out all the time. No lock. The room looked the same, glaringly white, except now it was a storage room for empty beer cans, gin and vodka bottles, blankets, and pillows.

"Isra, let's hurry and get out," she said. "What if those homeless guys come back?"

The bathroom was trashed. When I opened the door, a bunch of bottles clattered like a wind chime. The mirror was so dirty I could barely see myself in it. I rubbed some water on the mirror and saw myself, if somewhat blurry. I didn't bother to look closely.

Hanan ran into me in the hall. "We have to get out. I'm freezing, and someone's gonna find us. I can feel it."

I saw myself looking out the window, seeing all the decay around us, Mom yelling at me to stay away, and Baba looking off in the distance when I stuck my head out to get a better look.

We spent the next two days in the hotel room, watching TV and eating junk food. I didn't check my texts at all and kept my phone on silent. Hanan didn't have school that week, but on Monday she had to leave anyway when Amu called and demanded that she come home from her "friend's house." "It's not a lie. We are friends. We just happen to be cousins too," she said, and added sulkily, "I don't want to go back home. It's so boring over there."

I didn't know what was so exciting about being here. All I did besides eat and watch TV was cry and reminisce about Yusef and feel remorse about how I wasn't calling him.

Hanan came back as early as she could on Tuesday. "Baba knows that you left Yusef," she said. "He says he talked to him."

"He talked to Yusef?"

She nodded. "Yusef called him. He wanted to know if Baba knew where you were."

I shook my head and sucked my teeth. Yusef had gone to Amu. He knew how much I hated him. He knew I would never tell Amu anything.

"He asked if I knew anything about it. I said you had told me, but you left town to take a vacation." She sat down on the bed. "He wasn't going to believe you hadn't told me, and if he knew you were here, he would know I was going to see you."

Some time passed, and Hanan and I snacked and she watched a show on HBO her parents would never let her watch. I thought about what it would have been like if the twins had lived, where Yusef and I would be now. I'd probably be exhausted and resent Yusef for only taking the fun parts of raising children and leaving me with the breastfeeding and diaper changing and exhaustion, though he promised he would be a helpful father, especially with two babies at once. We would have a huge fight, or fights, and I might be able to keep my emotions in check enough to cry only after he was out of the room, unlike when I was pregnant. For months I crumbled over anything.

And he'd try to make me feel better every time. Even when I threatened to cut off his balls.

Then *Summer of Sam* came on. I nearly gagged watching that guy running around to get his sodomy fix from any woman he met. Do that many people do that stuff? *I did it a few times, albi, but I don't need it.*

I changed the channel.

"That guy's such a perv," Hanan commented. "How are you paying for this anyway? If you need some money, I'll just take a little from Baba's stash. I know where it is." She bit into another cherry cordial from the box of chocolates we had opened.

"I have some saved." I had used three hundred dollars already. I needed to look for an apartment and another job to get by, but I didn't want to think about that. It felt so final.

We were over. I'd be living alone. Twenty-four, and I hadn't managed to start a career or even have babies. All I had was a failed marriage.

Hanan and I had an evening slump. She was asleep with chocolate smeared on the corners of her face, and I was lying down with my back to hers, my hands on my belly. I could feel that I had lost more weight. I was hardly eating; I would have some junk food and then feel burnt out for the rest of the day, too tired to eat or to do anything but lie down and feel horrible about myself. I thought I'd be the type to balloon up after having kids or during a tragedy, but instead I was becoming someone who my grandmother would approve of. A woman who slimmed down when she left a man so she could get another in a minute.

I heard a hard knock on the door. Hanan woke up with a start. "Don't come in, please!" I shouted. I had put the DO NOT DISTURB sign on the door handle.

"It's me."

Hanan and I looked at each other. We recognized his voice. "Holy shit!" Hanan whispered.

I got up immediately and tried to fix my hair by running my fingers through it. When had that ever worked for me? I sighed and looked in the mirror. My hair was insanely frizzy. I didn't know what I felt. Scared, excited, stomach-sick.

"I have to do this some time," I said. My legs were jelly when I walked to the door.

He looked worse than I did. His hair was disheveled, his eyes bloodshot and red-rimmed, his whole face sagging. He seemed to have aged at least ten years. Neither of us knew what to say for those first few seconds. He shook his head at me, frowning. "It's been five days, and you haven't once called to let me know you were alive," he said. "What are you doing here?"

I had been asking myself the same thing the entire time. I couldn't come up with an answer.

"You're not gonna let me in?"

I looked down at the floor. My lungs felt heavy, too heavy for my chest to contain.

"There's someone else in there?" His voice broke and his eyes were wide and bright.

I moved out of the way to let him in. Hanan was scurrying around, picking up the trash. "It's okay, Hanan. Just leave it there."

His face softened, and he sighed. "Do you mind if I talk to Isra alone?"

She dropped the fast food bags on the floor. She looked over to me.

"We just need to talk," Yusef insisted.

"Are you sure you want me to leave?" She picked up her purse.

After she let herself out, Yusef said, "So I'm such an asshole that she doesn't even trust me alone with you?"

"I didn't say anything bad about you."

"Oh, sure. That's why Sana thinks you should be in the witness protection program because I'm—"

"Sana doesn't know where I am! I called her, and she wanted me to go back, so I stopped talking to her." I was close to tears. "Don't worry. No one thinks you're the bad guy. You got way more people on your side, as usual."

His eyes filled up. "Isra, I thought because . . . Look, I'm sorry about the babies and the miscarriage, but how can you just leave? All your shit is still at home, what was I supposed to think? I thought someone had come and kidnapped you. I was that stupid. I didn't think you would ever leave me."

I went to the window. I couldn't look at him. "It's not about that, okay? And if I'm such an evil bitch, why didn't you just say good riddance when I left?" I turned back around. It was always easier to look at him angrily rather than remorsefully.

"Because I'm such a fucking idiot that I still care about you. I still love you. Even when Sana told me that you said you were leaving, I was worried about you. I kept on thinking, 'Where's she going to sleep? What if someone hurts her?' I can't just detach like you. I see you didn't give a shit about what was happening to me. You can't even call me, can't even try to work it out with me." He fell on the bed and covered his face as he wept.

I placed a tentative hand on his back. He didn't seem to notice. "I am sorry about how I left, and I didn't mean for Sana to be the one to have to tell you."

"How else was I gonna find out? You didn't even leave a note." He wiped his eyes. The rims had turned an even brighter red, like fresh blood when the skin breaks.

I didn't know what to say. That I had wanted to see him again. That I was afraid to see him, afraid that I would be sucked in again when I didn't think I should be.

He looked up at me accusingly. "Was it ever love with you? Did you love me? I used to think you were just being modest, or you were insecure, but was it just games, ways to fuck with me? Because I know I would never have left you like that."

I took my hand from his back. "That is so unfair. I waited for you for seven years so I could fuck with you? And it turns out you were having plenty of fun, and you forgot about me soon enough."

"God, Isra, those girls didn't mean anything to me. You broke it off with me, remember? You wouldn't give me a number, a place to meet, nothing. I just respected your boundaries, and you had plenty of those."

I stomped my foot on the floor. "What did you expect me to do? Become your child bride at fifteen and live with you and your parents? If Amu found out I was 'whoring around' with you, he would have kicked me out, sent me to foster care, or had me eating out of the trash. I'm not his daughter. He wasn't going to forgive a sin like that. The stakes were a lot higher for me, and you refuse to see that." I pressed my eyes shut. I wanted to bring up how he said he would hold our daughter to the same standard of purity, but I wasn't that mad at him even then. "And don't act like you didn't enjoy screwing around with 'whores' before you settled down with your virginal wife!"

He stood up to meet me just above eye level. "All right, Isra. You're right. I'm a disgusting pig. But I didn't think I was hurting you. If you had told me these things—"

I snickered. "You wouldn't have done it? Yeah, right." And I did tell him. He just didn't understand.

He covered his forehead and eyes and shrieked. "You don't get it, Isra!" Now he held his arms out to the side. "I've given more to you than anyone else. I share things with you I wouldn't even think about sharing with anyone else. Nobody's had me the way you have, and you just throw it away, again and again."

"You don't get it! I gave you everything, and even that's not enough for you!"

Our fight was so long it had its own intermission. I went on about how we had to live our lives according to his standards because he never saw my side of things; he went on about how he wanted to take care of me and do his best for me, but I didn't appreciate it. When we both didn't have the energy to duke it out any longer, I sat on the bed and hid my face in my bent legs, my knees pressed to my forehead. Yusef sat on the floor next to the tiny round table, his head resting against one of the legs, silent for nearly an hour.

"Did you blame me for what happened?"

I looked up, but my eyes went right back down to my hands. "No. I mean, I was on the pill, and you knew and kind of accepted it."

He craned his neck and blinked slowly. "I just wanted a—"

"No, it's not bad. I can just be so bitter sometimes, and it made it hurt so much more when I wasn't on guard."

He came over to me and pressed me to his chest. We both cried. I could feel some of his tears drop on my hair. When I composed myself enough to speak, it came out in choked bursts. "Yusi, I left . . . I left because . . . I feel like such a failure. I never thought that they would die." I squeezed his shoulder and looked up at him. "I'm so, so sorry for leaving like that. I was such a coward. I don't know what came over me." But I did know what it was; the desire to flee, to escape, had been there since I could remember. This was just the first time I couldn't resist.

He took my hand from his shoulder and kissed it, closing his eyes tight.

"How'd you know I was here, Yusef?"

He didn't open his eyes. "Your amu figured out where Hanan was going. He called me while I was at the hospital. Baba had a heart attack last night."

"Oh, Yusi. . . ." I didn't know what else to say. I wiped the tears from his cheeks and told him how much I loved him.

"If I didn't come here, you would have come back home?"

"I don't know what I was thinking that day. I felt better that morning, but then in the afternoon, I just . . ."

He looked away, wiped his tears. "I just want you to be there, even if you're pissed, sad, or whatever."

And I heard myself tell him that I would be.

CHAPTER TWENTY

When I was seven, Mom and Baba resumed contact that went beyond Baba's occasional visits to see me. Mom had decided that she had to quit her job because her cancer had spread, and she needed someone to take care of me when she was gone. We didn't move in with Baba at first. He usually came over to our apartment to visit and watch me when Mom needed to sleep or something. For the first month or so, I got sick a lot, colds and stomach aches. Baba believed that I wasn't being properly nourished, and his solution, as it was to everything stomach-related, was tea with maramiya.

When Baba made me a cup, he made some for himself and Mom. During teatime, while I lay down on my stomach on the floor or the couch, my parents would discuss her medical treatment and "plans for the future." These conversations were a lot different from the ones I remembered as a little kid, when Mom and Baba would shout at the top of their lungs and Baba would leave for a few days, or sometimes a few months. Mom took him back a couple of times after that, but she would be mad about it for a while, and Baba would tell her that he didn't need her and could go back home where he would be loved and respected and could find a good Palestinian wife. "Then why'd you leave in the first place?" she would say. "If you want to go back, don't let your daughter and me stand in your way."

But after visiting Falasteen, I knew how he could have felt loved in a way that he never had in the United States and yet would want to leave. Maybe love couldn't be conquered, but it could be driven into retreat. My family in Palestine loved me more than Amu and Amtu, but I couldn't imagine myself staying.

Now they talked things out rationally, even when they disagreed. It was temporary, though. Once we moved in with Baba, they would be around each other enough to drive each other up the wall again. "Munir, I don't understand why you don't just move in here," she said. "That would really work out better. That apartment you live in scares the shit out of me. You can't have a child there."

"No, no. I will open my home to you, but I want to stay there. I don't like this place."

I could see Mom's temper simmering, but she looked sideways at the wall, her green eyes sad, her face thin and pale, cheekbones protruding far out from her face. She sighed. "It's full of drug addicts and criminals," she said. "Do you want your daughter living there?" Those were fighting words, but she said them in a calm tone, and Baba didn't have any retaliation.

He didn't waver, though.

We had just gotten back from one of her treatment sessions, so Mom was feeling especially tired. When we got to the stairs, we noticed that the door of our apartment was wide open. "I know I closed the door. I locked it," she said. She jogged up the steps, and I did my best to keep up with her.

When we examined the door, we found SAND NIGGER'S WHORE spray-painted across the outside of it. Mom's face bleached to an almost pure white, but she didn't cry in front of me. I thought these people were pretty stupid, thinking that Baba was black. My kindergarten teacher had thought the same thing because of my hair and Baba's, and she didn't know where Palestine was, so I told her that Baba came from a place that was overrun by European invaders who claimed they were the original inhabitants of the land but actually dispossessed the people who were. I didn't understand what all that meant at the time, but that's what Baba said, so I passed it on when people asked, until Mom told me to stop. My teacher gaped at me and said, "All right, Isra," but she never looked at me the same again, and she avoided speaking to me.

"They're dummies!" I said, trying to lighten the mood.

Mom jiggled the door handle, and it only made a muffled sound. "They broke the lock. How are we supposed to live here without a lock?" Her face contorted some more, and it wasn't any better when we got into our apartment.

There was a spray-painted picture on our living room wall of the three of us on a camel, and we all looked like stick figures with head covers. Then, across the wall, all three of us were being overrun by the camel we had been riding earlier.

Mom's face looked hard and still. She didn't seem close to tears anymore. It was the face she got right before she was about to yell at Baba but a thousand times worse. Her breathing came in bursts. "You know, I don't understand why people can't just leave us alone," she spit out, glaring at the picture. "Is our life any of their business?"

On the kitchen table Mom found a note and slammed it back down before she went to the phone to report this to the police and to the apartment manager so they could get the place fixed up. I read the note. Nothing was in it that wasn't on the door or the walls. Putting all this together, I figured out they did know that Baba wasn't black. Everyone thought of camels when they heard about the Middle East, but Baba had never mentioned them to me before.

But then, there were a lot of things Baba never told me.

The apartment manager claimed that he was just about to get off work, so he would call the maintenance man to come check it out first thing in the morning. Until then, he advised us to stay with friends. I knew friends would end up being Baba. I had been to his apartment once before. It smelled, and there was a lot of noise all around and dirty people hanging out on the street asking for change. Everyone glared at us, too, hating Mom and me before they even knew us.

The cops weren't much better. There was a tall Mexican guy and a short white guy. They surveyed our apartment and asked Mom a bunch of questions while I sat on the couch, wishing I could become invisible with Mom and we could float away, out into the sky. We would have our own universe, where there wasn't death and cops and stupid people breaking into your apartment and painting ugly pictures on the wall.

"Is there anyone you know who had a problem with your . . . preference for Middle Eastern men?" the white cop asked.

"Well, yes. Half the people in the complex."

"Maybe they all teamed up to do this," the Mexican cop said, laughing.

Mom glared at him. She crossed her arms and looked right at them. "You know what? Fuck both of you. I don't need any more people to judge my life. You won't even find the dipshit who did this, anyway. You just think it's funny."

"Ma'am, you're becoming emotional," the white cop said. "We'll do our best to find out who's done this to your residence, but we can't do that if you're impeding the process."

She shook her head. "He's from a different continent, not a different planet. And I don't want you in my 'residence' any longer."

"Suit yourself." The Mexican cop put his notepad back in his pocket, and the white cop adjusted his holster and sneered.

Baba took forever to come to the apartment. In the meantime, Mom lay down on the couch with her hands over her eyes and cried about what a failure her life had been and how Baba was the biggest mistake she had ever made. I stretched out in the space between the couch back and her legs, resting my head on her now-skinny butt. She assured me that I was the only good thing that came from her ill-fated union with Baba, and patted my shoulder. "He was a good man," she said. "When we first met, he wasn't so worthless. I never thought he would become this."

Her mentioning Baba in the past unsettled me. I knew nothing about how they met or how long they had been together before they had me, or if they were even together before Mom found out she was pregnant. I wanted to ask her more about the past, so maybe I would feel like I didn't just emerge from the collision of two unwilling lives to make me into a girl who everyone thought should be riding a camel and wearing a head cover but speaking like a white girl.

But Mom's green eyes were heavy, her thin hair a mess, and her mouth was still set tight, the same look she had nearly the whole time since we had gotten to our wrecked home.

That was a new thought, thinking something good about Baba. He had always been the one who came and went, destroying the peace in our house with his presence and his demands, and his insults about how much I wasn't his daughter.

He came while Mom was snoring on the couch, her thin arm covering her eyes from the remaining daylight. Baba had seen the door, and now he looked at the walls. He clicked his tongue and shook his head. "Isra, what will we do about this?"

I was stunned that he cared to know my opinion. I was seven. Adults never asked me what to do. They made the decisions for me. "I guess we have to go to your house," I said.

He rolled his eyes, disappointed. "Well, we must put everything away, then." He picked me up and walked with me to the bedroom. "We will let your mother rest until we are done."

We didn't have suitcases, so we put everything in big trash bags. I sat on the bed looking at him, at the curls he had on his head like mine but much shorter, at his deep brown eyes, his straight nose. I figured if he could ask me what I was supposed to do about all this, I could ask him a question I had been thinking about for the last couple of months. "Are you and Mom boyfriend and girlfriend again?"

He looked at me, one eyebrow raised. "Boyfriend and girlfriend?" he repeated, and laughed sadly, shaking his head. He said a few things in Arabic to himself, or maybe to me, and sighed.

I nodded. I instantly regretted asking the question. Nothing set my parents off more than having to define their relationship, and I was sure they were the only ones who did that. Plenty of people at school had parents who were divorced or broken up or together but not married, but they knew that much—if their parents were together or not.

He sighed. "It is very complicated, Isra, but there is . . . Your mother will not be around much longer, so it is best that we do not start this again."

I nodded and fixed my eyes on the sunset from our bedroom window, asking no more questions.

THE UNIVERSITY PRESS OF KENTUCKY
NEW POETRY AND PROSE SERIES

This series features books of contemporary poetry and fiction that exhibit a profound attention to language, strong imagination, formal inventiveness, and awareness of one's literary roots.

SERIES EDITOR: Lisa Williams

ADVISORY BOARD: Camille Dungy, Rebecca Morgan Frank, Silas House, Davis McCombs, and Roger Reeves

Sponsored by Centre College

 CENTRE
COLLEGE